Kiki
Coto

Edward Avanessy

Kiki Coto
Copyright © 2021 by Edward Avanessy

This is a fictional story and as such all the
names, locations, and events are imaginary,
and the creation of the author.
If there are any similarities of names
to actual individuals; present and past,
are by chance and unintentional.

Tellwell Talent
www.tellwell.ca

ISBN
978-0-2288-5365-7 (Hardcover)
978-0-2288-5364-0 (Paperback)
978-0-2288-5366-4 (eBook)
978-0-2288-6427-1 (Audiobook)

To my angelical wife and soulmate Anni, without you, I would be lost and could not write this book.

CHAPTER ONE

He runs toward the white church on top of the hill while holding a baby girl in one hand and a gun in the other.

He is well-built, athletic, and wearing a high-ranking police uniform with a bulletproof vest. He appears to be in his late thirties. Several thugs are chasing him, along with some uniformed police officers.

The church is still in the distance, and a cornfield is midway. He thinks if he reaches the cornfield, he may have a chance. He can see cars passing by him on the distant dirt roads on both sides. He knows they are encircling him. The thugs are shouting profanities at him, but he cannot hear what they are saying. He is outrunning them even though he is zigzagging to avoid the shower of bullets coming at him. His leg gets hit, but he keeps on running. He reaches the cornfield, and the stalks of corn are almost as tall as him. He feels a little safer and starts shooting at the thugs, hitting several of them. At least three are down, but there are so many of them. He continues running toward the church while gasping for air.

The thugs start burning the cornstalks from behind and from the sides. He knows they are waiting for him on the other side of the cornfield. He sits down, says a prayer, and puts the little girl on his lap. The little girl is scared. She clings on to the officer. She has a heart-shaped birthmark on her shoulder. The officer is not going to move. The smoke gets thicker. It is difficult to breathe.

The thugs position themselves on the front side of the cornfield where it is not burning—the only way out—and start shooting randomly. He covers the little girl with his body as the bullets shower all over his legs, hands, arms, and shoulders. He is losing a lot of blood, and as he falls on his side, he is still trying to protect the little girl.

The gang leader, a bearded man wearing a cowboy hat and dark sunglasses, approaches him and shoots him several times. The thugs leave.

* * *

Richard felt frightened. He opened his eyes and saw his mother standing over him.

"You had that dream again?" asked his mother, Cathy. "I did not wake you up this time. Did you see any more than before?"

"No, I woke up at the same time as usual."

"Don't worry; it is just a dream. You will grow out of it," Cathy said. "Now hurry up and get ready for school."

There was a bed in one corner, an L-shaped desk in another, and a shelf beside the desk with books, papers, electronic devices, and speakers spread over it. A violin box stood neatly in another corner of the room.

Richard rushed to the bathroom and brushed his teeth while his younger sister, Mary, knocked on the door, asking him to hurry up. Back in his room, he picked up his backpack, stuffed it with some books, then headed downstairs, placed his backpack beside the entrance door, peeked outside, and saw his friend waiting for him. Richard ran to the kitchen, where his father, Philip, was sipping his coffee while going through the daily paper. Philip was a calm man who did not involve himself in the morning chaos. Cathy was eating breakfast. Richard grabbed a piece of toast and ran toward the door.

"Richard, dear, I made you breakfast," said Flore, the maid.

"I'm late. Mike's waiting. We're going to play football before class," said Richard.

"Don't forget you have violin practice this afternoon. Come straight home and be careful playing, so you don't hurt your fingers!" yelled his mother.

"Yes, be careful of your fingers. You can break your head, neck, and every bone in your body, but if you hurt your fingers, you cannot play violin," said his sister, Mary. Then she turned to her mother and asked, "Why don't you insure his fingers?"

Flore was now running toward the door, saying, "Kiki, don't forget your lunch." She handed Richard a neatly folded sandwich bag. Richard left.

Hearing the name Kiki, Cathy gave an ambiguous look to her husband. Phil shrugged.

After Richard left, Cathy told her husband, "I'm very worried about him. What if there's something wrong with him, and he needs help?"

"Nothing is wrong with him. He just has a good imagination. He'll grow out of it," replied Phil.

"He's a teenager, and he still has the same dream he's had since he was a little boy. I think we should take him to a shrink."

"He doesn't need any shrink. I won't let some shrink give him all kinds of drugs and ruin his life. He is just a little sensitive and passionate, that's all," responded Phil.

"I agree with Phil," said Flore. "Richard is a very good boy, and he does not need a shrink."

"You are just saying that because he dreams about some Mexicans," Cathy said. Everybody laughed. Phil gets ready to leave for work.

Richard and Mike chatted while walking toward the school. Mike was a little big for his age and did not like studying that much, but he was very good at sports. Richard was very good at his studies and was also a talented violin player. While Richard and Mike didn't have much in common other than being on the same path to school, they had become close friends. After finishing his toast, Richard took out the sandwich and gave half to Mike as was their routine, and they kept eating while chatting. Richard talked about his dream with Mike as usual.

"I want to see how the dream ends. I want to hear what he whispers to the little girl."

"First of all, you say that the police officer was shot many times, so obviously he dies. That's the end of it. Besides, even if you hear what they say, you still won't understand because they speak in Spanish. Maybe you should learn Spanish, so when you hear what they say, you will understand," said Mike while giggling and ducking a couple of steps to the side so Richard wouldn't strike him.

While passing by a poster of a football player on a billboard, Mike said that one day it would be his picture on that poster and asked Richard if he, too, wanted to be a professional football player.

"I don't know," said Richard. "My dad says that all kids our age want to become football players, but only one in a million succeeds, like a lottery. He wants me to become a lawyer like him, but my mom says that I am a talented violin player and should pursue music."

"But what do you want to become?" asked Mike.

"I don't know. I like violin, but I don't know if I like it *that much*. I also would like to become a lawyer, but my father is a lawyer, and I don't think he makes that much money."

"But lawyers usually make good money," said Mike.

"I am not sure what I want to become. I feel there's something I have to do. I don't know what it is, but I feel it is related to the dream I keep having. I don't know; maybe there really is something wrong with me. Sometimes, I hear my parents talk about taking me to a shrink. Only Flore defends me and tells my parents that it is normal to have these kinds of dreams."

"I am more comfortable with her than with my mom. Flore seems to understand me," said Richard.

In the afternoon, during violin practice, Yelena, the violin teacher, informed Richard and Cathy that she had arranged a violin recital in three months on a Saturday afternoon.

"I am going to invite several teachers and staff from the music conservatory. Everyone who graduates from the conservatory becomes somebody in music," said Yelena in a heavy Russian accent. "If you perform well, they will remember you when you apply to the school."

CHAPTER TWO

It was a day off school, and Mary was going to a friend's house. Cathy suggested that Richard should go to his dad's office. Phil replied that it was a good idea; Richard could do his homework while he met clients, and then they could have lunch together in the park.

They went to Phil's office. Voski, Phil's secretary, was already in the office. While Phil was meeting with clients, Voski brought some homemade cookies for Richard from the office kitchen, and Richard started doing his homework. A client came out of Phil's office and thanked him for a job well done at a very fair fee. While he was waiting for Voski to prepare his bill, another client went to meet with Phil. After a couple of minutes, Voski printed the client's statement and called the client to the counter. The client was very grateful. He mentioned to Voski that he was delighted that Phil was his lawyer and that Phil charged less than any other lawyer. Then he paid the bill and left. Voski started talking with Richard and explained that she liked working for Phil because Phil was a very kind person and helped everyone, and she was happy to be a part of it.

"At the end of the day, I feel like I have accomplished something and not just exchanged my time for money. Your dad is a small city guy in a large city. Not too many people can keep their integrity when they are given the opportunity to make money by cheating people."

After meeting several clients, Phil and Richard got a couple of sandwiches and went to the park. They talked about different things, including Richard's school and the subjects Richard was studying. Phil talked about a park in the town where he grew up and said that this park resembled it. He remembered playing in that park with his childhood friends or going for a run through it. He mentioned that one of the reasons he opened an office in this location was because it was close to the park.

"Why did you move to Los Angeles?" Richard asked.

"To go to law school. And then I decided to stay in Los Angeles after meeting your mom and falling in love with her,"

"So, why are you sometimes fighting with each other?" asked Richard.

"We are still two different people, and we have our disagreements. Most of our fights are about your Uncle Bill," replied Phil. "Your mom loves your uncle."

"And you hate him," jumped in Richard.

"No, I don't hate him. I just don't respect him. His God is money and power. He will do anything for money. He has sold his soul for money; he is involved in all kinds of criminal activities and has built his fortune from crime money."

"Why don't you tell Mom these things?" asked Richard.

"First, I don't want to disappoint your mom. And second, I don't want her to throw me out of the house," replied Phil. "Your Uncle Bill covers his tracks very well. All his businesses appear to be legitimate. He does his criminal activities through corporations that are registered under other individuals."

"While waiting for you, I heard a couple of clients telling Voski that you are charging less than others. Why don't you charge a little more for your services, so Mom will be happier and will not compare you to Uncle Bill all the time?"

"I am charging fairly, and I do not want to charge more just because I can. And no matter how much I make, it will not be enough for your mom as it will never be as much as your Uncle Bill makes. We have a comfortable lifestyle, even if your mom doesn't think so, and I am against unnecessary luxuries," Phil explained.

Then, Phil told Richard that sometimes when he was stressed, he would go to that park and walk through the pathways to spend some time in nature and calm down.

CHAPTER THREE

Every Christmas, Bill Acrebond, Richard's uncle, threw two parties in his mansion: one for family and friends, and another, in a different time for politicians, business associates, and the top executives in his corporations. There was a banquet size hall in his mansion for these parties. In addition to regular staff, he brought staff from his hotels, restaurants, and sometimes his farm to help with food preparation and serving guests. Phil, Cathy, Mary, and Richard were invited to the party for family and friends and. Phil reluctantly attended.

When they arrived, they were greeted by valet parking attendants, and their car was moved by one of the valets. Inside, they were seated by a young man in a suit and bow tie, who was very articulate and polite but also very serious. He smiled at Mary. He locked eyes with Richard for a second, but soon he realized that another server was having trouble carrying a heavy tray and ran to help her.

He picked up the tray from her hands and very politely told her, "You should not take so many plates and glasses on one tray."

"Did you see that the waiter was staring at me?" Richard asked Mary.

"No, I didn't see," answered Mary. "But I think he is in love."

Cathy listened to the conversation and said, "His name is Gabriel, and he doesn't like to be called Gabby. He is one of the best employees Bill ever had. The girl is Gloria. They have been working for Bill for several years now. Gabriel's parents died when he was small. Bill brought him here and raised him like a son. Gloria's parents asked Bill to give her a job on his farm. Sometimes, she helps in the house during receptions."

"He looks a couple of years older than Richard," said Phil. "Is he going to school?"

"Don't start again," replied Cathy.

George, Bill's son, who was almost the same age as Richard, approached Richard and asked him to join him and his friends in the game room. There were video games, pool tables, and all kinds of other games in the room. George introduced Richard to some of his friends. At this time, he realized that the pool table had become free and asked Richard if he wanted to play, and they started playing. A couple of younger kids, Robert and Danny, the children of Terza, who was Cathy's assistant in the restaurant where she worked, came close to the pool table.

"Can we play, too?" Robert asked.

George replied, "Yes, right after we finish."

They stood close by, waiting for their turn. Robert was almost the same age as Richard and George, but Danny was much younger. The game became heated as Richard and George turned out to be equal forces. A crowd gathered around, and people started cheering—some for

George and some for Richard. As a result, pool became the most popular game of the day.

Richard won, and the crowd cheered for him. James, the police chief's son, and his friend took the pool cues and set the balls to play. Robert protested and reminded James that it was their turn.

James laughed and said, "Get lost."

"Sorry, James, but Robert is right. It's their turn," said Richard.

James laughed even more, thinking that Richard was being sarcastic and making fun of the brothers, so James began making fun of them, too.

But Robert stood his ground. "We were here before you guys, and it's our turn."

James swore at Robert and pushed him to the ground. George stepped in and defended Robert and Danny by asking James to step aside and wait for his turn.

"I can't believe it," said James. "You're taking their side? They are nobodies, just pieces of shit."

Richard interfered and said, "They are my friends."

The truth was that he barely knew them. He only knew that their mother was his mother's assistant in the restaurant.

"It doesn't matter who you are. I don't like bullying. They are our guests, and you will treat them with respect," George said.

"You're crazy, George," said James as he kept setting the table.

George put his hand on the pool balls and said, "James, step aside and wait your turn."

The chief's son was now really pissed off. He would lose face if he backed down. He pushed George aside, but George pushed him back.

One of the maids informed a couple of the guards about the commotion. By the time the guards came down, a big fight had already started between James and his friend on one side and George and Richard on the other. Many people, including Bill, Phil, Chief of Police Scott Timmins, Cathy, Terza, Renzo, were in the game room.

James yelled, "This piece of shit started it!"

Robert replied, "No, he started it. It was our turn, but he bugged in."

Robert's father, Renzo, quickly realized that they were dealing with the chief of police. He told his son, "You should have been nicer and allowed them to play first and waited for your turn."

Before his son replied, George said, "Robert is right. It was his turn, but James bugged in and bullied him. I can't stand bullying. Everyone needs to be fair and kind."

Renzo was looking at George with fascination and adoration. He could not believe the son of the cruelest individual in the world could be so kind and fair.

James picked up one of the cues, threw it on the ground, and left the room with his friend. "Let's go. This is crazy," he said.

Renzo apologized to the chief and Bill for his son's behavior and congratulated Bill for raising such a fine young man. Then he left the room with his sons.

The chief pulled Bill to a corner and asked, "How did this happen? How is George going to carry on your legacy and replace you with his stupid ideologies? You raised a softy; he is going to ruin everything you worked so hard for!"

"I assure you that when the time comes, he will become more logical and practical. He was raised by some Mexican nannies who put some stupid religious and ideological ideas in his head. Very soon, he will realize that the real world is different from childhood fantasies. He will realize that we are all working for a noble cause that is above all ideologies. Especially when he reaps the benefits coming from the organization, he will forget about his stupid ideologies. Spirituality, humanitarian ideologies and religion are common diseases of the poor. These are their weaknesses and the reasons they stay poor. I know how to cure my son of this disease. Besides, it does not matter who is at the top. There are professionals, strategists, and planners at work in our organization who draw the grand design of things to come and provide us with precise directions and activities to achieve higher goals. If George does not wise up when he is older, someone else will replace him. We have to carry on with our goals. We will become the strongest organization of all and maintain our status at the top," continued Bill. "We all have to sacrifice when we are dealing with a greater cause. Our cause is above everything and everyone."

Bill and the police chief went upstairs and were joined by their trophy wives.

"I want to start a charity. I'm looking for a cause for the charity that people will donate the most to. What is your opinion, Bill?" said the chief's wife.

"Who is going to run the charity?" asked Bill.

"I am, of course," replied the chief's wife.

"No, you can't," replied Bill. "There are several requirements to become the head of a charity. To run a charity, you have to look like a saint, talk like a saint and act like a saint and be the devil you are. You have all these qualities. One thing that you don't have is connections, and that is the most important thing. The reason my charities do well—they are like money printing machines—is because I have many connections in different developing countries, starting from the villages' elders to the mayors, ministers, and others. Every time they build roads, water purification systems, schools, churches, or any other construction, I give them a small amount, and they provide me with a certificate that says my charity built all those things. They also provide me with photos and videos. If it is a big project, I go there for a couple of hours and take photos with local people. When I publish and distribute all those photos and videos, people close their eyes and open their wallets. Why don't you work for me? With your misleading, kind face, and as the chief's wife, you can bring in millions every year. I will give you an excellent commission. This way, you don't have to go through all kinds of trouble starting a business and failing. You can work leisurely and still make very good money."

Bill saw a couple of people entering the room, excused himself, and walked toward them.

The chief became angry with his wife for bringing up the charity with Bill. "What did you expect him to say? Did you expect him to encourage you? Help you to establish your charity and become his competition?"

"I will not listen to him. I will do what I want," replied his wife.

"Not anymore. Now that you brought up the subject and Bill objected to it, if you do it, he will consider it to be war against him. Believe me, you don't want to fight him," replied the chief.

"Then maybe I will accept his offer, collect donations for his organizations and get my commission," replied his wife.

"Under the circumstances, I think that's a good idea," replied the chief.

CHAPTER FOUR

The days passed, and Richard kept practicing his violin. Every time he played sad music, he remembered the little girl in his dream with the dying police officer, and this memory made the sad notes even sadder. His parents liked what they heard, and his teacher Yelena was very hopeful that a star was about to be born. Everything appeared to be going in the right direction. There was the promise of a bright future for Richard as a musician, a violin player, perhaps even a songwriter, too, but Richard was getting more anxious as it came closer to the day of the recital. He was still not sure what he wanted to become in life, and he was afraid that there would be no going back after the recital.

On a Friday evening after his violin practice, a couple of weeks before his recital, Richard felt tired and anxious. He texted Mike that he was on his way to see him. Richard arrived at Mike's apartment and rang the bell. As he walked through the entrance doors, Gabe and Sally, the building superintendents, started asking him questions: what is your name, who are your parents, who are you going to meet in this building, and do you know anyone else besides Mike in this building? Finally, after asking many questions, they realized that he was Bill's nephew.

Sally said, "You are okay, you can come here anytime. This is one of Bill's buildings, and both the building and the neighborhood are very safe. That is why we are asking all these questions. Is your mom still the manager of Razzmatazz restaurant on Broadway, in Glendale? You have a nice uncle, giving your mom a good job, do you know that?"

They were talking about Bill like they were partners or equals. This continued for a couple of minutes until Mike came down, and then they left.

"My mother calls them the 'Duo gossipers.' She told me not to talk to them and respond to any questions they ask by telling them, 'I don't know.' She also said I should be nice to them as they are looking for trouble," Mike explained.

Richard talked about his anxieties and worries as they went to the mall together. He explained that he was not sure he wanted to become a professional violinist or play violin as a hobby. He was worried that after the recital, there would be no going back. He felt there were more important things in life than playing violin.

"Don't get me wrong, I like playing the violin, but I am not sure that is all I want to do."

At the mall, they watched a movie and then returned home. On the way back, they saw people lining up for a busy sandwich shop. They checked their pockets but didn't have enough money to buy a sandwich. Richard suggested they could go there another time on their lunch break.

*   *   *

As soon as the lunch bell rang on Monday, Richard and Mike whisked out of the school and started walking toward the new place they had discovered. As they were passing by another school, they saw several students gathered together. As they got closer, they realized that a couple of the students were trying to get something from another student while they kept hitting him and swearing at him. The victim was about their age. The students were asking him to open his hand and give them the money. The victim was groaning with pain but resisting.

"What is going on?" Mike asked.

"None of your business, get lost," one of the thugs answered.

"Why are you hitting him?"

"Didn't you hear me? Get lost," the thug answered.

"He stole our money, and we want it back," said the other one.

Several other students were looking on while laughing and giggling as if they were watching a show. They were not intervening to stop the quarrel, but they were not leaving, either.

Mike grabbed the victim's hand and said to the thug holding him, "Let go!"

A fight broke out, and they started hitting each other while the victim walked away. The two thugs realized that they could not win the fight, so one of them drew a knife and threatened Mike. Richard kicked him, and he stepped back. Now angrier, he attacked Richard with full force.

In the confusion, the knife landed right in the middle of Richard's right hand. The thugs ran off, and the audience spread as blood gushed from Richard's hand.

Mike called 911 and took off his shirt to tightly cover Richard's hand. The police and ambulance came as the students started gathering again, and some teachers rushed to find out what was happening.

The paramedics tried to stop the blood while the police questioned Mike. They asked what the assailants looked like, who else saw the incident, and many other questions. Mike told them there were many other students besides the two assailants, and he started looking in the crowd, trying to find them. A man came forward and introduced himself as the school principal.

"What is going on?" he asked the police.

Mike recognized him as one of the passersby who changed his direction and crossed the road to avoid the commotion.

"You should know who they are as you must have seen them while walking by," Mike said to the principal.

"I did not realize they were fighting, and I did not see anything," the principal responded.

Suddenly, Mike recognized several students, who had been cheering during the fight and pointed them out to the police.

They denied seeing the fight, except for one of the girls, who seemed to want to talk and said, "Well..."

But the principal rolled his eyes and signaled for her to shut up.

Then she continued and said, "Well, I just came by, and I didn't see anything."

But as soon as Mike described the victim, the principal said, "I know the guy. He's one of our students. A real troublemaker. I'm going to expel him."

Mike explained, "The other guys were trying to rob him, and he was resisting them."

"There is always something with this guy. He always ends up in trouble," said the principal.

Mike described the assailants.

The principal said, "I don't recognize them. I think they are from a different school."

The principal, having answered all the questions, stepped back into the crowd and signaled to the girl who wanted to talk to the police to follow him.

They stepped away, and before the principal spoke, the girl said, "Dad, you know who they are. It was Ramsey and Mika. Why didn't you tell the police or let me tell them?"

"Are you crazy?" replied the principal. "I have less than ten years to retire. I don't want any headaches. I don't want to get shot or see you get shot. These thugs have strong connections; you think the police don't already know who they are? They realized you wanted to talk but were happy that you shut up. Don't put yourself or me in trouble."

The girl became upset. "There were many other students present. If everyone would talk, the thugs could not do anything."

"You can dream that everyone is united against the thugs, but while you are awake, keep your mouth shut because things work differently in the real world," said the principal.

The ambulance took Richard to the hospital. Mike called Richard's home. Flore picked up the phone with an ominous feeling, as though she was expecting bad news.

As soon as Mike told her about Richard's accident, Flore became very worried and said, "My Kiki! Is he okay!? What happened to him?"

Mike explained that it was only his hand. Flore thanked Mike and called Cathy while getting ready to go to the hospital. While Richard went to the hospital with the ambulance, the police took Mike to the hospital in their cruiser for more questioning. On the way to the hospital, Richard called his mother. Cathy told Richard that Flore had told her already, and she was on her way. Cathy first called her brother, Bill, to brief him regarding the accident and ask him to go to the hospital. Then she called Phil and gave him the news and told him that she had already informed Bill and he was on his way to the hospital too. Before Phil said anything, Cathy explained that Bill had good connections, and with him present, they wouldn't have to wait long in emergency.

When they reached the hospital, a nurse was examining Richard while waiting for the doctor. A couple of minutes later, the chief surgeon introduced himself, saying that Bill had called and had asked him to examine Richard. He explained that Bill was a friend and a benefactor of the hospital, and so he was going to take good care of Richard. While the chief surgeon was examining Richard, Bill arrived with two people—either assistants or bodyguards. Bill and the chief surgeon shook hands and talked to each other like old pals. After completing his examination, the surgeon turned to Bill and said, "It is not a serious injury. I will stitch him up soon, and in about a month, he will be as good as new. I want to assure you, Bill, that this is nothing serious, and Richard should gain full function of his hand soon."

"Richard is a violinist. Can he continue to play violin?" Cathy asked?

The surgeon became grim, thought for a moment, and replied, "I hope so, but I am not sure. He may lose some very fine functions of the hand, but other than that, he will be as good as before."

One of the officers quietly motioned to one of the individuals who came with Bill to step aside and explained that the two guys who did this were Ramsey and Mika. The guy approached Bill and whispered in his ear. Phil noticed these secretive conversations.

Mike was sitting in the emergency section with his mother, who came to the hospital after Mike called her. When the surgeon told Richard's mom that he might not play violin as well as before, Cathy started blaming Mike and asked him why they went to that part of the city. Richard explained that it was his idea and not Mike's fault. One police constable said to Cathy, Phil, and everyone present that Richard and Mike were lucky to be alive.

"They could just as easily be dead. I am surprised the thugs left without inflicting more serious harm."

Bill pretended that he didn't know the officer, but he nodded to him as a sign for a job well done. The police asked Richard and Mike to go to the police station the next day to look through mug shots to see if they could recognize their assailants. Flore raised the concern that the thugs may come after Richard and Mike. Cathy and Phil realized that she had a point and were worried. Bill assured them that he would make sure they were not in trouble and explained that he was confident the police would not let any harm come to either of them.

The medical staff took Richard for surgery. After a while, the surgeon came out and informed them the surgery was a success, and as he had said earlier, he expected a full recovery.

*   *   *

The next day, Pedro, one of Antonio Donatelli's employees, who was working for Bill as a consultant, was sitting in a coffee shop with Ramsey and Mika. He explained that one of the guys in yesterday's stabbing was his boss's nephew and warned them that they were off-limits.

CHAPTER FIVE

Richard was not in any rush to get out of the house the following morning. In fact, he was sitting at the table and eating his breakfast. He was very quiet and sad. Flore, while making breakfast for everyone, pouring coffee, and cleaning, kept making the sign of the cross and thanking God for being with Richard and keeping him safe.

Cathy became angry and said, "What are you thanking God for? Can't you see that my baby's dreams are shattered? He may not be able to play violin again. He could have been a great musician!"

"I am thanking God for saving Kiki from a bigger disaster."

"Why are you always calling him Kiki, and what bigger disaster could there be than this?"

"She means that this is a blessing in disguise," said Phil calmly.

"Yes, a blessing in 'discuss,'" said Flore.

"Oh, don't tell me you believe in this shit, too," said Cathy to Phil.

Phil kept reading the newspaper without paying any attention to what Cathy was saying.

"I told you to insure his fingers. Had you listened to me, we would have been millionaires by now. If a celebrity could insure her ass, why couldn't Richard insure his fingers?" said Mary as she laughed.

Even Richard couldn't help but smile at Mary's comments.

When Richard left home for school, he saw Mike sitting under a tree a couple of houses away, waiting for him. He appeared to have been waiting for a while. As Richard approached, Mike stood and started walking alongside Richard.

"Why didn't you come to the door and ring the bell?" Richard asked Mike.

"I wasn't sure if you were going to school or staying home to get some rest."

"I don't know what I am going to do with my life now that I cannot play violin," said Richard. "It's what I've done all my life."

"But you said earlier that you weren't sure if you wanted to become a professional musician," said Mike.

"Yes, I did say that, but now that it appears my wish is coming true, I am not sure if this is what I wanted, either."

When they arrived at the school, several of their friends gathered around to ask about the fight and to make both Richard and Mike cheer up and feel better for surviving a dangerous fight.

After a couple of weeks, the cast and stitches came off, and Richard slowly began to move his hand by exercising with light weights and handgrips. Yelena resumed her visits. While she expected Richard to underperform due to his accident, she was still hopeful that with each visit,

Richard would play better and eventually fully recover. She even tried to teach him some new techniques. However, deep inside, she was also very worried that Richard may not recover completely.

But after three months, the doctor examined Richard's hand and happily declared a full recovery. Richard explained that while playing the violin, he sometimes had difficulty playing specific tunes. The doctor shrugged off Richard's concerns as temporary and the result of not exercising for a long time while recovering from the accident.

Several months passed, and Richard still couldn't play as well as before. Yelena lost hope that Richard could ever fully recover. Richard was also aware of his shortcomings but kept trying.

One afternoon during practice, Yelena became frustrated. Richard was playing a piece he used to play perfectly. Yelena stopped the practice and called for Cathy.

"Richard can become a very good violin player, but he will never be a star," Yelena explained.

Richard threw the violin and bow on the ground and left the room.

"Be respectful to your instrument!" Yelena yelled after Richard.

Cathy yelled for Richard to return to the room and asked Yelena to calm down.

"It may take more time for Richard to recover fully. You should both keep practicing," Cathy said.

Richard declared, "I will never play violin again!"

"I teach violin only to those who have the potential of becoming a star. You should hire another teacher," said Yelena.

Richard rushed out of the house and started running aimlessly. After a while, he slowed down and found himself in the schoolyard, where Mike was playing football with some friends. Seeing Richard, Mike ran toward him.

"I can't play violin anymore," said Richard.

"What are you talking about? I've seen you play after the accident," said Mike.

"But I will never become a professional violinist," said Richard. "I have practiced all my life, and now it's all over."

"When something like this happens, my mom says it's God's will or a blessing in disguise," said Mike, and then he asked Richard to join them and play some football.

Richard had more time on his hands now that he was not practicing violin. He hung out more in the schoolyard with his friends and with classmates after school instead of rushing home to practice violin. Sometimes, his friends were short one person for playing football, and they would ask Richard to fill in.

Richard played very rough and pushed himself to the limit. He had found a venue to redirect his anger and frustration and became defiant and insensitive toward everything and everyone, ready to start a fight in the blink of an eye.

One day, the football coach saw him playing and liked what he saw. He asked Richard his name and told him to come to his office on Monday during lunch break. The coach lectured Richard about football.

"You have a talent for playing football, but to become a good player, you will need discipline, dedication, and the willingness to work very hard. Are you up to it?"

"Now that I am not practicing violin all the time, I can concentrate one hundred percent on football," replied Richard.

"That's what I needed to hear from you," said the coach. "You are on the team. Go get your gear."

That afternoon, Richard walked home with Mike and told him about his conversation with the coach.

"I told him exactly what he wanted to hear, and I am on the team," said Richard. "The truth is I am not sure if I like it that much, but it is better than nothing. I can't go on doing nothing."

"If you are not sure you like it or not, why don't you do something that you like?" asked Mike.

"Well, I don't know what I want, so this should do."

Richard became a football player from that day on. He talked and dreamed football, and he was constantly exercising and practicing.

One Sunday morning, Richard went down to the kitchen to eat breakfast. Everyone was present in the kitchen. Flore served Richard his favorite breakfast—hot cereal with nuts.

"Why are you serving me cereal?" Richard asked Flore.

Flore, very surprised, told him, "This is your favorite breakfast."

"I don't eat this anymore. My coach told me to cut carbohydrates and eat more protein. Give me a couple of eggs," said Richard, starting to prepare protein mix.

While cracking and preparing the eggs, Flore asked Richard, "Do you still see that police officer in your dream?"

"I am not a child anymore. I have not seen that dream in ages," said Richard.

"But did you finally find out the name of the police officer?" asked Flore.

"No, I did not," said Richard. "And I don't care."

Cathy angrily looked at Flore and signaled with her hand not to talk about it.

As usual, Richard ate his breakfast and quickly left the house.

"I told you that he did not need a shrink," Phil told Cathy.

"Why did you bring up the dream? I was happy he stopped having it," Cathy asked Flore. "Why did you remind him?

"There was a police chief in our village named Kiki. He captured an American drug trafficker, who bribed the judges and the police and was charged with a much lesser crime. He was given a couple of years in jail but got out in eight months. Everyone in our village knew he killed Kiki. He came to our village, bribed the police officers working for Kiki, and killed Kiki and his family. They found the bodies of Kiki, his wife, and his nine-year-old son, but not his two-year-old daughter," said Flore.

"Don't tell this to Richard. I don't want you to confuse him any more than he already is. I'm glad that he stopped seeing that dream," said Cathy. "Probably you told him the story when he was small, and that is why he started seeing those dreams."

"I agree with Cathy," said Phil. "Don't mention it to him."

"What is the name of your village, and how long ago did this happen?" asked Mary, who wanted to become an investigative journalist and was already acting like one while still being in grade ten.

"It is called Juarez, and I was nine years old when this happened, so eighteen years ago," said Flore. "Like all the little girls in the village, I was in love with him. He was such a nice man and so handsome, everyone in the village cried when he was killed," continued Flore.

Mary immediately opened her device and started typing and clicking, and in a couple of minutes, she said, "I found him. His name was Enrique Coto, known as Kiki Coto. He was the chief of police in Juarez, but his killer has never been found."

Cathy excitedly exclaimed, "Now I am sure that is what happened! You told this horrible story to Richard when he was a baby, and that's why he was having nightmares for so many years! Thank God he is over it."

"No, Cathy, I never told this story to anyone. Richard did not hear it from me," said Flore. "I don't even know the details of his murder."

"Please don't remind him anymore," said Cathy.

*   *   *

Richard received admittance to several universities with scholarships for playing football. He chose the closest Ivy League university. In deciding what to study, Phil tried to convince him to choose a more practical field of study. He explained to Richard that in case he did not get drafted into the NFL, he should have an alternative to lean on and be able to make a living.

Richard chose criminology, thinking that it was an easy subject to study, and jokingly said that if he didn't get drafted, he would apply to the police academy. Phil didn't object to criminology and was even somewhat happy with Richard's choice.

CHAPTER SIX

Renzo was having dinner with his wife Terza, and his two sons, Robert and Danny, when the phone rang. Renzo took out a phone from his pocket but realized that it was another phone ringing. He took out another phone, but still, it was not the phone that was ringing. Finally, the third phone was the correct one.

He said hello and listened for a couple of seconds, and then asked, "Do you know what it is about? Okay." He hung up the phone looking a little worried.

"Who was it?" Terza asked.

"Why do you have so many phones, Dad?" Danny asked.

"Tony wants to have a meeting with me tomorrow morning."

"Which Tony?" asked Terza.

"Antonio Donatelli," replied Renzo.

"Was it Antonio himself?" Terza was surprised as he was a big boss in the organization.

"No, it was one of his neophytes, Jack," said Renzo.

"What is the meeting about?"

"Dad, why do you have so many phones?" Danny repeated.

"He didn't say why he wants to see me. As for your question Danny, one phone is for family and friends; the other two are for business," Renzo explained.

"They're burner phones," said Robert.

Renzo looked at Robert, a little surprised and angry, but did not say anything. They continued with their dinner, but the phone call had killed the mood. After dinner, when Renzo and Terza were alone in the kitchen, Terza told Renzo that she was worried about the meeting.

"If they ask you to do anything besides what you are doing now, don't accept," she said.

"First, I have to see what it is. And don't forget that I can't say no to Bill."

Robert was in his room, searching the name Antonio Donatelli on his device. There was no mention of his name on any website. He clicked on Acrebond Group, and Bill's photo came up with the description of the businesses under Acrebond Group, including construction, hotels, restaurants, food processing plants, charitable organizations, and other businesses. He entered Antonio Donatelli's name into Acrebond's website. While there were many executives, managers, and assistant managers, there was no mention of him.

The next morning, Renzo put on his best suit and went downstairs to the kitchen to have a coffee. Hearing his footsteps, Robert went down, too.

He poured some cereal, and while he started eating, he casually asked his dad, "Are you sure this guy, Antonio Donatelli, works for Bill? There is no mention of him on Acrebond's group website or any website for that matter. It's like he doesn't exist."

Renzo was taken aback by Robert's comments. He looked at Robert for a moment, then composed himself and said angrily, "You have no business poking your nose in things that do not concern you. Your only job is to study and get a good education."

"But you're meeting someone who doesn't exist," said Robert.

"Did you see my name in Acrebond Group?" Renzo asked. "Two nonexistent employees of Acrebond Group are going to have a meeting. He exists all right; he is Bill's assistant. I see him in our meetings a couple of times a year. But if you could not find him, it means he was successful in his intention of not wanting to be found."

Renzo headed out while he still had some time to kill, just to end the interrogation from his son. The meeting was in one of the larger Razzmatazz restaurants that had a full basement with different offices. Renzo entered the restaurant. The attendant greeted him and told him that they were waiting for him in the manager's office. He went downstairs and entered the room where there were two people: the individual who called him last night and one of Antonio's assistants.

"Where is Antonio?" inquired Renzo.

"He was busy, so he sent me instead," replied Jack.

Renzo was a little disappointed that Antonio could not come, but he immediately relaxed as he thought the issue might not be as serious as he thought. They sat down, and Jack introduced Pedro as his assistant and asked Renzo if he wanted a drink. Renzo replied that he had just had a coffee and the water on the table was good enough. Jack asked Renzo about his family.

"How are the boys? Robert and Danny, am I right? How is your wife? Is she happy with her job at Razzmatazz on Broadway?"

Renzo became uncomfortable. He realized that Jack was acting like his boss or superior, reminding him that he had a lot to lose, so he'd better do as he was told. He thought that Antonio was his boss. Now Antonio did not attend the meeting, and this jackass was acting like his boss.

"They are all okay. Let's get to business, shall we?" said Renzo in a disappointed tone.

"Of course," replied Jack. "You remember Alex, the head of our operations in Chicago? He's in the hospital, and we need you to go there and look after things until he's out."

"Yes, I know Alex, but we don't have operations in Chicago."

"Alex went to set things up there, but he got shot last week by already established businesses there."

"There are so many more qualified people besides me. I am a surveillance engineer. I don't set up branches. Why did Tony choose me?" asked Renzo.

"Everyone else is busy. Besides, it is only for a couple of weeks," replied Jack.

"I have paid my dues to Antonio and Bill by taking risky assignments before. Now I have a family with two young boys. Who is going to look after them if something happens to me?" asked Renzo.

"Nothing is going to happen to you. What happened to Alex was an accident because he was not careful. You have done these things before, you have experience, and you will be okay. Besides, you know that Bill always takes care of his own people, no matter where they are."

"I just set up surveillance equipment. I got shot for Bill. I went to prison for Bill, I paid my dues, and I deserve to have a family and be on the safe side," said Renzo.

"Here is your ticket. You fly to Chicago in two days, on Saturday morning. Sam will meet you at the airport, fill you in, and provide you with all the necessities. But remember, do not tell anyone where you are going or what your assignment is."

Renzo picked up the ticket and left. Jack called Antonio and briefed him about the meeting. He explained that Renzo was not happy, but he had agreed to go.

"We will find our mole soon," Jack said.

*   *   *

Renzo returned home and explained the situation to his wife.

"I think they have a mole in Chicago and are sending me there as bait to catch the mole."

"Just tell them you can't go, and if they insist, you should quit. We don't need them anymore. I can find a job in any restaurant I want, and you are an engineer, and there are so many things you can do," said Terza.

"You know that's not possible. Bill kills people for fun. He is looking for an excuse to order a hit. I tried my best not to go, but I have to."

"This is all my fault," said Terza. "You were out of work for only a couple of weeks when I casually told Cathy that my husband needed a job. She told me that you should go and see her brother. She didn't even ask what it was that you were doing. I should have suspected and not told you to go and see Bill."

"This is all in the past, Terza. We can't do anything except try and keep our kids safe from Bill," said Renzo.

"That horrible Acabar," replied Terza, using Bill Acrebond's criminal nickname.

During dinner that evening, Renzo told Robert and Danny about his trip. He praised his boys for being good students and having high averages and asked them to continue the good work and avoid trouble. Renzo asked his children never to use drugs, not even once. He explained that by using drugs, people damage their brains and abandon their true life's purpose and waste their lives.

In Chicago, Sam was waiting outside the airport. On the way to the hotel, he provided Renzo with a couple of handguns and told him that on Sunday morning, they would have a meeting so Renzo would get to know everyone. When they arrived at the hotel, Sam handed the car keys to Renzo and told him that he had another ride and would see him the following morning. Meanwhile, Robert was worried for his father and was checking the local news in Chicago every day.

A week later, Jack knocked on Renzo's door. Terza opened it, and as soon as she saw Jack, she started crying and asking about Renzo.

"Renzo is okay. There was an altercation with police, and he is now in police custody, but everything will be okay," Jack reassured her.

Terza started swearing at Antonio and Bill while crying. "Renzo did not want to go, but you forced him!

He knew something bad was going to happen. He paid his dues, and you should not have used him as bait!"

Jack was surprised that Terza knew about using Renzo as bait.

"Renzo was not being used as bait. Who told you that?"

"Renzo guessed," Terza replied.

"It's not true. I understand your frustration, but please control yourself. I did not hear all this swearing because it will be very bad if Bill finds out," Jack said.

"What is worse than this? Renzo did not want to go. You forced him to go, and now he is in police custody."

"You have two sons. You should think about their safety and take care of them. And as for Renzo, the whole organization is behind him and will help him come home as soon as possible. We will get the best team of lawyers to defend him."

Renzo called home whenever he could and talked to his wife and two sons. Every time he spoke with his sons, he asked them to stay away from trouble.

A couple of months later, Jack reported to Antonio that Renzo would probably get a six-year sentence and asked Antonio who would replace Renzo.

"I thought we had the best lawyers in Chicago. What happened?" asked Antonio.

"Our competitors owned the judge; that's what happened," replied Jack.

"I see, then give his job to a couple of his assistants."

"His assistants can do the IT part of his job, but he has a couple of warehouses leased in his name and was doing occasional deliveries," replied Jack.

"He has an older son, doesn't he?" asked Antonio.

"Yeah, he just turned eighteen," replied Jack.

"Then change the leases to his son's name and give him some delivery and safekeeping jobs. We are going to pay him while in prison anyway," replied Antonio.

"We caught and neutralized our mole thanks to Renzo, and now we are a go for our Chicago operations," said Jack. "Shouldn't we get someone else for warehouse leases and occasional deliveries?"

"Renzo always objected to the idea of introducing his sons to the business. He should have known that this is a family business, and his sons were born into this family. He shouldn't try to keep them out. We need more soldiers all the time. A couple of leases in his son's name and occasional deliveries won't harm anyone. You know that Bill always insists the children of employees should join their parents in the family. This way, he will be introduced to the business slowly," replied Antonio.

As a courtesy, Jack flew to Chicago to personally break the news to Renzo about Robert's involvement in the business. Jack assured him that they would take care of him and his family while he was in prison and try to transfer him back home from Chicago as soon as possible. Renzo was aware that he was going to serve time and was not happy about it.

"I knew this was a setup to catch a mole in the organization. I do not deserve this after so many years of loyal service," he told Jack.

"There is danger for everyone in the organization, and you are lucky that it was not worse than this. But even if it was worse, you should be happy and honored to sacrifice for the organization, an organization that will always stand behind you," Jack explained.

Then Jack broke the news about Antonio's decision to involve Robert in the operations.

Renzo became furious and shouted, "No way, you will not do such a thing! He's just a kid! He has his whole life ahead of him! You are not getting him involved and ruining his life, too!"

Jack calmed Renzo and asked him to sit down. "For the IT position, Antonio decided to put a couple of your assistants in charge, and it is only a couple of the leases that will be under Robert's name and occasional deliveries. You had the leases under your name for many years. Did anyone ask you anything about it? And you know that all deliveries are escorted discreetly by police cruisers," Jack said.

"I still don't like it. Leave my son out of it," replied Renzo.

"You talk like you are ashamed of your organization. Let me remind you that everything you have is because you are a member of the organization. Everything your wife and children have is because of the organization."

"I am a surveillance engineer. I could have found a job anywhere I wanted. I started working for Bill, thinking that it was a regular and legitimate IT job. When I realized that I was installing surveillance equipment to blackmail politicians, judges and others, I wanted to resign, but he threatened to expose me. If I can't quit my job, it means that I am working for a criminal organization. You are talking about the organization like it is a spiritual establishment," replied Renzo.

"It is much more than a spiritual establishment," said Jack. "We take care of each other, we keep everyone safe, and if anyone intends to harm one member, the whole organization is behind him. It cannot get more spiritual than that. Besides, you are paid much more in Acrebond compared to any other organization."

"What are you talking about? You kill people for money all the time. You get murderers free using dirty judges that are on Acrebond's payroll. You get people addicted to drugs all the time," Renzo said in disgust. "Is this spiritual to you?"

"But we only kill those who do not belong to our organization and those who intend to harm it or its members. You are either with us or against us. If you are against us, then we have the right to eliminate you."

"You are getting school children addicted all the time for money. You waste thousands of lives every year. You destroy thousands of families every year. Had I worked somewhere else, even if I had been paid less, at least my family and I would be free people and would not be forced to commit crime from the fear of my family getting harmed."

"People either belong to our organization and therefore belong to our family, or they are against us. There is no in-between. To become stronger, we have to expand, like what we are trying to do in Chicago. We have to forge ahead with full force. I am getting the feeling that you do not want to belong to the organization anymore," said Jack. "Just think about the wellbeing of your family seriously. There is no revolving door in Acrebond."

"Yes, I know, you harm family members to force people to do as you say. Once you get out, you are dead. That's the reason I stayed this long," replied Renzo.

"You are right. When you leave our organization, you become an expatriate. There is too much to lose from an expatriate. We cannot leave loose ends. You know that," stated Jack.

Renzo realized that he could not push too much. He started begging Jack not to get Robert involved.

"The decision has already been made. I promise I will personally look after Robert. There is nothing to worry about. Wouldn't you prefer the whole organization be behind Robert instead of him being alone and vulnerable to danger?"

Renzo realized that if he disagreed, Robert might be murdered. So he reluctantly accepted for Robert to have a couple of leases registered under his name and occasionally make some deliveries. He asked Jack not to get Robert involved in anything else.

"Well, the plan is to get Robert involved very slowly, so he can grow with the organization. Always with police escort, of course."

Renzo again jumped up and started yelling and screaming that he did not want Robert to be a part of the organization and explained that Robert had high marks and would attend university.

"I want to talk to Bill!" he demanded.

Jack replied, "It is a big mistake even to say Bill's name. Bill is not involved in any activity. His name is not on any corporation except his law firm, the real estate development, a couple of businesses, and charitable organizations. The extra time he gets, he spends on lobbying and strengthening his political connections. He is a busy man. You should never repeat his name or associate yourself with him. There is a chain of command, and I am your contact. Besides, if Robert wants to study, we won't stop him. He will get a position in the organization according to his education and expertise."

"When I started working in Acrebond, I was taking my orders from Bill directly. I know who Bill is. Don't talk to me like he is a prophet. I demand to talk to him!" said Renzo.

"My guess is that you weren't smart enough to advance in your career like Mr. Donatelli and be able to meet Bill whenever you wanted. Prophet or not, Bill is one of the fairest and kindest men I know. Everything I have is from him. He looks after his people, and I will do anything for him, but I can't even see Bill or say his name. Only Mr. Donatelli can meet him."

"Everything you have is from blood money. This organization was built on murder, drugs, and other crimes. Do you know how many people Bill has personally killed and still kills through so-called loyal employees like you? In his early days, he would even hold up tourists in Mexico with his gang. He would kill the men, rape the women and take their cars and other belongings. His brothels, the ones where his name is not on them, force young girls to have sex with politicians and judges while he is recording them in action to blackmail them. That's how he strengthens his political connections. How can you call a murderer and a rapist a prophet?"

"I think you have completely lost your mind. You are becoming too soft, too crazy and dangerous for your own good. Bill would never hurt anyone who is a member of his organization. On the contrary, he always looks after his own people. He is even looking after you and your family while you are in prison. What more do you expect? Maybe you purposely got yourself caught so you could sit on your lazy bum while the organization takes care of you," replied Jack.

"So, it is okay to kill and rape innocent people as long as they are not a member of the organization?"

"If it weren't for Bill, you would have been sentenced to life in prison. If that is what you want, it can still be arranged."

Renzo realized that he had put himself and his family in danger. He apologized to Jack and asked if he could at least talk to Tony.

"Mr. Donatelli is a busy man. But I will convey your request."

Jack called Tony that night and explained that Renzo wanted to talk to him. He explained that Renzo was not happy with the decisions regarding his son, and he was going crazy. He did not mention the details Renzo said about Bill and the Acrebond organization.

The next morning, Jack visited Renzo again and explained that Mr. Donatelli had agreed to talk to him but cautioned him not to name names, not even Mr. Donatelli's. Ten minutes later, Jack's phone rang—it was Tony. Jack said hello and passed the phone to Renzo. Renzo was calmer today. He had had time to reflect on yesterday's conversation, and he was a little worried about the things he had said.

"I understand your situation, but I promise that I will look after Robert, and in the case of deliveries, I will make sure that a friendly cop escorts him the whole time. I also promise to replace Robert as soon as I find someone else. Jack will be your contact from now on," Tony told Renzo.

Renzo became very sad but realized there was nothing much he could do and agreed with the proposed duties for Robert.

CHAPTER SEVEN

Renzo called his son. "Someone by the name of Jack is going to call you soon. You need to do as he says. You will have to sign a couple of leases and occasionally deliver some packages. There is nothing to worry about, Robert, but do not tell your mom about this. Promise me that you will stay away from trouble and keep up with your studies."

Robert became worried. He could not sleep or study. After a couple of days, he relaxed a little, thinking that no one would call. A week later, on his way home, his phone rang. He answered, and it was Jack. In addition to sounding young, Jack acted even younger, using a slang style of talking. He told Robert that his father had asked him to call, and they had to meet. Robert was relaxed. He treated Jack like one of the guys and asked him where and when they should meet.

"How about now, in the bar patio to your right?"

Robert looked around, surprised, and saw that a guy sitting on a patio was waving at him. Robert became alarmed as the guy looked a little older than he sounded, but still, he was not worried. After all, Jack was a young guy, and he couldn't be too much trouble. Robert cautiously got closer, trying very hard not to show any anxiety.

"Hi," Robert said.

"Hi," Jack said very politely. "Have a seat. Do you want a beer?"

Robert was a little hesitant as he tried to guess how much a beer would cost in that joint. "It is on the house," continued Jack.

"Sure, why not," Robert said. "Do you own the place?"

"No, I can't waste my time in this boondoggle, but I know the owner, and he has a running tab for me. It is a business expense, don't worry," replied Jack.

One of the servers approached to take their order.

"Magi, I want to introduce you to a friend of mine. This is Robert," said Jack.

Magi looked at Robert like he was a trapped jackal that soon would be skinned alive and asked Robert what he wanted.

"A beer," replied Jack.

Jack started making small talk with Robert. He was being very respectful and trying to appeal to Robert's masculinity and wisdom, and Robert was trying to act his part as set out by Jack. Robert started acting and talking like he was already a gang member—exactly where Jack wanted him to be. Jack went on to the main subject and explained to Robert that he needed to take over a small part of his dad's responsibilities, including leasing a couple of premises for storage and occasional deliveries.

"What type of storage facilities are they?" asked Robert.

"You don't need to know. You will be subleasing them to other people. It is their problem."

"How do I find people to sublease?"

"All you have to do is sign a couple of documents. Everything else will be taken care of," replied Jack.

"What would I deliver and where?" asked Robert.

"I don't know. I don't even think your dad knew. The merchandise comes in sealed packages. When necessary, you deliver to addresses provided to you. It is set up this way to distribute responsibilities so that everyone is safe, in case, you know what I mean," replied Jack.

At this point, with all the compliments and preparations Robert had received, he had no other option but to say, "Yes, I know what you mean," while taking a small sip of the beer and acting like he completely understood what Jack was saying.

"Your dad had many responsibilities. This was just one of them. It was a very small part of his job. We have distributed most of his duties among others. But as we are confident that he will be out soon, we want to keep something small for him so he will have something to start when he is out," said Jack.

"I can take more responsibilities, if necessary, for my dad," replied Robert.

Jack held back his laughter with difficulty, realizing that he had stroked Robert's ego too much, and continued to say that if he could think of additional duties, he would inform Robert.

Robert agreed and asked, "What is the next step?"

Jack gave him a lawyer's business card and asked him to go and see him the following day.

"I have class in the morning," Robert said.

"You are the boss, go in the afternoon after your class. All you have to do is sign on some dotted lines; the lawyer will take care of the rest. We have several business locations that are purchased under the names of different people who are not related to the organization. We then lease the places to other people, who again, are not related to the organization. Then these locations are subleased to people who cannot be found, let alone be traced to anyone, because they don't exist," Jack explained.

Then he took a picture of a man from his wallet. 'Jose Adoklyn' was written at the bottom. He gave it to Robert. "Memorize the features and the name and if anyone asks who is subleasing the space from you, give them the name and his physical features."

"This looks like a drawing," Robert remarked.

"Yes. A fine work of art. It does not match anyone in the police database. That was the difficult part," Jack said.

Hesitantly, Robert asked, "If I get caught, who will believe that I subleased the premises to someone who does not exist?"

"You will never be in the location of the storage facility to get caught, so don't worry about it. But in case you are questioned about it, do not say a word and ask for your lawyer. Our lawyers will take care of you. We have friendly judges who will completely believe you when your lawyer presents signed leases by Jose Adoklyn," Jack reassured Robert.

"What kind of a judge in his right mind will believe such a ridiculous story? Won't they investigate, ask questions and find out the truth?" asked Robert.

"Any other judge, or anyone else, would not believe this story. But all our friendly judges need is an excuse, and Adoklyn is the best excuse."

"Won't the police get suspicious because I am so young?"

"Police are dealing with young businessmen all the time. Some kids, sorry, some men as young as you have their own franchises already," replied Jack.

"What is a franchise?"

"They start with a city block, and then they expand it to a larger area. They buy the merchandise from us; they sell it in their area and keep all the profit for themselves. In return for buying the merchandise from us, we provide complete support, including police presence and legal services, and most importantly, friendly judges in case it becomes necessary."

"What happens if someone decides to buy the merchandise from other suppliers?"

"You have a long way to go before owning a franchise. When the time comes, you will know," replied Jack.

"Do you kill them?" asked Robert.

"Not me personally," replied Jack. "Listen, the chances of you getting caught are very remote. The premises are in the vicinity of friendly police stations and are guarded and monitored by police twenty-four seven. Even if you get caught, a friendly judge can dismiss the charges as the premises are subleased and occupied by someone else."

"Your dad's pay is deposited into his account every month. But you will receive a signing bonus as well a monthly bonus, too. Tomorrow afternoon, I will be waiting across from the entrance of the building where the lawyer's office is and will see you when you leave."

"How do I get paid for the rent from subleasing the premises?" asked Robert.

"What rent? I just told you that your dad's pay would be deposited in his account every month. That's how you get paid," explained Jack.

"If they ask me how I get paid from the sublease, what should I tell them?"

"Oh, I didn't realize your question. You get paid cash," replied Jack.

"If they want to see the money, what should I tell them?" asked Robert.

"You smoke it, you gamble it away. That is none of their business, okay? I have to go. Wait one minute and then leave," replied Jack.

*   *   *

That evening, Robert asked his best friend, Shane, to go with him to see the lawyer. He explained that he needed to do some work for his dad now that he was in prison. *They usually hung out together, so why not*, his friend thought. He would get to go downtown to a real lawyer's office, so he accepted.

The next day after school, Robert and his friend went to the address on the business card. It was a big building in a busy section of the city. They were both nervous, but Robert was more nervous than his friend.

"This is the first time I am meeting a lawyer," Robert told his friend. "I feel I'm doing something illegal. But a lawyer wouldn't do something illegal, and my dad wouldn't ask me to do it. I am doing this to help my dad and my family," Robert said, trying to justify this unusual and suspicious meeting.

"Don't worry," Shane told him. "If we see that something is not right, we will run."

"But there must be something wrong because my dad asked me not to tell my mom."

"Don't worry about it. Moms are always overprotective," replied his friend.

Robert thought, *don't moms love and care for their children more?* But he was embarrassed to say it out loud, so he said, "Obviously, I'm doing something that my mom would not approve of. Am I going to be in trouble?"

"Moms don't approve of anything," replied his friend.

Robert held himself together, head high, and became determined to do it for his father and family, even though his mother would not understand.

They arrived at the floor where the law firm was and were disoriented for a second. There was a big area like a lobby in front of the elevator. For a moment, they thought that they were still on the first-floor lobby. Robert turned around and checked the number on the floor. It said forty-eight, and the address for the suite was 4800, so it should have been right. They walked very slowly toward the reception desk and Robert told one of the ladies behind the reception that he was there to see Mr. Andrew Ramstone. The lady asked him very casually to have a seat while she called Mr. Ramstone. While Robert liked the courtesy extended to him by the receptionist, he was worried about her casual treatment. For her, he was a regular client.

He turned to his friend and said, "You see how casual she was? Are all their clients young guys like us?"

"Ask the lawyer if he has more jobs like this for me too," Shane said. "And by the way, if he asks you to sign something, always ask for a copy. When we were buying our house, my dad asked the lawyer for a copy of everything he signed. He told me that it is very important to have a copy of what you sign."

A couple of minutes later, a very well-dressed, courteous, professional-looking gentleman walked toward them, shook hands with both of them, and asked Robert to follow him.

Inside the meeting room, the papers were ready. Mr. Ramstone asked Robert to sign different documents and then told him their meeting was over. Robert was surprised. He was expecting a lengthy meeting with lots of discussion and signatures. They shook hands again, and as Robert started walking toward the door, he remembered what Shane had said about always asking for a copy of what you sign.

He turned back and asked, "Can I have a copy of what I signed?"

Mr. Ramstone replied, "Yes, Jack will get it."

"But I want a copy for myself and for my dad if he asks."

Reluctantly, as if it was a waste of his time, Mr. Ramstone took the documents and asked Robert to go with him. He gave the documents to the receptionist and asked her to make a copy and return the original to the file.

"Which file?" asked the receptionist.

"Donatelli," replied Ramstone.

Robert shook with fright when he heard Donatelli's name as he remembered his mother crying and swearing at him after his dad went to jail. But he tried to keep his composure.

Ramstone realized the name upset Robert. He asked him, "Is everything okay?"

"Yes, fine," answered Robert.

Ramstone left, and the receptionist took copies and gave them to Robert. As Robert and Shane were leaving, Shane asked Robert what it was that took so little time.

Robert replied, "Nothing, I just signed a couple of documents."

"Let's see what it is," demanded his friend.

"I guess we could check it out," replied Robert and gave the envelope to his friend.

As soon as they stepped out of the elevator, Robert saw Jack standing outside the building and asked his friend to tuck the envelope in his backpack. Outside, Jack greeted them and gave a small envelope to Robert. He told him that he did well and the envelope was the signing bonus that he had promised.

"I did what Mr. Ramstone asked of me," Robert said.

"I know. Do you need a ride?" Jack asked while pointing to his black sports car.

Robert and his friend accepted the invitation enthusiastically. Jack took them to Robert's home and stopped one hundred yards before the house.

"Can we have a minute of privacy?" Jack asked Shane.

Shane left the car, and Jack reminded Robert, "In case, for any reason, you are arrested by an unfriendly cop, you should remember not to talk under any circumstances and ask for your lawyer. The lawyer will take care of everything." Then Jack gave Robert a phone. "This phone is only for contacting me. Don't use it for anything else; just charge it once in a while."

As Robert took the phone, he remembered the evening his father had received a call, and he was looking to see which one of his phones was ringing and how shortly after, he went to prison. Robert became frightened, turned pale, and his hand started shaking.

"What happened?" asked Jack. "It's just a phone."

Robert wanted to say no to the phone and to Jack but realized that his father might get in trouble.

"Are you okay?" asked Jack.

Robert pulled himself together and, with great effort, replied that he was okay, took the phone, and got out of the car. Before Jack drove away, Shane approached him and asked if he would have other jobs like this for him, too. Jack gave him a card and asked him to call next week. Robert's friend pulled out the envelope, took out the contents, and started scanning the pages very fast.

"I think you are the owner of a couple of properties."

Robert did not reply.

"Didn't you hear? I said, I think you own a couple of properties!" yelled his friend.

"No, not owner, it is supposed to be a couple of leases," replied Robert in a sad voice.

"What happened to you? Are you okay? Did he say or do something? Why didn't you tell me earlier?" asked his friend.

"No, he didn't do anything. He just gave me a phone and told me that I should not use it except to answer it when he calls."

"Oh, you got an extra free phone," replied Shane. "That's cool."

"Yeah, but several days before my dad went to jail, we were having dinner when my dad's phone rang. He tried two phones before he answered the right one. I think it was a phone like this. It was given to him to answer when he was given a dangerous mission. My mom got very upset and worried. When Jack handed the phone to me, I felt that I was in trouble, like my life as I knew it was over. I don't want my life to be over," replied Robert.

"What are you talking about? It's just a phone."

"Maybe you are right; it's just a phone. I can't wait till my dad comes back and gets me out of this," replied Robert.

Shane was still going through the documents and said, "Yes, you are right; it says lease agreement on top. Let's go and see what they are for. Maybe we can hang out there sometime?"

"Absolutely not. My dad told me never to go there."

"Where is the small envelope that he gave you? Let's see what's inside that."

Robert said nothing, but his friend insisted. Robert reluctantly said, "It is a signing bonus." His friend got excited and told Robert that he was going to call Jack soon.

Once inside his home, Robert took out the envelope, looked around for a safe place to hide it, and decided to put it at the bottom of a drawer under his clothes.

Shane kept bugging him for a few days until Robert agreed to look at the address on the leased property and go and see it from afar, just one time. He took out the envelope, wrote the addresses of the two properties on a piece of paper, and headed out, leaving the envelope on his desk. They went to the first address. It was a coffee and sandwich shop on the first floor. The address said basement unit. They went to the back of the building, but the door was closed. Hesitantly, they went inside the coffee shop, found a free table, and looked at the menu. The prices were very good, lower than everywhere else. They ordered two hamburgers. The place was busy, and the customers were mostly factory laborers from the nearby factories. Before eating the hamburgers, Robert's phone rang. It was his mother. He signaled to his friend to keep quiet and answered the phone.

His mother, in a very angry and frightened voice, asked Robert, "Who gave you this envelope!? Why didn't you tell me before signing it!? Come home immediately!"

When Robert arrived home, his mother was crying and swearing, and Jack was trying to comfort her.

Seeing Jack in his house shocked Robert, and he became very scared and asked him what he was doing there?

"Your mom called me, and I came immediately," replied Jack.

Jack kept on explaining that Renzo was aware of this arrangement and had approved of it. "There is no danger to Robert. He does not have to do anything."

"Until you ask him to deliver some packages for you and he gets caught. Renzo is in jail because of you. You want to put my son in jail, too?" said Terza.

"No, it is just a lease. Robert has subleased just the basement, and in return, subleased it to someone else. He is not responsible for anything at all," explained Jack.

"He's right, Mom. They are just selling hamburgers and coffee," replied Robert.

"Didn't I tell you not to go there?" asked Jack.

"They are stashing and selling drugs from there. And the person you are supposedly subleasing to does not exist. They do it this way, so if police who are not on Bill's payroll find the drugs, they cannot connect it to Bill. But you will go to jail for possession of tons of drugs. No judge will accept the phony setup of leasing and subleasing to a ghost," said Terza.

"Wow, this has nothing to do with Bill. Don't even mention his name. We are just trying to make a living and create some jobs. Besides, we make sure that a friendly judge is on the bench. And if an unknown judge gets the case, we postpone it for different reasons until our judge gets the case. By then, our friends in the police department puncture enough holes in the case that our judge easily tosses it out. You see, Robert, when you join the Acrebond family, you are completely safe and set for the rest of your life," replied Jack.

"You mean the Acabar monster family. You just told me it has nothing to do with Bill. Isn't Acrebond Bill's last name? Besides, if it is so safe, how come my husband is in jail?" asked Terza.

"Please, don't use that nasty Acabar word anymore. Bill helps us when we need his help because he is a kind person, but he has nothing to do with our operations. And Renzo was out of our territory. But soon, he will be transferred to our territory, and besides, Renzo could have fought his way out. Instead, he froze," replied Jack.

"You mean instead of surrendering, he should have shot the police officers and got life in prison," said Terza.

"There were more people in the warehouse. Everybody fought their way out except Renzo," said Jack.

"I don't care how many officers and judges you own. Renzo is not a murderer, and Robert will have nothing to do with you or your dirty Acabar organization."

"Okay, I will talk to Renzo tomorrow," said Jack and left.

That evening, Jack had a lengthy telephone conversation with one of their contacts in Chicago. He gave him all the instructions and asked him to go and talk to Renzo the next day. His suggestion to Renzo would be to continue the agreement, but Renzo should instruct Robert not to tell his mom or leave any evidence of their agreement in Terza's home.

At the same time, Terza was talking to Robert. She was asking Robert to promise her that he would never talk to Jack or Andrew Ramstone again, that dirty lawyer of Bill's, or have anything to do with the Acabar criminal organization, as it was called on the street.

"This is how they get people in. Slowly, they give small packages to deliver, then larger packages, then they ask you to murder people, and before you know it, you are a full-fledged criminal with no way out. The minute you walk out, you or your loved ones are murdered," she explained to her son.

"So, why are you working in Bill's restaurant if you hate him so much?" asked Robert.

"When I started working there, I did not know who Bill was or even that the restaurant belonged to Bill. I introduced your dad to Bill because Bill's sister was working there too, and when she found out that your dad was looking for work, she suggested that he go and see her brother. In the beginning, it was just security cameras and system installations. Little by little, it became surveillance and bug installations. When your dad wanted to quit, he was threatened that he would be arrested for installing the systems that landed one of the politicians in trouble, and he lost an election as a result. It was either continue working for Bill or go to jail for the rest of his life. I would quit tomorrow if I could. But if I quit, it may look bad for your dad," replied Terza. "I want him to get out of prison, so I can quit."

Robert finally promised his mom that he would not have anything to do with these people. "I will tell my friend Shane not to call Jack, either."

"What did you say? Did you introduce Shane to Jack?"

"Well, I asked him if he would accompany me to the lawyer. He agreed, and we went there together. He asked Jack if he had a job for him and got his card," replied Robert.

Terza immediately called Shane's mother and explained that Shane was in danger of getting involved with gangs and told her about the business card. While talking to Terza, Shane's mother went to his room, found the business card, and tore it to pieces. After finishing her phone call with Terza, she had a lengthy conversation with her son and made him promise not to talk to Jack or anyone in the Acabar group ever again.

The next morning, Renzo called Robert. He was very angry at letting his mom find out. He instructed Robert not to go to the place and not to talk with anyone about it, even his friends.

"Lives depend on you and your promises."

"But I promised Mom I would have nothing to do with these guys," said Robert.

"Unfortunately, I am one of these guys for now. But don't worry, at this stage, you are safe. You are not considered a member of the family yet, and as soon as I get out, you will be completely out of the picture," replied his dad.

"You mean Acabar," replied Robert.

"I told you, no names," said his dad. "Son, do not say anything on the phone that is not necessary. Take this conversation seriously. You don't have to do anything. Just don't keep any document with you in the house. Otherwise, your mom will find them again. Just memorize Jose Adoklyn's name and features, that's all."

CHAPTER EIGHT

A couple of months after Richard was admitted to university with a scholarship, George called and invited Richard for a night out with his friends to celebrate his admittance to the same university as Richard. They went to one of the Razzmatazz locations where George had reserved a private room with a big table. There were several of their friends already present, and the rest arrived one by one.

Richard was surprised when he saw James, the police chief's son, enter the room, and how George was very friendly while greeting him. The chief's son realized that Richard was surprised seeing him at George's party and explained to Richard that their friendship was much deeper than a simple disagreement.

"We were younger then. Our parents are friends with each other, and they do business together. There is a lot at stake," explained James.

The drinks and shots kept coming, the music was loud, and everyone was talking loud. After a couple of hours, when everyone was completely drunk, one of George's friends stood up.

"Congratulations to George for his admittance to one of the best universities! A toast to George!" After sipping from his drink, he continued jokingly, "It is a mystery to me that George has been admitted to an Ivy League university with such a low average, while some of his classmates with much higher averages were not admitted to the same university!"

James stood up and defended George. "The university must be very proud to have someone of George's caliber attend their school!"

George tried very hard to take things lightly. Around midnight, he signaled to Richard, James, and a couple of other close friends whose fathers were friends with Bill, to leave.

He explained to the rest of the group, "We have to attend a private party at home. Stay as long as you want, and eat and drink as much as you want as I will take care of the bill."

On the way out, he told his small group of friends, "My father was right; these are a bunch of jealous losers. Let's get out of here."

*　　*　　*

During George's fourth year of university, Bill called him to his office and started a lengthy speech. Bill explained to George that as he was finishing university, he should be getting himself ready to take on more responsibilities in the organization.

"Nothing comes for free in life. Your great-grandfather worked hard and built this business with his bare hands.

Then your grandfather worked very hard and expanded the business into an empire. I have worked all my life to become somebody in this country. Now our friends include the police chief, judges, district attorneys, politicians and many others. Of course, we take good care of our friends. That's how friendships continue and get stronger. You will soon learn how much each of them gets paid, but for example, Judge Éclair's pay from me each year is many times that of his official wages. You have responsibilities to carry on, and it is time for you to stop with stupid ideologies and other childish ideas. Find your place in this society and own your duties and responsibilities. Nothing good comes from being good or kind. People will step all over you. As a good father, I must sometimes discipline my children. We have to keep the order of things so we won't be destroyed. Unfortunately for us, if we suspect that anyone in our group is cooperating with the enemy, like police or our competitors, we have to eliminate them and we have the best soldiers for these purposes.".

At the end of a lengthy speech, Bill told George that he couldn't stop his education with just a Bachelor's degree and that he had to continue with a profession.

"Yes, I was thinking about it," replied George. "But I have not decided on any specific discipline."

"How about law school?" asked Bill.

"How about it? I cannot pass the entrance exam, and even if I pass, my marks are not high enough to get admitted to any law school," replied George.

"Here, I have not one but two law school admittances to two of the most prestigious law schools in the country. Your choice," said Bill.

George opened the envelopes, looked at the contents one by one, and didn't know what to say. After a while, he asked, "How did you do it? I didn't even apply to any of them."

"This is the least I can do for my son," replied Bill. "I have helped many politicians send their children to the best law schools and medical schools. Of course, I will do it for my own kid. Very soon, you will learn how to do this among many other things, and you will be doing it yourself."

"Aren't you afraid we will get caught?" asked George.

"Everything is being done through middlemen and so-called consultants or lobbyists, if you want a fancier word for it. In addition, once in a while, we catch a couple of rogue players, who are trying to do the same thing that we do, and put them in jail for a couple of months so the public will be satisfied and believe that everyone else is legitimately accepted to these law schools and medical schools. We are safe; our name is only on our law firm, a construction company, the hotel chain, a couple of factories, and a couple of charities. We are known as philanthropists."

"I have friends who attained higher marks than I did, and they were not admitted anywhere. How can I continue my friendship with them when they find out that I am a hypocrite and a phony?" replied George.

"There is Acrebond blood in your veins. You were born to rule not to kill yourself studying and be friends with some losers. Don't compare yourself with the general population, and stop wasting your time with a bunch of losers."

"All my life, I have tried to be kind and fair. I always preached about justice. How can I face my friends knowing that they consider me a phony and a hypocrite?" replied George.

"Believe me when I say that every single one of them would give anything to be in your shoes and have access to the life choices you have, including going to the law school of your choice. You need to be friends with people at your level."

George left his father's office, promising him to let him know his choice of law school. George was faced with one of the most important decisions of his life. He had always preached about fairness and justice, and now he realized that nothing about his life was fair. The house he lived in, the luxurious life with all the maids, the cars he drove, all of it came from crime money. He remembered being stopped for speeding a while ago, and the police officer gave him a friendly warning and sent his regards to his father. Would he accept all the advantages provided by his father and the Acrebond Group's money and power, or would he lead an honorable life? If he refused to benefit from them, his marks would mean that he could only be a clerk or a laborer like some of his classmates. Then he realized that he couldn't even be that. If he never worked in his life, he could still live a life of luxury. His father arranged good and comfortable government jobs for the friends and families of his associates. He could certainly arrange a management position in one of the many government offices for him. And all he would have to do, like thousands of them, was to show up, and the money would be deposited in his account every month. What difference would that make from attending one of the best law schools in the country? In both cases, he would be taking someone's right to that position. Unless he turned his back on his father completely, moved out of his dad's house, went to another city, and got a job according to his credentials?

"I cannot do that. I am no Buddha," he told himself.

The burden of guilt was heavy. The decision he made today would affect the rest of his life. So far, he had no say in what kind of life he would lead. He was born into this family; as a child and a young individual, he had to carry on living. So far, he had not committed any crime. But now, he had the choice. He could either hold his head high and live poor or become a hypocritical criminal and live like a king.

But how can I continue my friendship with my friends? How can I have a friendly conversation with them? They will all consider me a phony. Just thinking about accepting the law school admittance made him anxious. *What if one of my friends tells me that I am a phony? What can I reply? I have respect among my friends. Heck, I don't even care for their respect as long as I know I am right. Now, I have to live a lie. I have to keep my distance from my friends, so I won't read in their eyes that I am a phony and a liar.* He struggled with these thoughts for days.

He imagined being a lawyer and winning big cases with some humbug judges and district attorneys. He imagined how respected he would become in society. Every time he won, the papers would write about it. *What is better: to become popular, wealthy, famous and successful through criminal means and activities, or not commit crime and stay anonymous or even hated by the members of the criminal organizations you oppose?*

He thought about it for several days, until one day, while he was driving alone and deep in his thoughts, his phone rang. It was one of his friends informing him that several of his classmates were going to a bar to celebrate Michael's admittance to law school. He asked George to join them. George was tired of all the thinking, so he accepted the invitation and went to see his friends. Everyone was at the bar already, drinking and cheering for Michael. George sat down, said hi to the guys sitting beside him, and ordered a beer. Michael saw him, raised his glass, and toasted George for his admittance to two of the best law schools.

"Fortunately, I was admitted to only one of them and didn't have to make a difficult choice," Michael said. "Have you finally decided which one you are going to?"

George was very surprised and did not reply to the question. Instead, he just said, "Thanks," and sipped his beer.

From the corner of his eyes, he could see the mocking smiles and gestures of his friends. He excused himself and went to the washroom. After leaving the washroom, he headed to the exit. Michael was standing outside the restaurant exit door, waiting for him.

"What's the matter?" asked Michael. "Why aren't you happy? Why are you leaving?"

"I'm not in the mood. I shouldn't have come," replied George. "I am not sure I will be attending either of those law schools you mentioned. How did you know? I didn't tell anyone. Why did you mention it in front of everyone?"

"Your dad told my dad. They are friends, remember?"

"Oh my God, now everyone knows," replied George.

"Are you crazy? The best thing has happened to you, and you are not sure what to do? How do you think I got in?"

"What do you mean?" asked George.

"Your dad, of course," replied Michael. "Even the undergrad admittance was with your dad's help."

George realized that his undergrad university admittance was also his father's doing. Otherwise, he could not have gotten in with his low marks. He remembered that his friends knew that, and they had made fun of him, but he was too busy with his bullshit ideologies to realize it.

Michael put his hand on George's shoulders and started walking inside while explaining to George that he should be proud of who he is and the family he belongs to. George stayed for another hour, finished his beer, said goodbye to Michael and a couple of others, and left.

George was now facing an even more difficult decision. So many people were benefiting from his father; why shouldn't he? He could go to the law school arranged by his father and still be himself—a nice, fair and just individual.

Then he told himself, "I don't even believe myself. What happens to all those who are more deserving but could not get in because my dad arranged for me to get in?"

CHAPTER NINE

Everyone in Richard's family was getting ready to go to George's birthday party and the celebration of his acceptance to law school. Richard, who was now in his fourth year of university, usually did not participate in family outings anymore since he had become a football star at his university, but today he was very excited and selected one of his best outfits. He had several prospects for joining NFL teams. All he had to do was choose which team he wanted to join. Cathy was very happy for Richard.

Richard left home feeling proud of being a football player, but once they arrived at his uncle's mansion, Richard could not help but feel small again. There was a huge gate at the entrance to the house with a couple of armed gatekeepers. The house was in one of the city's most expensive areas, and the land was so vast that he could not see where it ended. When he was younger, he didn't pay much attention to the details; he just knew his uncle was filthy rich. What he didn't know then was how rich.

Guards at the entrance to the building greeted everyone while they subtly checked the guest list and made sure that everyone entering had been invited. There were several guest houses, each bigger than Richard's house.

The mansion was like a palace. Richard was not sure how many bedrooms it had and did not want to know.

Many guests had arrived, and the valets took the cars to the parking lot one by one. Phil stopped the car on the side, behind the other vehicles, and they started walking toward the house entrance. Richard saw a couple of familiar faces. At first, he did not recognize them, but then he realized they were Gabe and Sally, the superintendents of Mike's building.

There was a commotion at the entrance. People were yelling and shoving. Cathy recognized Robert in the middle of the commotion. The chief's son James was yelling and pushing him, and he was yelling and pushing back. Finally, Robert angrily took his car, which was still waiting to be parked, and went around the circular drive and towards the main gate very fast.

One of the maids was walking with her three-year-old daughter, whose balloon became loose and floated toward the long driveway. The little girl escaped from her mom's hand and ran to catch her balloon as Robert sped toward her. Everyone walking toward the entrance of the house stood still, not knowing what to do, and were frightened by the prospects of the accident about to happen but not Richard. He ran toward the little girl, jumped at the last second before the car hit her, grabbed her like a football in one hand, and flipped to clear the speeding car with the other.

Richard almost cleared the car, except one of his ankles was clipped. Robert stopped the car and got out. Everyone gathered around, trying to take a peek and see what happened to Richard and the little girl. The little girl ran toward her mom crying, without any clue what had just happened. She was frightened that a stranger had grabbed her and flipped her over. Seeing the little girl run, people started applauding and making joyous sounds. Then they started applauding Richard and saying, "Bravo!" They didn't even realize that Richard had been hit. Robert drew closer to Richard and thanked him for saving the little girl's life and a lot of headaches for him. People were talking all around them.

"He is lucky the car didn't hit him. Otherwise, he would be dead in a split second for nothing," one woman said.

"He is Bill's nephew and a football player; that's why he could clear the car," a man said to his wife.

"He is a stupid football player. Why did he put his life and career in danger for her? If one of them dies, one hundred more will cross the border the next day," the wife replied.

"A Mexican was killing another Mexican. Why would this stupid guy interfere? Let them kill each other," a woman said to her friend.

All these conversations were happening in the first couple of seconds after the accident while Richard was disoriented from the spin he received when the car hit his ankle. As soon as Richard stood up and people said that he was okay, he hit the ground.

"Oh my God, he broke his foot," said one woman to another. "How stupid could he be? Why couldn't he mind his own business? Was it worth ruining his chances of being a great football star for nothing?"

George was close by. He immediately called an ambulance and realized that several others were making the same call.

Cathy started swearing at Robert and said, "Why were you driving so crazy? Where is your mom?"

James, who had just approached closer to the scene, started yelling and screaming at Robert, "You are a coward and a troublemaker!" Then he turned to explain to Cathy, "He was not invited, but he wanted to force his way in, and when we stopped him, he drove like crazy!"

Then James began to yell at the guards at the door. "How did this loser get in!?"

"Don't call Robert a loser!" Cathy yelled at James.

"When we saw Renzo's car and Robert driving, we assumed that he was invited as usual. By the time we realized that he was not on the list, he was already inside," one of the guards told James.

"What is the list for if you are making assumptions? Are you stupid?" replied James.

Cathy started crying. "All this for not letting one individual in. He is Renzo and Terza's son. Why wouldn't you let him in? Had you let him in, this wouldn't have happened!" she said.

Cathy looked around for Phil's confirmation of what she said. She saw Phil a couple of steps behind with a tear in his eye. Cathy realized that while Phil was standing behind her physically, he was far away in his thoughts, in a different world where everything made sense and nothing hurt. She now realized the seriousness of the situation and the consequences of the accident. She started crying harder and dropped to the ground to get closer to Richard. Several police cars and an ambulance arrived.

After covering Richard's ankle in a temporary cast, they took him to the hospital. They separated Robert from the crowd, and a couple of officers questioned him while the rest of the officers were analyzing the accident scene and questioning the crowd. By the time Cathy, Phil, Mary, George, and many others arrived at the hospital, Richard was being X-rayed and examined. A little later, Flore arrived, followed by Terza.

Cathy held her face in her hands and fidgeted while waiting for the bad news they were about to receive. Mary was sitting, quietly shedding tears for her brave but unlucky big brother. Flore was praying and making the sign of the cross. She looked around and decided that the most likely person who would talk to her was Mary.

She approached Mary and asked, "What happened?"

One of Richard's friends sitting beside Mary stood up and gave his seat to Flore. Mary described the incident.

Flore made the sign of the cross again and said, "Kiki saved the little girl's life. God was present, and he was with Kiki and the little girl."

Cathy took her hands away from her face, looked at Flore, and said, "Please pray for my Kiki."

It was the first time Cathy had called her son Kiki. Flore realized the complete surrender and helplessness and the pain Cathy was going through. While the tears rolled down her cheeks, she asked Cathy to join them in their prayers. Flore realized that Phil was looking very sad, with his eyes full of tears. She called him to join them, too. Terza came closer and held hands with Cathy and Mary.

At the sight of Terza, Cathy jumped a little but composed herself and held hands with Terza.

While making the sign of the cross, Flore started, "En el nombre del Padre, del Hijo, nuestra Madre María y el Espíritu Santo." (In the name of the Father, the Son, our Mother Mary, and the Holy Spirit.)

And at the end of her prayer, she finished with the same words she started with and made the sign of the cross again. After the prayer, Terza apologized for Robert and explained that since his father's imprisonment, Robert's behavior had changed.

"Especially since Bill gave Robert some of Renzo's work. He is not used to living dangerously and looking over his shoulder all the time. He has been studying all his life. He does not know anything else. This is too much for him."

"That is impossible," replied Cathy. "Bill wouldn't do such a thing, I'm sure. He will be here soon, and we will ask him. Why didn't you tell me about it earlier? I realized that you have been acting strangely in the past several months, but I thought it was because Renzo went to prison, and you are worried about him, and you feel lonely."

"I was able to make peace with Renzo going to prison. It is Robert that worries me a lot. He is not continuing his education, he is always angry, and he is seldom home. It is like I lost both my husband and my son at the same time. At least Renzo is safe in prison. When other prisoners know he is an Acabar, sorry, I mean Acrebond, they don't bother him. But I am worried for Robert every day. I am not sure if he will be alive by the next morning. I am up until he comes home. I am praying every night the police won't knock on my door to give me bad news."

Bill came in, kissed Cathy, nodded to Phil, and then went to reception. Ten seconds later, the hospital president came out and shook hands with Bill, and started talking. Cathy, Phil, Mary, Flore, and others rushed closer.

"Has Dr. Coxic finished examining Robert?" the hospital president asked the nurse.

"Let me check," she replied.

She called Dr. Coxic's nurse and informed her that everyone was waiting for him.

"Dr. Coxic will meet them in room 5B," the nurse said.

Everyone headed to the elevator.

"Immediate family only!" announced the nurse.

Terza and Richard's friends stayed behind. When they arrived at room 5B, everyone was experiencing *déjà vu*. Richard, on the other hand, was joyful. They realized he was under the influence of painkillers, but Richard's happy face made everyone feel temporarily happier. Dr. Coxic came in, and after brief greetings, started explaining about the X-ray with a pointer.

"The lateral malleolus, just above the anterior tibiofibular ligament, is broken. As well, the posterior talofibular ligament is torn."

"Can you say it in English, doctor?" asked Bill. "Is it his ankle that is broken?"

"Well, it is the ankle area. It is a very sensitive area of the fibula that takes longer to heal. But it will heal."

"And how long will it take to heal completely?" asked Bill.

"My brother is a football player," said Mary. "Can he continue playing?"

"Well, Richard told me that he was a football player about to be drafted for the NFL," replied the doctor.

Hearing the words "was a football player," Cathy started crying.

"Well, in my opinion, there is a fifty-fifty chance he can play professionally. But as a non-professional football player, I think there is a ninety-nine percent chance that he will recover completely," continued the doctor.

"How long before we find out?" asked Mary.

"At least three months," answered the doctor.

"I may not be able to play football anymore. That is what I was told before you got here," said Richard.

"But, Kiki, I am glad you are not sad," said Flore.

"Between that beautiful angel's head and my ankle, I will choose my ankle every time," replied Richard.

"Hallelujah, my Kiki has found God," said Flore while making the sign of the cross.

The media talked about Richard's heroic act of saving the little girl's life. Most of the media referred to Richard as Bill's nephew, George's cousin, and a promising football star, without mentioning Phil, Cathy, or Mary.

The following morning, Cathy called Bill. "Have you given some of Renzo's work to Robert? Terza said that since Robert started doing Renzo's work, he has fallen behind in his studies."

"Renzo was not working for me. He was an independent contractor installing security systems for businesses and residences. I was indeed giving him some work, but he was not working for me exclusively. He was a surveillance engineer and a good one, but as far as his son is concerned, what could a high school graduate and college dropout do for me? What you are saying does not make sense. Probably he is hanging out with a bad crowd, and that is why he stopped studying," Bill replied.

Cathy felt embarrassed for even thinking about it. She apologized to Bill and promised herself never to doubt her brother again.

Richard left the hospital after a couple of days but would go for physiotherapy every day and tried very hard to recover completely. He was often exercising at home in addition to the physiotherapy. After a couple of weeks, George called and invited Richard to Razzmatazz for a drink. Knowing that Richard did not drive yet, he offered him a ride.

On the way to the restaurant, Richard asked George, "Which law school did you decide on?"

"I have not decided to go to any of them," replied George.

"But weren't you celebrating your law school admittance a couple of weeks ago?" asked Richard.

"That was my manipulative and exploitive dad who decided to put pressure on me by making it a done deal, hoping that I would be forced to accept one of the schools after celebrating my admittance. Now, if I decide not to go, I will appear to be a lazy bum. No one will think that I didn't go because of my principles. But I don't care what everyone thinks. I will go to law school only if I conclude that my good deeds from becoming a lawyer will surpass the bad deed of taking the opportunity from a more deserving individual."

All of George's friends were at the restaurant. They started asking Richard about the accident and his chances of playing football professionally.

One asked, "What would you do if you couldn't play football?"

Another friend replied, "His uncle will get him into the best law school as he did for his son."

George was offended but realized it was a friendly joke and pretended he did not hear the comment. It was *déjà vu* for George, like getting admitted to undergrad, celebrating in the same restaurant. A couple of hours passed, and everyone was drunk, and the jokes about George's law school admittance were more frequent. George realized that everyone was aware of how he gained his admittance to law school. When his friends were sober, they never said anything about it, but they knew, and by not confirming the fact, he was acting like a fool.

He stood up, raised his glass, and told everyone, "I am proud of my father and his power and influence. I will go to one of the universities I received admittance to."

Michael opened a bottle of champagne in his honor and splashed it on him. "I baptize thee, Acabar," he jokingly told George.

Richard and George left the restaurant soon after. George was half drunk and drove quietly. Richard had just witnessed a battle between good and evil and the capitulation of good. Richard could see that George was struggling and trying to make sense of what had just happened. He could see George's gradual metamorphosis into a pretentiously conceited and lordly person.

The burden of guilt pressed against George's heart the moment he made his final decision to take his dad's offer and go to the law school arranged by his dad. He felt a heavy turmoil inside. He did not realize that evil had entered his heart, and like a dark blanket, had covered his soul and cut him off from the Holy Spirit and the universe. Richard witnessed the death of humanity in George.

"From now on, I will only associate myself with successful people," said George.

He used the word 'successful' as his dad had told him, rather than dishonest people as he had called them before. But deep inside, he knew that associating with honest people would make him ashamed, anxious and pretentious. While dishonest people competed against each other to be more dishonest, bigger thieves, and more dangerous criminals. He could be proud of who he was when he was with them because, among criminals, his father was one of the biggest criminals of all.

CHAPTER TEN

As days passed and Richard faced the harsh reality of not being able to play professional football, he became depressed. He did not socialize much with his friends. He talked to Mike and other friends less and less until they didn't contact each other anymore. They only occasionally saw each other in a mall or a bar and said a quick hello.

Several times when he was very depressed, he tried to drink and forget his sorrows, but the feeling of getting drunk and losing control scared him, and so he would stop. Richard had more free time since the accident. Each day, he spent a couple of hours doing physiotherapy and a couple of hours exercising at home, but not much else.

During her regular phone calls to her brother, Cathy would tell Bill that she was worried about Richard.

"I am worried that his depression may become permanent. Can you talk to him?"

Bill agreed and called Richard a couple of days later to invite him to his law firm's headquarters on Broadway Street for a chat. Richard reluctantly agreed and went to the meeting. After introducing Richard to several of the firm's partners, Bill took Richard to his corner office with its breathtaking city view. He told Richard that he had one of the biggest and most successful law firms in the city and explained that the reason they were so successful was that they made things happen.

"Nothing is impossible with our law firm. I know that your father is a lawyer too, but he is going by the books, and he is practicing corporate, real estate, and family law, while we are practicing criminal law, and our practice is completely different from other lawyers. Ours is called the law of winning and making money. The money is in criminal law. When you save someone from life in prison, they pay anything you ask. All we have to do is estimate the client's wealth and ask for half. Most of our top lawyers make more than the average football player. Next year, George is going to law school, and very soon, he will be making top dollar. Let me know if you decide to study law, and don't worry about admission. I can register anyone in any law school; as long as you breathe, you are in. You know, family is very important to me and you are my favorite nephew," said Bill.

"I am your only nephew," replied Richard.

"I told you that you would make a good lawyer," said Bill with a laugh. "And if after several years, you decide you don't want to continue as a lawyer, we will help you become a judge. We have helped many lawyers who could not make it as a lawyer to become judges. How is that for options?"

"But, Uncle Bill, I have not been studying seriously for the past four years. I was only studying enough to get passing marks so I could play. I will have a lot of catching up to do."

"I just told you, as long as you breathe, you are in. I will get you admitted to any law school you desire," said Bill. "As I said, we make things happen around here."

When Richard left, Andrew Ramstone asked Bill if it was a good idea to bring a relative in.

"What if he obtains sensitive information? He is your nephew, he can be trouble, and there is nothing you can do."

"I will do anything necessary. The success of this institution is the most important thing to me. It is above my family and friendships. I did not let my stupid father stand in my way. I surely won't let my sister do that, either. If Richard becomes a good soldier, he will then become a member of *this* family and we will treat him like one of us. Otherwise, he will be like any other liability," replied Bill. "I am recruiting a soldier, not a relative."

At the dinner table that night, Richard told his family about his meeting with Bill.

He excitedly asked, "Did anyone here know that a good criminal lawyer makes more than most football players?"

Phil became worried and irritated. Although he did not want to upset Cathy, he felt that for the sake of their son, he could no longer hold back the truth.

"Bill meant that when he keeps criminals out of prison with the help of dirty district attorneys and even dirtier judges, the criminals pay whatever they are asked, and from the proceeds, he pays his lawyers and those same district attorneys and judges. It's dirty money. A murderer walks free, and justice is not served for the victim. Stay away from your uncle. You don't know what he is involved in and what other criminal activities he is carrying on. If you work for him, you will become a criminal like him. If you refuse to cooperate, you will become a liability. If you want to be a lawyer, just study a little harder. After you graduate, you can work for me, and in a couple of years, take over my practice."

Richard started to explain, but he was interrupted by his mother yelling at her husband to stop lying about her brother.

Richard continued, "If I want to become a lawyer, I would like to make good money like Uncle Bill."

"All you need is a comfortable living, and you can do that honestly and with dignity. You don't need to become a criminal. You are not going to take anything with you to the other side when you die, only your soul if you can preserve it," replied Phil.

"We have a house because of him. He is paying me twice as much as I would get if I worked anywhere else, just to help us. Where is your gratitude?" asked Cathy.

"He took your dad's entire inheritance and gave you his half of this old house," replied Phil. "Besides, we don't need his handout. You can quit your job anytime you decide. We will be okay."

"My dad's company was bankrupt when he died. He rebuilt it from zero again, but he gave me his part of the house anyway," said Cathy.

"How could your dad's company be bankrupt when six months after your dad's death, Bill started a government contract worth over a billion dollars?" asked Phil.

"Maybe because he is smart, unlike you, that's how," said Cathy.

"Or maybe the large government contract that your father was working on was already signed when your dad died," said Phil.

Mary, trying to change the subject, asked Richard, "So, if you don't want to become a lawyer, what are you going to do after graduation in case you're not drafted?"

"I don't know yet," replied Richard.

"But I told you that you need something to fall back on, just in case," said Phil.

"Yes, Richard, I think you should consider law school," said Cathy.

Mary and Richard looked at each other with satisfaction while Richard gave the thumbs up to Mary for averting another fight.

The days and weeks passed, and Phil kept on worrying about Richard. On the one hand, he was worried that Richard would become more depressed and do something stupid like using drugs or worse. And on the other, he was worried that from desperation and the rosy picture Bill painted for him of his criminal activities, Richard would join Bill's criminal organization and waste his life for money. Phil could not talk to Cathy about it as she could not be objective. Sometimes, he talked to Mary.

One day, after giving it some thought, Mary suggested that her father tell Richard that the filing and administrative system in his office were archaic and needed updating.

Phil was very happy with the suggestion and told Mary, "Under normal circumstances, I wouldn't change a thing in my office as I am completely comfortable with the way things are, but if it makes Richard busy and maybe interested, then it is worthwhile getting Richard's help!"

One day, Phil asked Richard to go to his office.

"The administrative system needs an update. It is completely manual and archaic. Voski has some knowledge of new systems, so if they are set up for her, she can follow them, but she can't set up a new system herself," Phil explained to Richard.

He convinced Richard that instead of hiring someone to do it, Richard should do it and get paid. Richard refused at first and told his dad that it was better to hire a professional.

"But a new system will have glitches and will need updates all the time, especially at the beginning. And every time a new guy comes to fix it, they may get confused and screw up the system. But if you do it, you will be aware of everything and can fix and update it without any problem. You can also teach Voski and me how to work with it," Phil argued.

Voski enthusiastically confirmed everything Phil said. "The system must be upgraded, and I would not trust anyone else but you to do it, Richard, because I would know that in case of any questions or problems, you will be there to help."

Finally, Richard reluctantly said, "I'll think about it."

Voski took that as an acceptance and thanked Richard.

After Richard left, Voski said to Phil, "I am nervous about the upgrades. I'm not sure if I can ever get comfortable working with the new system, but I will do anything for Richard. I hope that Richard will start working on the project, keep busy, and who knows, he may become interested in law and forget his accident and become the same old happy Richard again!"

One day when Richard was not there, Mary told her dad, "I could update the system myself, but I think that we should wait, and hopefully, Richard will eventually agree to do it."

Phil admired Mary's wit. "That is exactly what I am hoping will happen!"

Finally, after flailing for a couple of weeks, Richard agreed to look at the system and decide if he could or wanted to do it. After a couple of days, he dragged himself to his dad's office. Voski was very cheerful and pleasant as usual and was very kind to Richard and happy that Richard was keeping busy. She was always trying to cheer him up. She brought a different treat for Richard every day—a cookie, a piece of pie or cake, all homemade. First, Richard analyzed the existing system, then researched and studied different upgrades. He purchased two new electronic devices and slowly installed new programs. Then he started studying and practicing the programs so he could teach Voski and his dad.

It took Richard almost six months until he finished updating the system. During this time, Phil would often discuss cases with Richard, ask his opinion and sometimes ask him to file documents with the court. He had become interested in law, but he did not want to admit this to his dad. He had a feeling that he had been tricked into liking law, but he appreciated all the efforts by his dad and Voski. On the other hand, what he accomplished gave him a sense of pride and confidence. After all, people had to study these programs full-time in college to learn the basics, and he was an expert in several months.

One day, the inevitable happened. His dad took him to lunch and casually asked him if he had considered becoming a lawyer.

"Indeed, I have, but I am afraid that I will not get into law school," Richard replied.

"You should try and do your best," Phil said.

"I have been getting passing marks while playing football all the time and almost not studying at all," Richard explained.

"If you try a little harder, you will succeed," Phil assured him.

"Okay, I will give it a try, but I'm not promising anything," Richard said.

"You have to make up your mind, though, because the application deadline is fast approaching," said Phil.

Richard started studying for the law school admission test.

CHAPTER ELEVEN

Robert was asking Jack for more money all the time, and Jack was giving him more responsibilities according to his pay increases. Robert was not anxious and worried like before. He was very comfortable carrying small packages in his car and his pockets and delivering them to different individuals and places. He knew most of the 'friendly police officers,' as Jack called them. He sometimes stopped and chatted with them with his pockets full of merchandise.

One day, Robert was stopped for drunk driving, and he told the police officer that he was working for the same employer as him. The officer happened to be a friend of James, the chief's son, and on Bill's payroll. He pretended that he did not know Bill or Acrebond Group and gave Robert a speeding ticket instead of one for driving under the influence. The officer immediately called James and described the situation. James told his dad, who told Bill. Bill called his top management to a meeting.

"We are getting sloppy and careless, and our organization is in danger. If every punk associates himself with us, people will start treating us like a bunch of criminals. We are a very respectful and ethical organization, and we have noble humanitarian plans. We are like a small nation in its infancy. All nations advance because their people obey their government without any question and work together as one body. Nations fall behind when their people oppose each other and their government all the time, and the government has to deplete their resources to fight their own people's opposition. I don't know who this punk thinks he is to associate himself with us, but this has to stop. Who is this guy, anyway?" asked Bill.

Scott Timmins, the police chief, whispered in his ear, "It is Robert, Renzo's older son."

"Who is his handler?" asked Bill.

"It is Jack," said Antonio Donatelli.

"I don't know any Jack. Who is he, who is Jack's handler?" asked Bill.

"He works for me," replied Antonio.

"Take care of it!" ordered Bill.

"Let's give him one more chance, considering that his dad is in jail and was very useful to us," Antonio requested.

"If you want to give him one more chance, it will be at your peril," replied Bill.

That night, Jack had a meeting with Robert and explained to him that he should never again associate himself with Bill, Antonio, or Acrebond Group. Jack made it clear that Robert was an independent contractor and was not working for anyone. Robert promised that he would never again say their names and would mind his own business and stay out of trouble. Robert was getting paid well by Jack and took on more responsibilities by delivering more packages. He did not go to school anymore. He spent more time in bars and was drinking all the time.

One night, he started a fight in a bar.

When the guards stopped the fight and threw him out of the bar, he started yelling, "Do you know who I am!? I work for Bill!"

The bar manager called Jack and described the situation. Several days later, police found Robert's body in an alley. The coroner determined it was an overdose.

CHAPTER TWELVE

The next evening, Cathy was reading a book, and Phil was doing some work when the phone rang. It was Fabrizio, Bill's director of hotels and restaurants. He informed Cathy that Terza's son had committed suicide and she could not come to work for several days. He asked Cathy to arrange the work schedule for other employees accordingly. Cathy obtained the funeral information from Fab, thanked him for calling her directly, and said goodbye.

Cathy was sad that her friend's son had died. She told Phil about the incident and explained that usually, one of Fabrizio's secretaries or assistants would call regarding absenteeism and employee schedules, so she was surprised that Fabrizio called.

"Poor Terza," said Cathy. "Her husband is in jail, and she had to take care of the two children all alone, and now Robert is dead. She must be devastated. I can't imagine what she is going through."

Cathy called several employees and made the necessary arrangements to cover for Terza for several days and herself for being absent on the day of the funeral. Cathy also called Terza to offer her condolences and to say she would help her in any way that she could. Terza's voice was hoarse from too much crying. She talked to Cathy in a very unfriendly and official manner and told her that she did not need any help, as though Cathy was a disturbance. Cathy was sad and puzzled by Terza's behavior. She had acted like Cathy was a stranger, but Cathy did not make too much of it, thinking for a mother who had just lost her son, anything is acceptable.

At the funeral, there were not many relatives of Terza's. Terza was holding her nine-year-old son's hand very tight and keeping him very close to her as though she was afraid someone would snatch him away. She was crying and not talking to anyone or shaking anyone's hand. People started leaving one by one. Cathy stayed at the cemetery with Terza and several of her friends and relatives. Finally, Terza's sister and a couple of other relatives grabbed Terza and pulled her up from her son's casket. Terza was half-conscious and leaning on her sister while another relative was holding her up on her feet and walking toward the car, sometimes dragging her.

Cathy approached and tried to hug her, crying herself, but Terza pulled back, looked away from Cathy, and continued walking without acknowledging her. This time, Cathy was taken aback and offended. Especially because Terza's sister and other relatives did not acknowledge her either. She walked to her car, sat a while and again tried to blame the odd behavior on her son's death. She started the car and drove away, hoping that in a couple of days, when she returned to work, it would be different.

The days passed, and even after a week, Terza was not back at work. Cathy thought that she was not able to cope with the loss of her son. She called Terza several times, but there was no answer. She thought of going to her house to find out when she would be back but remembered the treatment she had received at the funeral, so she refrained from going to her house. On the tenth day, she called Hector, one of Fabrizio's vice presidents who overlooked the operations of the Razzmatazz restaurants.

"Will Terza be back, or should I look for another assistant?" she asked.

"I will call you back soon," Hector told Cathy.

One hour later, Bill called. "Cathy, can you wait a little longer for Terza to come back? Obviously, the death of her son is devastating for her, and she is not able to cope with it, and who can blame her? You should spread Terza's workload among other employees. I will talk to Fab regarding higher wage expenses for the next quarter as there will be more wages paid to cover Terza while she is also getting paid."

Then the conversation became family-related, and Bill asked about Phil, Richard, and Mary before saying goodbye.

Cathy was surprised. She would not expect Bill to know which branch of Razzmatazz Terza was working at, let alone to handle her absenteeism personally and not through Hector or even Fab. She thought about it for a minute and then attributed Bill's behavior to his extreme kindness during a time of crisis for one of his employees.

During dinner, while very sad, she talked about Terza's loss and spoke with pride about Bill's attention to a simple employee while managing a multibillion-dollar enterprise. Everyone became very sad.

"I could not believe how Robert changed so drastically in a couple of years. From being a kind and serious teenager to a drunk and irresponsible adult," said Richard.

"What did Terza say about his death? Did she confirm the overdose?" asked Phil.

"I haven't had the chance to talk to her yet," replied Cathy.

"Didn't you go to the funeral?" asked Phil.

"Yes, but she was not in any shape to talk about it."

"Wasn't Robert yelling at Bill's house entrance, saying that he was working for Bill?" asked Richard.

"He was obviously drunk," replied Cathy.

"Or maybe he was telling the truth," replied Phil.

"What could he possibly be doing for Bill? He had not even finished college," Cathy said.

"Don't ask a question if you don't want to know the answer," replied Phil.

"If you know something that I don't, tell me. I want to know."

"I am not in the mood for another fight," replied Phil.

"You don't know anything. You just grab any opportunity to put down my brother!"

The days passed, and Cathy was waiting for Terza to go back to work, so she could know what was going on and how her brother was involved, but Terza did not return to work. One day, Hector called and informed Cathy that Terza would not be coming back to work.

"Why?" asked Cathy.

"I don't know. She called and said she doesn't want to work here anymore."

Cathy called Terza several times, but it went to her answering machine. Again, Cathy blamed it on her son's death and thought that Terza was probably going through depression, until one day, one of Razzmatazz's regular customers asked Cathy why Terza was let go.

Cathy replied, "She wasn't let go. She quit."

"But I saw her working in Joe's Deli a couple of days ago," replied the customer.

Joe's Deli…why would she leave Razzmatazz, a prestigious restaurant, and work in Joe's Deli, a fast-food joint? Cathy wondered. Cathy became sad and worried. Could her husband be right about her brother? Was her brother in any way responsible for Robert's death or Renzo being in jail? *There must be another explanation, for sure.* Cathy had to find out the answers.

She left work early and headed to Joe's Deli. She parked beside the store and observed for a couple of minutes. There she was. Terza was behind the counter, serving customers and cleaning tables. She was pale, had lost weight, and her hair was scattered all over with black spots under her eyes.

Terza was a manager in Razzmatazz, making at least three times what she would be making at Joe's Deli. All she was doing was scheduling the staff hours, ordering, making payments, and other managerial duties. There must be a very good reason why she accepted this job. Maybe Hector fired her, thinking that she was grief-stricken and she could not perform her duties as well as before. If that is the case, I will be going straight to see Bill and demand he hires her back.

She climbed out of her car, took a deep breath, and hesitantly and cautiously walked toward the deli. As Cathy entered the deli, Terza saw her and went to the kitchen while telling another employee if anyone asked for her, she was not there.

Cathy approached the counter and said to the employee, "I want to see Terza."

"She is not here," replied the employee.

Without saying anything, Cathy went behind the counter and walked toward the kitchen.

"Hey, lady, you can't go there!" yelled the employee.

Cathy did not flinch and pretended she could not hear her.

Not having anywhere to hide, Terza turned her back and, with a heavy and grief-stricken voice, trying to hold back her tears, asked Cathy to leave.

"Please, Terza, I just want to talk to you for a minute and find out what's going on. We have known each other for so many years. We are friends, and if Hector fired you, I could ask Bill to rehire you," said Cathy.

On hearing Bill's name, Terza reacted like she had been hit by lightning. "The last time you talked to Acabar, Robert died. The only one I have left in this world is Danny. Do you want to kill him, too?" she asked in a frightened voice.

Cathy started crying while mumbling, "What are you talking about? I am not a monster. My brother is not a monster. Please talk to me, Terza. Do you think someone killed Robert because of the accident?"

"Please don't play dumb. Please leave. Just don't tell your brother that you talked to me and don't even mention my name. Leave and don't come back again. Let me be," said Terza.

Cathy kept begging Terza to talk to her, and Terza kept asking her to leave.

When Cathy turned around to leave, while trying not to burst into tears, Terza told her in a commanding voice, "Remember, we did not talk. Don't lie and tell your brother that we talked."

Cathy turned around again and said, "Why are you saying these things? Why shouldn't I tell anyone that we talked?"

"Just leave and don't come back," said Terza.

Cathy came out of the deli and called Bill from her car. "Why did Terza stop working at Razzmatazz?"

Bill assured her, "I do not know anything about it. Fabrizio's assistant, Hector, makes these decisions. I promise to find out and let you know." But before hanging up, Bill asked, "What did she tell you? Did she talk to you? Did she tell you that she was fired, or did she quit?"

Cathy replied, "It's very strange. Terza would not talk to me, not a word."

After she hung up, Cathy pondered Bill's last question, "Did she talk to you?" and remembered Terza emphasizing, "Remember, we did not talk. Don't lie and tell your brother that we talked." But she dismissed the importance of Bill's question as a coincidence. *Most probably, Bill wanted to know her side of the story,* she thought.

A couple of hours later, while Cathy was at home, Hector called.

"Bill wants you to hear this directly from me. As you know, Bill never gets involved in the day-to-day operation of any of the businesses, and he does not know anything about it. The company did not dismiss Terza. We tried very hard to get her to change her mind and stay at Razzmatazz. We even promised to give her a raise in pay, but she did not accept. You should promote one of the more experienced senior employees to the assistant manager position."

Cathy thanked him and said goodbye. She wondered why Terza would accept a more difficult job with probably less than half the pay and quit Razzmatazz. Maybe she was also brainwashed by the conspiracy theory, like Phil, that Bill is the reason for all the bad things that had happened to her family. She did not move from where she was sitting. She was perplexed and utterly confounded, not moving at all while staring at the wall.

Mary called her several times. "Mom, Mom?" There was no answer. Finally, Mary yelled, 'Mom!!'"

Cathy jumped. "Why are you yelling, Mary?" she asked.

"Because I called you several times, but you did not listen."

"Sorry, I didn't hear you. I have a lot on my mind."

"What is bothering you?" asked Mary.

"It is work-related. I don't want to bore you," replied Cathy.

CHAPTER THIRTEEN

Richard was studying very hard for the law school entrance exam. He soon realized that it was not as difficult as he thought, at least not for him. He was encouraged by his ability to get high scores in past sample exams. He kept remembering what his uncle had told him—that some of his top lawyers were making more than a football player. He was hoping that he could work for his uncle without offending his dad. While setting up his dad's bookkeeping and filing systems, he became aware that his dad was just making a fairly good living which was nothing compared to the lawyers working for his uncle.

He started studying even harder and finally wrote the exam and got a decent mark which allowed him to be considered for a local law school. Richard was not happy that he received only one admission and from a local law school, while George was going to an Ivy League law school. But Phil explained that the important thing was how well he studied and how much time and energy he had dedicated to it. He explained that without his dad's help, George would not get admitted to any law school.

Cathy overheard this conversation and said, "You are saying bad things about my brother again!" And then she left the room.

Phil became sad.

"Don't worry, Dad. You know Mom, she gets angry whenever you say something bad about her brother," Richard told his dad.

"I am not worried because she got angry. I am worried because she did not get angry enough. She did not have her usual vigor. Something has happened; she knows something. I was always worried that she would find out who her brother really was and that it would devastate her. I don't want to see her sad," said Phil.

"So, why do you say bad things about him all the time?" asked Richard.

"Because, whenever someone is looking for a job, your mom introduces that individual to her brother. She does not know that her brother enslaves people and makes them commit crime. I want her to stop introducing people to Bill."

The law school would start in several months, and Richard kept working in his dad's office almost full-time. In the meantime, an injury lawyer introduced by Phil was working on Richard's accident case with the insurance company. Law school began, and Richard continued studying hard in his first year while still helping his dad and Voski occasionally with upgrading their system or correcting their mistakes.

Richard's used car needed repairs all the time, which was both a waste of time and money. Soon it would be summer, and Richard didn't have a steady income to purchase another car. Richard was aware that his uncle's law firm hired summer students and paid enough in one summer to buy a brand-new car for cash. He wanted to bring up his uncle's job offer with his dad.

Richard invited his dad to lunch, telling him that he wanted to discuss something with him and ask his opinion. They went for lunch. Richard explained that he was more interested in criminal law than real estate or corporate law, like his father practiced.

"And my car needs to be replaced. I'm thinking of taking a summer job in my uncle's law firm. After I graduate, I promise I will join your law firm. By then, I will have enough experience in criminal law that I will be able to practice."

"Son," his father replied. "I am glad we are having this conversation in a restaurant without your mother present. There are so many things about your uncle that you don't know, heck there are so many things about him that I even don't know. But what little I do know scares me. All I can say is stay away from him. I don't know how he got his law degree, but he is not practicing law, as you understand it. He has many judges, district attorneys, law enforcement officers, politicians, and court clerks on his payroll. He bribes those who accept bribes and blackmails those who don't accept bribes. He started this for his own criminal activities but realized that he could use the same connections to keep other criminals out of prison and charge astronomical fees for his services. His law firm does not take regular cases, only murderers and big drug dealers. He makes evidence and witnesses disappear.

That is how he keeps on winning his cases and keeps the criminals out of jail."

"They are just a group of people cooperating and helping each other for the benefit of the individual members," argued Richard.

"Of course, it is okay for different groups and communities to put their resources together for the betterment of its members and to help each other in different aspects of life. But when the congregation and the cooperation of a group of people results in benefiting its members at the expense of the nonmembers and when members are allowed and even encouraged to commit crime against nonmembers, you know it is a criminal organization regardless of the number of members, how popular and powerful it is even though you were born into it or joined them later," Phil explained. "Even their own members become like slaves and prisoners in the organization as they have to do, say, and think according to the organization's rules and regulations. In other words, they have to forego their individuality and their soul for some monetary gains. The richest of them are poorer than the poorest with a free soul. Another way of knowing if you are a member of a criminal organization is if you cannot quit being a member of that organization. At the Acabar Group, a bunch of lazy bums enslave other people and live off their hard work like parasites. If you work for your uncle, you will soon become aware of some criminal or classified information, as criminals call it. Then you will be forced into becoming a member of the Acabar criminal organization, and if you leave, you will be a threat to the organization, and your life will be in danger," warned Phil.

Richard jokingly argued that he was his uncle's 'favorite nephew' and, as such, he would not be in danger.

"The lives he has destroyed, the murders he has committed, he could not have done them by having a conscience or empathy. Only an evil personality could have done what he has done, and he is doing it every day. If you witness your uncle partying with a judge who is the presiding judge in a current case where Bill's law firm is the defending lawyer, it does not matter who you are; you cannot leave that organization," replied Phil. "If you go to his inner circle parties and hear people's conversations about winning government contracts, manipulating elections and other criminal activities, you cannot just say goodbye and leave."

"I will be working there only a couple of summers to gain some valuable experience, get paid good money, and buy a car. I will not be witnessing these kinds of activities that you are worried about," said Richard.

"You know that I will help you with the car. But you will not be able to use any of the experiences you gain in your uncle's law firm. If you go to court and see that the witnesses don't show up, evidence is missing or replaced, such that it exonerates the criminals you are defending, or see the judge rejecting valid evidence for invalid reasons, can you use those experiences?" asked his father. "And besides, you have to choose what kind of a life you want to live—an honorable one as a free man away from criminal organizations with less income, or join a criminal organization and become a criminal yourself and have a lot of money? Sometimes, I am even worried about your friendship with George," said Phil.

"But George has not been involved in any criminal activity. On the contrary, he always talks about justice," replied Richard.

"Maybe he has not directly committed any crime yet. But it is only a matter of time before he gets promoted to committing crime. Additionally, he is living on criminal proceeds. The car he drives is more expensive than most people's houses; he gained admittance to the best university and one of the best law schools without studying. When he was a child, he did not know where all this money came from and could not do anything even if he had known. But now, he is aware of his father's activities and accepts all the luxuries he receives. That is a crime in itself."

"But he has no choice. That is his family," replied Richard.

"He could walk away from all the luxury. He could work hard as many others, find a decent job and not get involved with his father's activities. You know, son, when people die, from the poorest to the richest and from the kindest to the cruelest, it is like they never existed physically. The only thing that survives this physical body and is eternal is the soul, and the only thing the soul carries to the spirit world is how good or bad you were when you were in your physical body. The Great Spirit or God, however you call it, is in your heart. All you have to do is follow your heart. Don't worry about money; all you need is your daily necessities, which God will provide. What you should worry about instead is how much good or bad you will be doing in this lifetime. I know this may sound silly to you as you have been born and raised in a very big city where the law of the jungle rules—cheat or be cheated, grab what you can as the only thing that matters is money. But in the middle of all this chaos, some people stay out of this vicious loop, or as some call it, they stay out of the loop. They don't sin; they don't get into silly competitions over becoming richer than their neighbors or relatives, they don't try to appear richer than they are, and they don't attach themselves to criminal organizations. I was born in a small city. I came to this city to study and I was determined to go back when I met your mom and fell in love. But I consciously kept my small city's simplicity and honesty, something that to this date, your mom cannot accept and make peace with. You know, son, I also believe in destiny and a higher power. If, after all this, you still want to work for your uncle, then do so; there must be a reason for it. Maybe it is your mom's influence or maybe other reasons, but the final decision is yours. I can only tell you what I know. I can't force you to do what I think is right. But whatever you do, even if you decide to work for your uncle, please don't abandon Voski. She is still making mistakes and needs your support. She panics when you go away for a week."

Richard was listening quietly. After his father finished talking, he said, "You're right, Dad. I will not work for Bill. Deep inside, I know it is not possible to be so successful in court and win so many cases without committing crimes. Still, in my mind, I had not fully comprehended his criminal activities the way you just explained them."

So, Richard started working in his father's firm the first summer after studying for one year in law school.

Phil tried to get Richard involved with clients as much as possible. When a client visited, he called Richard to the meeting. After the client left, he did the client's work with Richard. Richard realized that for the time they spent on each case, his dad charged much less for clients who were poor and in need.

CHAPTER FOURTEEN

Richard and George met each other more often, now that they both were in law school. They had more in common and more things to talk about. One day in December, during the second year of Richard's law school, Richard, George, and a couple of other friends were out in a bar.

Since Richard's accident ended his football career, George was a little less boastful toward Richard. Before, when Richard was playing football, George would feel a little jealous, intimidated, and insecure. He knew that no matter how much money Richard made, it would be like pocket change to what he would be making, but he was afraid he would never be as famous and idolized as Richard would be by sports fans and especially by football fans had he continued his career. Now, George took pride in pretending to treat Richard as an equal since they were both just law students.

They were all drinking heavily, except Richard, who was drinking much less. After the accident, he was very careful, so he took a long time to finish a beer. During a very hot conversation, while George was utterly drunk, his phone rang. It was Bill. George tried very hard to talk normally.

"George, stop drinking," said Bill. "I am in a meeting out of town, and I need some information from a document that I keep in my home office. You need to find the document, scan it, and email it to me. You must go alone."

George told his friends that something had come up and he had to leave for a short while but promised he would be back. Even though everyone was drinking a lot, they said bye to George, considering him fully capable of driving and taking care of business. Richard realized that George was in no shape to drive and had difficulty keeping his balance. He was concerned and offered to accompany him. George declined the offer at first but then tripped and almost fell, so reluctantly accepted the offer after all. George pretended that he was doing Richard a favor as if he would break Richard's heart if he refused his offer. Richard insisted on taking his own car and leaving George's car in the restaurant's parking lot.

When they entered Bill's house, they were greeted by Gabriel, the head of the staff.

Gabriel asked George and Richard, "Do you need any food or drink?"

Richard replied, "No, we are going to take care of a small chore and head back out."

Richard gave George's car keys to Gabriel without George noticing and asked him to send someone to pick it up.

When they got to Bill's office, George instructed Richard, "Keep this confidential because my dad will get very mad if he finds out that someone other than me was in his office. What was it that we were looking for?"

"I don't know. I did not talk to Bill," Richard replied.

George started to dial Bill's number and signaled to Richard to keep quiet so Bill would not hear him. This time, he wrote down the name of the document. He shuffled papers and some files on the desk but could not find it. He gave the file name and description to Richard and asked him to help locate the file. Richard searched one side of the room, which contained a credenza and a shelving unit, and George took the other side with a couple of filing cabinets.

While George was looking for the document clumsily and slowly, Richard was methodically and carefully looking for the document. He picked up each file folder, and holding from the base, he flipped the pages, looking for the document. There were framed photographs between several files at the bottom shelf of the credenza. He flipped through the files, setting aside the framed photos one by one to not break the glass. He wasn't paying much attention to the photos. After a couple of minutes, as though lightning had struck him, he stopped and picked up the framed photos and looked at them very carefully, one by one. He reached a specific photo, and it made him jump back in fear. He tripped on the coffee table as he fell while holding the photo.

George yelled that he had found the document, but there was no answer from Richard. He thought that Richard did not hear him.

He shouted, "Richard, I found the file! Let's send it to my dad and get the hell out of here!"

George went to the scanner to scan the document. Richard was still looking at the photos very carefully in a frightened state. George sent the document to his dad and then came closer to Richard and found him staring at a photograph.

"What happened?" he asked Richard. There was still no response from Richard. George started laughing. "Richard? You are sleeping with your eyes open!"

Richard finally stood up and showed the photo to George. "Who are these people in the photo?"

George identified most of the people. Some he didn't know, but he identified one of them as his father, Bill. He then took the photographs from Richard and put everything inside the credenza.

"We have to leave. My father should never find out you entered this room and went through the files."

Richard could not hear a word George was saying. He stood there like a statue, dismayed and horrified while living through the nightmare he would see while asleep. He was miles away in a different lifetime, feeling the bullet wounds and searching his surroundings with his hands so he could find a rock to sit down on or lean against.

Now George started to get worried. He held Richard and helped him go backward a couple of steps and sit on an armchair. He then asked Richard, "What happened? You look like you saw a ghost?

"Can you show me that photo again?" asked Richard.

"No, let's go. If Gabriel comes and sees you in the office and tells my dad, I will be in big trouble for letting you in."

Richard tried to find the photo himself, but George reluctantly took it out and showed it to Richard.

He tried to put it right back, but Richard held on to it and asked again, "Who did you say this man was?"

"This is my dad," replied George.

"I'll be dammed. I know this guy," replied Richard.

"Of course, you know this guy. He is your uncle."

"No, I know him at this age, time, and place," replied Richard.

"Now, who is drunker? When this photo was taken, neither of us were born," replied George.

Then he grabbed the photo from Richard, put it back in the credenza, closed the door, and pulled Richard out of the room by the hand.

"Let's get out of my dad's office and get ourselves a couple of beers," said George.

They sat down in the kitchen and drank beer until Richard slowly came around and out of his deep thoughts.

Richard stood up and said, "I want to take a copy of that photo."

George insisted that they should not enter his dad's room, but Richard insisted it was very important for him to have a copy.

"We are lucky that nobody saw us the first time. I don't know why my dad is so secretive, but if he finds out, I have to listen to hours of lectures on how to conduct business and keep important information private," said George.

Richard kept on insisting, and finally, George reluctantly agreed, and they snuck back into the room. George was curious to see Richard's reaction again. They went toward the photos. George was laughing as he looked at Richard, expecting that Richard would freak out again and he would have a show to watch. But this time, Richard was calmer, still nervous but in control of his emotions. He looked at the photo as though trying to remember if he had seen it before. But the more he looked at it, the more he was convinced he had never seen it before.

He turned to George and asked if he could take the photo out of the frame to scan it.

George was still intoxicated and could not think straight. "Why do you want my dad's photo?"

"He is my uncle. I want to have his photo," Richard replied.

"I suppose there is no harm if you have a copy," answered George. "But can't you just take a photo with your camera?"

"I will be very careful," replied Richard. While removing the pins, he explained to George that there were only a couple of pins on each side. "I will take them out very carefully and put them back in the same place."

Richard took out the pins, removed the protective cover, and eased the photo out. He scanned it and emailed it to himself and then carefully put it back in its frame. They exited the room and saw Gabriel passing by. George explained that his dad asked for a document to be emailed to him, but Gabriel did not respond. He stared at them while passing by. George became worried that his father would find out that he had let Richard in his room.

Richard said goodbye and left. On the way out, he saw one of the guards entering with George's car. He got home to his room, took several prints of the photo and put them in a safe place between the pages of a big book, and then went to sleep.

*   *   *

The next day, he woke up early as usual and went to work. George arrived around noon with a hangover. They didn't talk about the photo—Richard was not sure if George even remembered. Or maybe it was so insignificant for him that he remembered but it was a non-issue. Richard thought that maybe Bill found out that he was in his room and was mad at George, and that's why George did not talk about it.

"Did Gabriel tell your dad about us being in his room?"

"Whose room?" George asked, but then he remembered last night's events. He started laughing at Richard's reaction to the photos and replied, "My dad did not say anything. Probably Gabriel didn't mention it, which is odd because he tells my dad everything. Maybe he was drunk, too," George said, still laughing.

That evening, Richard asked his family if they remembered his recurring dream. "I found out who the people are in my dream. At least, I found out who their leader is, the guy who was doing the shooting," Richard excitedly revealed.

Everyone seemed surprised and asked, "Who is the man?"

"It is Uncle Bill," replied Richard. "I saw a photo in his office, hidden under some papers in a credenza." Then he showed a printed copy of the photo to Cathy and asked if she recognized him while everyone gathered around Cathy to see the photo.

After carefully looking at it, Cathy guessed that maybe he was Bill, but she was not sure. "He has so much facial hair and a hat and dark glasses. I can't really tell if it is Bill."

"You are right; it is Uncle Bill," replied Richard.

"I don't remember this photo, nor Bill with so much beard, but you must have seen this photo when you were very small, probably in my arms, and you got scared and started having nightmares about it."

Phil looked at it and asked Richard, "What purpose can this photo serve?"

Mary looked at it and exclaimed, "Uncle Bill looks scary in this photo!"

"Why don't we go to my village, Juarez, show the photo and see what the elders remember?" Flore suggested.

"Don't be ridiculous," said Cathy. "I am telling you; Bill was not involved in any illicit activity. It will be a complete waste of time."

"This is the man who was shooting at the officer in my dream," said Richard.

"It will be a trip, and we will get to know Flore's family!" said Mary. "Even if we don't find out anything about Uncle Bill."

Richard looked at his father from the corner of his eyes, but he wasn't saying anything. Richard considered his silence as agreeing with Flore and Mary.

While Flore started saying prayers in Spanish and making the sign of the cross, Cathy relaxed and, in a very calm and caring voice, like talking to a small child, said, "Thank God, now we know why Richard was having those dreams."

"That was the first time in my life I had entered that room. I know I have never seen that photo before," said Richard.

"Uncle Bill looks kind of scary in this photo. You were probably too small to remember when you saw the photo. But it was imprinted in your brain, and it kept coming back in your dreams as a nightmare. I am glad the mystery is solved," said Cathy, and then she left the room.

Flore stood there not believing a word Cathy said but could not argue with the proposed theory so firmly presented. She looked at Richard and realized that he was puzzled, too. He did not agree with Cathy either, but he did not have a better explanation.

"Come, Kiki, come have some dinner," said Flore and started walking toward the kitchen while mumbling in a low voice, "This is just the beginning. God help us."

A couple of weeks later, Richard called his dad and asked to meet for lunch.

"Can we get sandwiches and go to the same park that we usually go to?"

Phil, realizing there must be something important that Richard wanted to talk about, happily agreed, and they decided to meet the next day. While having lunch, Richard explained that all those years, when he said he didn't see the dream anymore, it wasn't true.

"I would see it, and sometimes, if I got busy for a while and did not remember seeing it, I would feel guilty like I was betraying a loved one, and I would close my eyes and intentionally review the whole dream and meditate about it. I don't agree with Mom's theory regarding how and why I started seeing those dreams."

Phil replied, "I realized it a couple of weeks ago when your mom was theorizing how the dream started. I realized that you did not believe her explanation. So, what are you going to do now? You cannot ask your uncle about it, and even if you do, you will receive a stupid answer."

Richard looked at his dad without saying a word as if it was obvious what he should do and his dad should know the answer.

Phil looked at him, puzzled at the beginning, then slowly his expression started changing to worry and grief, and he said, "No, there must be another way."

"Remember what you told me when I was small? You said that whenever you are overwhelmed with problems and questions, you come here to the park, and after walking for a while, your mind gets clear, and you get the answer to your questions. It is like many invisible and wise people feed you the answers. All you have to do is send your questions and problems out into the open and forget about them, and the answer will be revealed to you when the time is right. Well, I have spent many days in a park like this in the last couple of weeks and I think the only way for me to get to the bottom of this mystery and find out why I am constantly seeing this horrible dream, what I am expected to do about it, and how is it related to Uncle Bill, is to get closer to my uncle. And what better way to do that than to go and work for him?"

"You know the dangers of working for him, son," said Phil. "The only reason he wants you to work for him is to exploit you and benefit from you, even if it means destroying your life."

"Yes, now I am even more afraid of him than after the explanation you provided last time," answered Richard. "I will be very careful, but beyond that, I am prepared for anything to find out how he is related to the character in my dream. I know that if I don't do it, I will regret it for the rest of my life."

"Don't accept anything to be registered in your name—shares, properties, leases, or anything else. Don't go to his private parties where politicians and judges are present."

"Why would he register anything under my name?" asked Richard. "Wouldn't he be afraid that I might sell it or keep it for myself?"

"Before you own anything, you will be signing documents transferring everything to him or a corporation he owns through another nominee owner so he can transfer to someone else if necessary. And, of course, he will make sure you know what he is capable of if you decide to cross him. And I assure you, being his nephew doesn't mean anything to him. He will even use Mary to make you do things for him. You should try to get a position in the Broadway Street office," said Phil. "He spends more time in that office than anywhere else, and he handles the biggest criminal cases there. Don't tell your mom why you decided to work for your uncle, and tell Bill your father wanted you to work for him, but you prefer to be where the action is and work in a larger firm. This way, when you want to leave, you will have the excuse that your dad needs you and wants you to join him."

CHAPTER FIFTEEN

That evening, Richard told his mother that he had decided to work in one of Bill's law firms if he could.

At first, Cathy was excited. "I am happy for you! I think you are making the right decision," she said. Then she remembered the conversations she had had with Terza and asked, "Is your dad aware of your decision? Does he agree with it? Not that it matters . . ."

Richard said, "Yes, I talked to Dad and convinced him that I will learn more and have a lot of opportunities by working for Uncle Bill."

"I'm sure that Uncle Bill will be very happy," Cathy said, and then she walked away.

Richard was very surprised and followed his mom. "Why are you not as excited about this decision as I thought you would be?"

"I am happy for you. I am sure your uncle will be thrilled, too."

Richard called Bill the following morning. "Is there room for one more law student in your firm?"

Hearing that Richard wanted to work for him, Bill got excited and said, "I usually don't do the hiring, but I am sure we can fit you into one of our offices."

"Do you think I can work at your Broadway Street office?" asked Richard.

"That is our best office. Our best lawyers are in our Broadway office. I see you have done your homework. Broadway office it is then," replied Bill.

A couple of days later, Andrew Ramstone, the managing partner of the Glendale office on Broadway, called Richard and set up a meeting. During the meeting, Ramstone introduced Richard to his colleagues and told them that Richard would be joining them as a law student.

Richard was now a little nervous about joining one of the most reputable law firms. While he studied very hard in law school, he was aware that Acrebond law firm only hired students from the top ten law schools in the country, and he was not sure if he would measure up to them. To get closer to his uncle and find out more about Bill's connection to his dream, he felt he'd have to work very hard when he joined the firm as a student and become one of the top-performing law students.

The semester ended, and Richard started working in Bill's law firm. He was given the usual law student tasks like researching, reviewing and summarizing files for Andrew Ramstone and others. He tried his best and spent more time working than anyone else in the firm.

After a couple of weeks working there, George approached Richard.

"Your hard work is disturbing other students. They feel obligated to work hard, too. Don't set new standards for law students."

From that day, instead of going early to the office and leaving late, he kept his standard hours and started socializing with the other students. However, he would take work home and catch up that way. Even Andrew Ramstone was surprised at Richard's accomplishments. He asked Richard how he accomplished so much more than other students within the same working hours. He also asked if he wanted to join him in court as an observer in a drug-related pretrial the following morning. Richard happily accepted and went to court with Ramstone.

The trial started, and the charges were read. There were large amounts of drugs found in the defendant's car. Andrew Ramstone stood up and informed the judge the police had illegally searched his client's car as the police only stopped the car for speeding. And then, for no reason at all, the police asked his client to get out of the car and started searching it. "Just because my client is an African American," said Ramstone. This indicated prejudice and bias. Therefore, the evidence should not be admissible, and the case should be dismissed. The police officer testified that he received an anonymous tip to search the car. Ramstone demanded evidence of the call, but the officer could not provide it. Ramstone reiterated his demand for dismissal.

The judge asked the prosecutor, "Is there any more evidence?"

Sean Wilderson, the prosecutor, replied, "No, Your Honor. We think that so much drug should be evidence enough."

"I have to accept the defendant's argument and dismiss the case," replied Judge Éclair.

Leaving the court, Richard overheard the police officer talking to James, the police chief's son. James was patting the officer's shoulder, thanking him for a job well done and telling him that he would see him tonight.

The summer ended and Richard had not learned anything about Bill or his connection and involvement with the people in his dream. But he was still happy. Bill's law firm, Acrebond and Associates, was the highest paying firm for law students. He had earned enough money for his car and even had enough for his pocket money for the entire year.

Richard finished the second year of law school and started working in the Broadway office again. It was the middle of the summer, and still, Richard had not obtained any clues regarding his uncle's involvement with his dream. He tried to become friendlier with George so that he could meet with Bill more often outside of the office.

One week before the schools opened, Richard stopped his summer employment with Bill to prepare for school. On that Sunday morning during breakfast, Richard reminded his family of the conversation they had had a year ago about going to Juarez.

"I am ready to go anytime!" Flore said with excitement.

"So am I! I want to see the real Mexico. We have been to several resorts, but they are all tourist destinations. I want to see the real Mexico!" Mary said.

"Unfortunately, I can't. I am busy," said Phil.

"Well, I can't let you two go alone in case you do stupid things and put yourselves in danger!" said Cathy.

Richard purchased the plane tickets and rented a van to be picked up at the airport on landing. Cathy arranged her absence at work but kept their destination secret and just said that they were going to a resort in Mexico and that her son had made reservations. They would all be back in time for the start of the new school year.

They arrived in Juarez and went to a hotel. Flore called her relatives to tell them she was in Juarez. She asked them if they were still living in the same place or if they had moved to give her their new addresses.

While having dinner that night, Richard made a suggestion. "I think Flore's relatives shouldn't be told that Cathy is Bill's sister. Otherwise, we may not get the truth from them."

"I disagree," said Cathy. "Bill is a nice man and would never do anything illegal."

"Please, Mom. I insist that we do it this way," said Richard. "Otherwise, the whole trip will be a waste of time."

"If they know Bill is our uncle, they may not speak freely, and we may not know the whole truth, but it will not be a waste of time. It will be a nice trip to Mexico that most people vacationing in Mexico have not seen," added Mary.

"All right," Cathy said reluctantly. "We won't tell them I'm Bill's sister. We'll just say Bill is someone we are investigating for."

The next morning, they went and saw Flore's relatives. The elders all remembered Kiki, the police chief, and they became sad when speaking about him. When they saw Bill's photo with his friends, they all said he was 'Acabar.' Then they said that Bill was the guy Kiki arrested, and after bribing his way out of prison, Bill had killed Kiki and his family. They said that Acabar, along with his gang and some of the city's police officers, surrounded Kiki's house and started shooting randomly. They found the bodies of his wife and son in the house. Kiki's body was in the burned-out cornfield close to the old church, but they never found his daughter, Gloria, and they didn't know if she was still alive.

"So, this is not Bill?" asked Cathy.

"Yes, Bill Acabar," replied one of the elders.

"It is Acrebond, not Acabar," said Mary.

"Yes, Bill Acabar," replied another elder.

"I think Acabar is Bill's nickname," replied Flore.

"Does it mean anything?" asked Cathy.

"Originally, it was how people in Mexico pronounced Acrebond. As Acabar is a familiar Spanish word and easier to pronounce for Mexicans," said Flore.

"While Acabar means 'to end or finish' in Spanish, but given that Bill is a murderer, by calling him Acabar, they meant someone who ends lives," replied one of the elders.

"If he killed a police chief and his family, why didn't the police arrest him again?" asked Cathy.

"No one dares to testify against him," said one of the elders. "Besides, there were police officers in his gang."

"I heard that he even killed his own father," said one of the elders.

"That is ridiculous!" exclaimed Cathy very angrily. "You have ganged up against me!"

The elder asked Flore in Spanish who Cathy was.

"I guess we can tell them the truth now. She is Bill's sister," replied Flore in Spanish.

Everyone was suddenly very scared. While trembling, they started apologizing and telling Cathy they were sorry for what was said and promised that they would never say anything bad about her brother. They asked Cathy not to tell Bill about the conversation. Bill still had a big operation in Mexico, and he could have them all killed. Flore translated everything for Cathy, word by word.

Cathy remembered Terza asking her not to tell Bill that she had talked to her.

She said to Flore, "Please assure everyone that we won't say anything to Bill. All we wanted was the truth, and unfortunately, we got the bitter truth."

After that, Cathy was very sad and silent. She left shortly after and told Richard that she had heard enough and she would wait for them in the car. On their way back, everyone was quiet. Cathy had learned the true nature of her brother. Instead of thinking of him as a nice, caring, and benevolent person, she now knew he was a criminal.

"Don't be sad, mom. We won't socialize with Uncle Bill anymore," Mary said.

"Don't call him Uncle Bill. He is a criminal. I disown him," said Cathy. "I was living a lie all my life. I was always proud of my brother. Everyone knew me as Bill's sister, but that made me happy and proud. It was like I did not exist outside that SOB's world. They even said that he may have killed my father. Can you imagine that? If this is true, every time that I talk to him like the nice man, I thought he was, every time I treated him like a brother, it was like I was approving of what he might have done."

"First of all, we don't know if he killed Grandpa," said Richard. "The guy said he heard that he killed his own father. He was not sure. So maybe it is not true. Even if, God forbid, it is true, you didn't know about it. How else would you treat him?" Then he asked his mom, "What are we going to tell Dad?"

"We will tell him everything we found out and give him the satisfaction to say I told you so."

"Do you remember the last time dad called Bill a gangster, and you got mad?" asked Richard. "Dad was surprised and sad that you only got a little mad. He became worried about you. Did you suspect something then? Did something happen?"

"No, I don't remember it," replied Cathy. "I don't want to talk about Bill anymore."

"Maybe he was a bad person when he was young. Maybe now he is a better man," said Mary, trying to comfort her mom.

When they returned to Los Angeles, they told Phil everything. While Phil always knew that Bill was a criminal, he did not think it was this bad. He cautioned everyone not to talk about it to anyone and suggested that Richard stop working for him. Richard argued that after two years of working for him, he had made a little progress, and at least he had gotten to know him better. He would be more cautious now, but he needed to keep close relations with Bill.

Richard finished the last year of law school, and against very strong opposition from his parents, he kept working in the Broadway office while getting ready for his bar exam.

CHAPTER SIXTEEN

There was a big Christmas party in Bill's mansion. The chief of police, with his top officers, were present. Also present were Judge Éclair, the public prosecutor Sean Wilderson, several court clerks, retired judge Alexander Parvello, Archbishop Matthew Rodriguez, and several politicians, including Earl Murphy, who had the final word in deciding who would get the government construction contracts and many other business associates of Bill. It was a work-related party, not a social one, and so the family was not invited.

The waiters and waitresses were touring around with all kinds of exotic foods on their trays, including black caviar, different types of wines and other drinks. Bill was mingling with all the guests, going from one group to another, chatting and making sure they were all well-fed and having fun. He spent more time with influential individuals. While talking to Earl regarding a construction bid that he had made, a waitress came with a tray of drinks. Earl immediately changed the subject so the waitress would not hear them talking about confidential government contracts. Bill started laughing and continued the conversation.

After the waitress left, Bill said to Earl, "The waiters and waitresses are my employees. During the day, they work as maids, kitchen help, gardeners, or security personnel. I assure you, Earl, they all have families, and they are handpicked because I trust them completely. As long as they do as I say and don't cause any problem, I will take care of them, and they know the minute they disobey me or think of turning against me, I will take care of them." Bill and Earl laughed.

Judge Éclair joined them. "What are you two laughing about?"

The judge turned to admire the beauty of a waitress passing by. Bill noticed the judge's wandering eyes and called for the waitress.

"Judge Éclair is tired, and he wants to get a short rest and maybe a good massage. Show the judge one of the guest rooms on the other side of the mansion," Bill instructed.

It appeared that 'getting a short rest' had a different meaning in Bill's vocabulary.

The waitress replied, "I understand." She told the judge, "This way, sir."

The judge told her, "Maybe later, thank you." Then he turned to Bill and jokingly said, "Nothing escapes your attention."

They laughed, and Bill said, "Remember, for the after-party, we are going to the gaming room in the basement to play, then you will be tired, and you can get a short rest."

The retired judge, Alexander Parvello, approached them, and Bill signaled to the others to stop talking.

Alexander thanked Bill for inviting him, said goodbye, and left.

"I do not want Alexander to know that we will be gambling later," Bill explained. "I told him not to retire, but he didn't listen. Maybe it was my fault. I made him so rich that he doesn't need to work anymore. He is very lazy. Can you imagine? All he was doing was taking a nap on the bench and reading the verdict given to him at the end. He is a nice man but useless now. I need to borrow Earl for a couple of minutes, excuse me."

Bill and Earl went to a room on the other side of the building for a business meeting away from the crowd.

"I have tendered a bid for a construction project, and you are in charge of deciding who will get the job," Bill told the politician.

"I am aware of the situation, but there are several bids for the same job," replied Earl.

Bill laughed and said, "I am sure you have already made up your mind that I will get the job."

"I would like to do that, and I hope that you want the job as much as I want to give it to you," said Earl.

Bill stopped laughing. "Make yourself a drink, Earl. And have some caviar, too. I need one minute with my assistant."

Then Bill went toward Doug, his chief lobbyist, waiting at the door to join the meeting. He put his arm on Doug's shoulder and took him outside the room.

"I think there may be a problem with Earl. He has become greedy, and he must be made aware he cannot fool around with us. But be very respectful and break the news to him very gently. We don't need any problems tonight. You can go up to $10 million."

Then they came back into the room.

"Doug is in charge of all the projects and negotiations. He will discuss the details with you," Bill told Earl. "Take a seat and have a chat with Doug, so we can come up with a solution on how the tender can be approved."

Bill left the room, and Doug and Earl began chatting like two old friends. They discussed past projects until it was time to discuss the project at hand.

"We are prepared to transfer $5 million to any account you provide," said Doug.

Earl started laughing. "I have offers for twenty times more than that," replied Earl and started walking toward the door.

Doug intervened and asked Earl to come back and sit, so they could continue talking.

"The only reason I favor Bill's bid is that I've worked with Bill many times before, but Bill was more generous in the past," Earl said.

"I can increase the offer to $10 million. There is not much profit in the project for us to be able to pay more than $10 million," Doug said.

Earl took a notepad from the desk and wrote out a ballpark figure.

"The budget is now approximately $900 million," he explained. "And as with any other project, it will go way over budget, maybe twice as much. I estimate that the final net profit to Acrebond Group will be approximately $400 million, so my share should not be less than $100 million."

"You should accept the $10 million offer and be happy that you are getting even that," replied Doug.

Doug's voice and attitude were slowly changing. Five minutes earlier, he'd had the tone of a professional businessman, but now he started talking like a gangster does to a hostage.

"If you give the contract to our competitor, all the newspapers and other media will receive documents showing that you have taken bribes on several occasions," warned Doug.

Earl was suddenly mad. "You're bluffing!" he said. "There is no such document."

"Our meeting is being recorded, Earl, as all our previous meetings have been recorded. Even with other contractors you thought were not Acrebond, they were, and the whole conversation between you and some people who cannot be tied to Bill has been recorded. They will all go to the media the day you give the contract to another company," Doug said. "You see Earl, the $10 million I offered you was a favor. I don't have to give you a penny, and you will still do as I say and give the job to us."

Earl, who had guzzled down a couple of large glasses of scotch while Doug was explaining the situation, realized that if he didn't do as Bill said, not only his career and political life would be over, but he would go to prison and his family would suffer greatly. He became furious, and while swearing at Doug and Bill, a letter opener grabbed his attention. He picked it up and attacked Doug in full force. Doug put his arm up, and the letter opener sliced his arm. Earl attacked again, and Doug defended himself by putting his hand underneath Earl's hand. Earl raised his hand again, and as he tried to strike, Doug grabbed Earl's wrist, twisted his hand and landed the letter opener in Earl's chest.

A couple of guards standing behind the door rushed in. Doug asked one of them to call Bill while he assessed the situation and checked Earl's vital signs.

Bill came in and was angry with Doug. "You weren't able to execute a simple task!?"

Doug explained the chain of events.

Bill was furious and told Doug, "You should have been very friendly and broken the news about the recordings and other documents slowly and gently. Now we've lost a big asset. We went through a lot of planning and hard work to get all these necessary documents. Now they are all worthless!"

"I had no choice. It was either Earl or me!" Doug explained.

"I can get ten people like you in a day, but a hooked politician is a priceless commodity!" Bill yelled. "The choice was obvious and simple, yet you could not figure that out. If you had died instead of him, Earl would have been much more cooperative. I told you that individuals are not important; it is the institution you should have thought about. But you just saved your skin at the institution's expense!"

Several close associates of Bill's arrived. One of the associates checked Earl's body for vital signs and very disappointedly shook his head, indicating there were none.

Another associate stopped the argument by saying, "Now is not the time to blame each other. We have to come up with a solution. Everyone, go to the next room for a conference and brainstorming."

They all went to the next room.

Doug started by saying, "The situation is clearly self-defense!"

Bill started swearing at Doug, and then he said, "You may prove that he attacked first, but that will also prove you were trying to bribe and extort him. It will also prove that I was in on it, too."

Doug confidently said, "We can select sections of the conversation where Earl is asking for money for a favorable decision."

"Any voice or video recording expert will instantly find out the recordings were tampered with, and then everything will be on you, and by you, I mean me— bribery, extortion, and murder," replied Bill. "Get lost for a couple of weeks or until your wound is healed."

Then Bill turned to another associate and said, "Tell the guests that the party is over and take the special guests to their homes with limousines from covered areas, so no journalist or photographer will be able to see them."

Then he attended to the inconvenience at hand. One associate suggested moving the body and burying it far away in the woods. Another disagreed and said people would have seen Bill, Earl, and Doug walking out of the party together. Another argued that they could simply say they had a ten-minute conversation, and Earl left from a different exit. Yet another agreed on moving the body and suggested changing the carpet the same night since he had a friend in the carpet business who could come and replace it before dawn. Everyone in that room, even the guards, was trying to provide opinions and look more important than their current status.

Slowly, everyone accepted the idea of removing the body and changing the carpet, when around 11:30 p.m., a guy talking on his phone entered the room where Earl's body was lying and started screaming to the person on the phone, "I found Earl and he is lying on the ground in a pool of blood!!"

Bill asked the guards to check and see who this guy was. One of them returned and reported that he was Earl's driver, and he was on the phone with Mrs. Murphy. Bill asked him to take the driver to another room. Then he went to the driver and told him that he wanted to talk to Ms. Murphy. He took the phone and explained that an accident had happened and Earl was injured, but the police and ambulance were on their way.

Bill gathered his associates again. "With the driver reporting the incident to Earl's wife, all the plans are out, and there is only one solution."

"Find a maid called Gloria and bring her to me," Bill told one of the guards. Then he explained to his associates. "The best solution in this situation is to set up the scene as attempted rape and self-defense. Roy, clean the letter opener handle of all fingerprints while in Earl's body."

The guard came back with Gloria.

"Gloria, an accident has happened, and I need your help and cooperation," Bill said. "Check Earl's pulse and see if he is alive and pull out the letter opener from his chest."

"No, you should call the police, said Gloria, very frightened.

"I need your help. There is no time for me to explain further, but everything will be okay. I promise nothing will happen to you, and I will take care of the situation. You will not get harmed. I will be very thankful and even bring your entire family to America, give them good jobs, and take care of them."

As soon as Gloria heard Bill talking about her family in Mexico, she capitulated, and her attitude changed, and she agreed with whatever Bill said. Distraught, she got closer to Earl's body while tears were falling down her cheeks. She stepped in the blood, checked the pulse on his neck, then pulled out the letter opener and posed as one of Bill's associates, Roy, took photos.

Everyone was standing on the opposite side of the room so that it appeared Gloria was standing alone in the room. While Roy was taking photos, Bill was on the phone talking to his buddy, Scott Timmins, the police chief, and watching Gloria standing there crying helplessly, which he thought would make his story more plausible. He did not realize that a couple of guards and other associates were also taking photos while trying to be helpful.

Bill was very proud of himself for coming up with such a genius idea in such a short time and under so much pressure. He felt absolute power while watching Gloria posing for incriminating photos. Bill had called Scott Timmins at around 11:42 p.m. The police chief told Bill that he was on his way and asked him to have one of the guards call 911 and report the incident in five minutes. Bill asked one of the guards to call 911 and report that someone was wounded. Then he approached Gloria.

"You will have to tell the police that Earl wanted to rape you and that you defended yourself by striking him with the letter opener."

"No," Gloria said while crying. "It is not true; I cannot do it."

"Nothing will happen to you," Bill again reassured her and then spoke about her parents and how he would take good care of her family.

Hearing the word 'family,' Gloria burst into tears and started sobbing. She remembered their deal: she did everything Bill said, or her family would get hurt.

The police arrived before Bill's friend, Chief Scott Timmins. Gloria was aware that her role was to take the blame and responsibility for the murder. She knew that the police were there to arrest her, but when she saw the police, she felt relieved because she knew the police would keep her safely away from the monster called Acabar and his gang. At that moment, being arrested and the prospect of prison was like freedom to her.

The head of the group asked one of the officers to handcuff Gloria and asked another officer to set up a room to interview the witnesses and record the conversation. The police chief arrived and took over the investigation. He decided the room assigned for holding the witnesses was too small and asked everyone to move to the bigger room. He instructed one of his own officers to set up recording equipment in the small room where the witnesses were originally held. The police chief asked the officers dispatched by 911 to secure the premises and stand guard at different doors.

The police chief and Bill took a few steps away from the crowd and whispered to each other for a couple of minutes.

The officer who had set up the room for interviews, later designated as a holding room, realized the recording equipment was turned on. He casually turned it off and packed the equipment in the container.

The police chief took over the interview. Everyone said they had not heard anything, except one of the guards, Cortez, who said he saw Mr. Murphy and Gloria enter the room, and he stood guard. A couple of minutes later, he heard a commotion and reported to Roy, and together they entered the room and saw Mr. Murphy lying down covered in blood and Gloria standing on top of him with what appeared to be a blade in her bloodied hand. The police chief asked both Cortez and Roy on separate occasions what time they entered the room, and both of them said it was 11:00 p.m.

One of the rookie police officers realized that one of the guys who had said he just arrived had blood on his shoes.

"What's your name?" the officer asked him.

"Evan," he replied.

"Can you remove your shoes?" the officer asked.

Evan looked down and realized there was a blood stain on his shoe.

"I was eating a hamburger. It is probably a ketchup stain," Evan said.

The police chief told the rookie to leave the guy alone. But the rookie insisted that according to guidelines, they had to take the shoes as evidence and bagged the shoes.

When they talked to Gloria, she was very confused. At first, she said that she had killed him, but then she said that she did not. She kept crying and praying. The police recorded everything and considered it a murder confession.

Earl's wife arrived. A police officer escorted her to identify the body and asked her to stay in another room where some maids and associates tried to calm her down. Bill, the police chief and another officer went to say condolences to Mrs. Murphy.

Seeing Bill, Mrs. Murphy asked, "you told me on the phone that an accident had happened, but you did not tell me how it happened. How did Earl die? Who killed my husband?"

The officer accompanying the chief took out his notebook and said to Bill, "I thought you said that you had just arrived and heard about the incident."

The chief signaled to him to stop talking. He quietly put the notebook and the pen in his pocket.

The coroner and his assistant indicated that Earl had died at or around 11:00 p.m. Some of the photos taken with Gloria holding the knife showed a clock on the wall displaying 11:40 p.m. Earl's driver walked in while on the phone with Earl's wife at 11:30 p.m. All the cell phone photos had the time registered on the photo and matched with the wall clock. They were all ten minutes after Earl's driver came into the room. The coroner's assistant, Addis Olizar, had several cell phone photos with the time. When Earl's driver saw the photos with Gloria holding the knife, he indicated to the police she could not have killed Earl because he saw that lady on the other side of the building serving drinks, and he had asked her where Earl was and got directions to the meeting room from her. She must have posed for photos after Earl was murdered. The police chief ordered his officer not to take notes on the driver's statement.

After examining the body, the coroner indicated the cause of death appeared to be the puncture wound in the chest by the letter opener but suggested that he would provide a full report after the autopsy.

The police officially arrested Gloria, along with Roy and the guard. They took them to the police station for more questioning and processing. They collected all the evidence, including the shoes, the letter opener, and every large or small item that was even remotely connected to the scene.

There were many reporters outside the gate. A police spokesman explained to the reporters that Mr. Earl Murphy had been stabbed to death and the alleged suspect was arrested along with some witnesses, and they were being taken to the police station. The officer did not answer any questions due to it being an ongoing investigation.

Gloria was crying all the way to the station, which made her look even more guilty. At the police station, they took official statements from Roy and the guard and downloaded all the photos taken by Roy. Then they released Roy and the guard and held Gloria to appear in court the next day.

*　　*　　*

The next morning, all the papers, radio, and TV stations were talking about the murder at Bill Acrebond's mansion and that the alleged killer was one of Bill's maids. They all announced that the motive was not yet confirmed, but some reporters said they had heard from staff that it was a love triangle.

Bill was on the phone till long past midnight. He summoned his camarillas for a conclave to chart a byzantine and Machiavellian scheme to deflect the adverse effects of the murder in his mansion. Midmorning, a fleet of dark-tinted limousines entered Bill's house, passing through the reporters surrounding the gate. As usual, they entered an enclosed section before the passengers climbed out of the cars. There were a couple of politicians, the police chief, the coroner, a couple of judges and several lawyers, and a district attorney—all summoned by Bill. After everyone settled in and served themselves coffee, sandwiches or pastries, Bill arrived. In these meetings, no maid or other employees were allowed. They were just told to have coffee and food for so many people and leave the hall.

Bill spoke in a perlocutionary tone as if he was talking to his maids.

He began, "Gentlemen, an unfortunate accident has happened. A simple business deal has gone horribly wrong due to Earl's stupidity and stubbornness and partly due to an underestimation of Earl's stupidity by Doug, our associate. The truth is that Earl attacked Doug, and Doug defended himself and killed him with the same letter opener. It was a special, custom-made letter opener that was much stronger and sharper than a knife but shaped like a letter opener, and only we knew that it was more than a letter opener. Earl accidentally grabbed that and attacked Doug, and I guess Doug panicked and plunged it into Earl's chest. While it is clearly self-defense, many questions will be asked that will make things much worse. Especially because there is a big government contract coming up and Doug is our chief lobbyist and negotiator, and Earl was the ultimate decision-maker. At the very least, we will lose the contract. Yesterday, in the nick of time, I had to make a quick decision and involve one of our maids. But we still have the chance to make changes to our strategy if necessary. Any ideas?"

Martin, the coroner, started explaining something about the knife and then asked, "Can we call it a knife?"

"It is indeed a knife," Judge Éclair interrupted the coroner. "But a knife has more serious connotations attached to it. A letter opener simplifies the matter and makes it more acceptable as a quarrel and an accident."

The coroner continued, "As I was saying, the letter opener hit the rib bone, broke the bone, and penetrated the rib cage. Now, that needs a tremendous force, and it's not possible that the very delicate lady we have in our custody did this."

"I sense that you have developed some affection toward her. Has she captured your heart?" asked Judge Éclair.

"There is something different about her. I can't pin my finger on it, but she is different. When she is in the room, the room appears to be bigger. I don't know how to explain it. I don't even know what it is."

"Is this going to affect your judgment?" asked Bill.

"Of course not," answered Martin.

"Let's get back to the topic of our discussion," said one of the lawyers. "What if we don't talk about the broken rib?"

"I have an assistant who saw that, and besides, what about the district attorney?" said the coroner.

"Don't worry about the district attorney," replied one of the lawyers. "You just take care of your assistant. Are you saying that you don't have control over your assistant?"

"You were given this job for a day like this. For years, you have been getting a fat check with all the benefits so that you could be helpful on a day like this. Now we have to worry about your assistant?" asked Bill.

The coroner, while trying not to show he was worried, stood up and excused himself, saying, "I have to make a phone call."

He dialed his assistant, Addis Olizar, and very worriedly asked, "Have you talked to anyone or reported your findings to anyone?" Then he breathed a sigh of relief and said, "Don't talk to anyone and put the report in the filing cabinet and lock it. Anyone asks you about it, tell them it is not completed yet."

Then one of the politicians started speaking. "Even if the broken rib is not mentioned in the coroner's report, it will not be acceptable for people, the politicians, and the media, that this was simply self-defense by a maid whom Earl tried to rape. No one will believe that Earl wanted to rape a maid; it is disgraceful to the family, appears too simplified, and smells like a cover-up. If it works, the girl will walk free. Earl's blood was shed. People want to see blood in retaliation for Earl's blood."

"Whose idea was it anyway?" asked one of the lawyers.

"It was my idea," replied Bill.

"You know better that it won't work," replied the lawyer. "If she walks, the feds will get involved and interrogate her and everyone else until they find the truth. But if she serves time, then no more questions will be asked, and no one will get involved."

"What do you suggest?" asked another politician.

"I was thinking that it should be more in line with, let's say, love triangle, jealousy, that sort of thing."

"Then it will be considered murder one, intentional murder," said Bill, who was listening quietly while trying to grasp the situation.

"Is it going to cause a problem if Gloria is convicted and sentenced to a lengthy time in prison?" asked Judge Éclair. "You know, the longer the sentence, the fewer people will talk, and the less your name will get involved."

"When I called for her, I was thinking of attempted rape and self-defense since she is the most beautiful maid we had that night, and it would have been more plausible if it was her being attacked. But I don't care if she gets life, or we can ask one of our contacts in prison to kill her," Bill said.

"That would end the story fast, and people will not get satisfaction. It must drag on for years until people start getting tired of it and forget about it, and hopefully, more important news will come up. Then we can wrap it up any way we want," said one of the lawyers.

"It will not necessarily be murder one. The scenario will be that the maid was under the impression that Earl was leaving his wife to marry her, and when she found out that Earl was not leaving his wife, she got mad. In the heat of the moment, she picked up the letter opener and attacked Earl without planning to kill him—that would be considered manslaughter. It will be more acceptable to people and less damaging to Earl's family," said Judge Éclair. "Let's take a few minutes' break."

"He thinks he is a real judge in the courtroom," said Bill. "But it is a good idea. Let's take a break."

"Well, let's see. He has put many innocent people in prison, he has let many criminals free, and when you see how serious he is acting in the courtroom, you would consider him a real judge," said one of Bill's assistants.

"Some people want to go to the washroom, and some want to get a coffee. If the discussions continue while everyone is not present, then everyone will not know the whole plan, and mistakes will happen," said Judge Éclair.

"That is what I call good judgment," said Bill's assistant.

"I know," said Bill. "Thomas Éclair has always been very helpful, and I don't regret for a moment spending so much money and effort and resources to help elect him as a judge."

During the break, Thomas Éclair went to the washroom, got a coffee, took a big éclair from the breakfast table, and then sat back down.

Bill's assistant approached him and asked, "Is there any correlation between your name and your preferred pastry?" They both laughed.

When the session started again, one of the lawyers asked, "What if she changes her mind and denies any involvement?"

"She has already confessed to the murder and signed a confession," said the police chief. "All we have to do is change the story to a love triangle and have her sign again."

"What about blood-stained shoes, or as I have heard, there were some photos of the crime scene with the maid that showed a clock at a different time than the time of the murder indicated by the coroner," continued the lawyer.

"The time of death can be easily changed," said the coroner.

"Not that easy," said Bill. "Earl's driver came in at 11:30 p.m., and he was talking to Earl's wife. The time of his arrival and the phone conversation is registered. But the photos show time of death at 11:40 p.m."

"Then we have to collect and destroy all time-stamped photos and the ones with the wall clock in it," said the police chief.

Then Bill assigned one of his assistants to be in charge of finding and destroying all the photos. He asked him to review all the cell phones of guards and everyone else and delete the images. The police chief said he would take care of the shoes.

"Okay, gentlemen, now that everyone knows what to do, let's wrap up this meeting and get started," Bill concluded.

Then he asked Éclair, the coroner, several of his lawyers, and a district attorney to stay. They moved the meeting to Bill's office, now that there were fewer people. Bill took the lead and started the meeting.

"We have three issues to discuss. First, how we will make sure that Éclair will be assigned as the judge in this case. Second, to make sure that Sean Wilderson will be the district attorney, and third, who can take the case as the defendant's attorney."

Éclair said, "I can manage to be assigned to this case."

Sean Wilderson said, "I think I will get it, but, Bill, call your friend, the chief deputy DA, Jarred Trendad, to make sure that I will get the case."

Andrew Ramstone volunteered himself. "I am not that busy, and I can handle one more case."

"Remember, I want the best outcome for everyone. I want Earl's family to feel that justice has been served, so they won't appeal or try to drag us into it, and I don't want our name to be mentioned in the trial," said Bill.

"Does it matter to you how long the sentence is?" asked Sean Wilderson.

"Of course not. We all sacrifice for the cause, so let Gloria do her share. I have been employing her and her kind for years. It is time for some payback," replied Bill.

"I suggest prolonging the trial as much as possible. With time, the public rage will subside, and hopefully, other newsworthy events will occur so that we can go through it with the minimum amount of media and public scrutiny," said Sean Wilderson. "Bill, can you ask your friends in the media not to talk so much about it? The less they talk about it, the sooner it will be forgotten."

"I have done that already. But if other stations keep on talking about it and some of the stations don't, they will lose business and credibility," replied Bill.

"It would have been good if you owned all the stations," replied Sean.

"I am working on it," said Bill.

Then Bill turned to the coroner and asked, "Is your assistant aware of the broken rib?"

"I don't think he knows yet," the coroner replied. "And I asked him to stop working on it and store the body and the autopsy results. I did not want to put too much emphasis on it by asking him if he has reached that point yet."

"Tell me if he knows too much, and he will be eliminated," replied Bill.

"But he is a very cooperative individual. Any time I ask him to change something in the report, he has done it without question," replied the coroner.

"But why should we keep worrying about it? Just one bullet, and it will be the end of the story," said Bill.

"I will check it today and let you know," replied the coroner.

The coroner left Bill's house and went straight to his office. He asked his assistant to show him the report. He scanned the report and reached the point where it talked about the broken rib.

He turned to his assistant and explained, "This is going to be a problem. Change the report and write instead that the letter opener went in between the ribs and punctured Earl's lung and heart."

"I can't do that," replied the assistant. "I studied for so many years. I don't want to lose my license and end up in jail instead."

"You don't know who you are dealing with. There are people lined up waiting for the opportunity to kill someone so they can become a member of the Acrebond

Group. They are competing with each other to get the opportunity. Do you want that?" asked the coroner.

"Then I will quit. You tell your boss that I had not yet completed the report, and there was no mention of the broken rib. Then you prepare the report and do it any way you want," replied the assistant.

"Let me fire you instead. I will tell Bill that you had not found out about the broken rib yet, and I fired you so you would not find out. But be careful not to talk about it with a soul. There is a lot at stake. Not only will you get killed, but you will cause me to be killed, too. If Bill finds out that I lied to him, he won't hesitate for a moment," replied the coroner.

"I don't want any trouble," replied the assistant. "I will take it to my grave."

"Just make sure that it won't take you to your grave instead," replied the coroner.

The next morning, the coroner asked for a meeting with Bill and explained that his assistant had not started the autopsy, and as such, he fired him for a different excuse so he would never know about it. Bill proposed to arrange an out-of-town job for the assistant so no one would suspect or ask questions.

"There is a job opening in Houston. I can call my contact there."

"But that job opening is for chief coroner. Addis is an assistant with no experience."

"I can arrange it," said Bill.

Then he took a notepad, wrote down the Houston contact information, gave it to the coroner, and asked him to tell his assistant to contact him.

CHAPTER SEVENTEEN

It was Saturday morning. Phil was reading the newspaper while having coffee. When Richard entered the kitchen, he saw the back of the page that Phil was reading. It was about Earl's murder, and there were photos of Earl, his wife and children. There was also a photo of Gloria being escorted to the police car.

"Can I have the paper after you're done with it?" Richard asked.

Richard grabbed a coffee while Flore was preparing breakfast. When Flore brought out the breakfast, Phil handed the paper to Richard. Richard started reading the article about Earl's murder and looking at the photos. While police were escorting Gloria to the police cruiser, her dress shifted slightly and exposed her shoulder. Richard noticed a small heart-shaped birthmark. It looked familiar. Richard mentally reviewed his dream and realized the little girl in his dream had the same birthmark. However, she was covered with dust and dirt in the dream, so it was not clearly visible.

"I'll be damned!" exclaimed Richard, very astounded and excited. "I found out who the little girl in my dream is!"

Everybody became excited and asked Richard who she was.

"It is Gloria, the woman accused of killing Earl."

Richard showed the photo and pointed out the birthmark on her shoulder. He explained it was the same shaped birthmark the little girl in his dream had.

"Are you sure, Kiki?" asked Flore. "I have goose bumps all over my body. So, it is true. She is Kiki Coto's daughter!" Without waiting for a reply, she added, "Now you know why you are seeing the dream. You have to save her from these animals and prove her innocence."

"I have to be on her defense team," said Richard. "But how? I haven't written my bar exam yet."

"It is risky business to be on her defense team. The whole trial is going to be a sham," said Phil. "This is what we were talking about earlier. You will be exposed to some confidential information that you cannot walk away from. There are big politics involved in this. Maybe you should quit working for your uncle before you get in too deep."

"Your dad is right, Richard. I think you should not get involved anymore," said Cathy.

"Can't you see? This is what I have been waiting for all my life. I cannot quit now, no matter what the consequences are!" said Richard.

"Son, if your mother says to stay away from your uncle, you should listen."

"Mom, you have to ask Bill to put me on Gloria's defense team," said Richard.

"Hallelujah, finally my son asks me to do something for him!" exclaimed Cathy. "But I will not do such a thing.

I don't want to talk to him at all, let alone ask something from him."

"Even if you don't ask him to put Richard on Gloria's defense team, you should still talk to him as before, so he won't suspect anything. Otherwise, it will be bad for Richard. I still think you should quit, Richard," said Phil.

Reluctantly, Cathy picked up the phone and dialed Bill's number.

"You sound different. Are you okay?" Bill said. "Is something bothering you?"

"I'm okay. I might be coming down with a cold," Cathy answered.

Mary picked up a sheet of paper and wrote *pretend you are happy, as before.* She showed it to her mom as she was talking to her brother. Cathy tried very hard to talk a little more happily and enthusiastically. Finally, she got to the subject of Earl and Gloria.

"Since Richard's accident put an end to his football career, he needs a push and some encouragement to get into law. Could he be on Gloria's defense team? Even in the smallest of positions, it would be a big boost to his ego."

Bill thought for a moment and then said, "I will consider it . . . I'll try to find a position for a first-year law associate. I think we can get him on the team."

Cathy thanked him, and after chatting a little more, they said goodbye and hung up. Richard thanked his mom, but neither Phil nor Cathy were sure if this was the right thing to do.

Monday morning, Bill and Andrew Ramstone were having a meeting and further strategized Earl's case.

"Have you decided which junior lawyer you want to help you?" Bill asked.

"I haven't as my assistant is helping one of the other lawyers, but I think he will become available soon," Andrew replied.

"Why not assign Richard to the case?"

"But Richard hasn't passed the bar exam yet, and he has no experience whatsoever," Andrew said.

"You don't need anyone with experience. The less experienced, the better, as there will be fewer questions. Everything has been decided and set to go, and all you have to do is follow it step-by-step. It is not like you need to do research or anything you would need an experienced assistant for. Besides, Richard has been working both in his father's law firm and here, so he has enough experience. And it is better if he gets experience on a sure case like this that he cannot screw up than a serious case, so he will be ready for the next case if we need him in the future."

Andrew reluctantly accepted Bill's suggestion and asked his secretary to call Richard for a meeting. When Richard arrived, Andrew explained that he had been chosen as his assistant for Earl's murder case. Richard was very happy and thanked Andrew. They briefly reviewed the case together.

"Our strategy is to argue manslaughter, an accidental murder. In a moment of heated anger, Gloria reacted when she found out that Earl will not leave his wife and marry her," Andrew explained to Richard. He did not mention anything about the cooperation from all sides.

"Make yourself familiar with the case, organize all the documents and make a glossary so that I can produce any necessary document instantly in court," Andrew instructed.

Richard thanked him, gathered all the documents, and went to his office to review and take notes.

After a couple of hours, Richard could not wait any longer to tell the good news to his dad, so he called him and told him, "Guess what? Richard Dudhaull is the lawyer's assistant in Earl's murder case!"

Phil congratulated him reluctantly and asked him to be extremely careful.

Richard came home and told Mary and Flore he was on the defense team and thanked his mom.

"What did you find out about Gloria?" asked Flore.

"Well, the interesting thing is that according to the police report, she was born in Tijuana and not in Juarez, and she has a brother and a sister. All her family, including both her parents, are alive," replied Richard. "How can that be?"

"Can you talk to her?" asked Mary.

"I think so, now that I am on her defense team," replied Richard.

Cathy walked in, and Richard told her about his findings.

"Thank God, she is not the girl in your dream. How could she be? She is real, and your dream is not real," replied Cathy. "So, you can now quit with peace of mind and give us some peace of mind, too."

"I've been thinking about it since you called," replied Phil. "This is a big case. Not only are all the media in the country talking about it, but the media in other countries are also reporting on it. While you are excited that you have been assigned to this case, ask yourself, why would Bill assign you instead of a more experienced assistant? And don't believe that it was just because his sister asked him for a favor."

Cathy did not say anything as though she had doubts regarding Richard's assignment to the case. The TV was on, and a reporter started talking about the murder in Acrebond's mansion. Cathy turned off the TV angrily and asked Flore if the dinner was ready.

"Yes, it is ready. I will serve it now."

"So, are you going to meet her?" asked Mary. "Can I come with you?"

"No, you can't," answered Cathy.

"Why not? I feel like she is family. I've heard about her for years in Richard's dream," said Mary while giggling.

"One crazy person is enough in this family. I can't handle two," replied Cathy. Then she turned to Richard and said, "I have changed my mind on this issue. I agree with your father on this. I also think that you should not be on the defense team. Especially now you have found out she is not the girl in your dreams. I can't believe I am saying that, mixing dreams and realities. Just ask your uncle to assign you to something else, or better yet, get out of there and start working for your dad."

"When are you going to see her?" continued Mary.

"No, I am not going to ask Uncle Bill to assign me to another case," replied Richard. "And I don't know when I can see her."

Everyone sat down for dinner.

"There are rumors that Bill, or one of his assistants, killed Earl Murphy and blamed the maid. Is that true?" Phil asked Richard.

"Yes, they say it was Doug, Bill's chief lobbyist, who killed him, but he is nowhere to be found," replied Richard.

"Can we not talk about murder at the dinner table?" asked Cathy.

While everyone was upset and they were all talking to each other, Mary said, "Excuse me, I have something to say." But nobody listened to her. She said it again but with a higher voice this time, and again, nobody noticed her. Finally, she yelled, "Excuse me!"

Then everyone quietened and looked at Mary, surprised.

Phil said, "What is it, honey?"

"Mom, for as long as I can remember, you were always very appreciative of Uncle Bill for giving his half of the house to you while Grandpa's company was bankrupt at the time of his death, and Dad, you always thought that Grandpa's company was up and running very successfully when he died.

After our trip to Juarez and the new revelations about Uncle Bill, I did my own research and investigation.

It was a very long and difficult process. But finally, I found the truth about Grandpa's company at the time of his death. It is not a nice thing, and I didn't say anything because I didn't want to upset you, Mom," said Mary. "But I think under these circumstances, you should all know. Especially because Richard is working for Uncle Bill."

"Do you have more bad news for me?" asked Cathy, very upset.

"Well, compared to what you found out on your trip to Mexico, it is not as bad," replied Mary.

"You are killing me; say whatever you want to say," said Cathy, frustrated.

"Well, I did some digging and found out that the government contract was signed by Grandpa six weeks before he died," said Mary.

"Oh my God," said Richard. "Does this mean that half of Uncle Bill's wealth belongs to us?"

"Well . . ." said Phil.

But before he could continue, Cathy said while crying, "Don't call him Uncle Bill anymore. I lost my brother on the trip to Juarez, and now I don't want to hear his name. I lost the only family I had."

Cathy turned to Mary and asked, "Are you sure the contract was signed six weeks before your Grandpa died?" Cathy realized that Mary's eyes were full of tears. "Why are you crying?" she asked but then remembered what she had said. "I'm sorry, Mary. I didn't mean what I said. I wanted to say that I had lost my only sibling."

"I found the contract, and I took photos of the important pages," said Mary. Then she went to her room, brought back a file, and gave it to her mom.

Cathy looked at a couple of pages, checked her father's signature, then said to Phil, "Are you happy now?"

"Of course, I'm not happy, and I'm sorry that my suspicions were true," said Phil.

Cathy picked up the file from the table and said that she was going to see her brother.

"Are you out of your mind? He will kill you!" said Phil. "You won't be able to get anything from him after so many years anyway."

"But I can shame him," said Cathy.

"Mom, if you confront Uncle Bill, all our ties will be cut off. Can you wait a while longer until I can find out more information about this case and see who this Gloria really is?" Richard asked.

"No, you should get out of there immediately," said Cathy.

"Just give me a couple of days," said Richard.

"No, get out of there right away," said Cathy.

"Kiki, why don't you go and see Gloria and talk to her?" asked Flore. "I can go and see her with you if you want me to."

"Not with this Kiki business again," exclaimed Cathy.

"I think I can do that," said Richard. "After all, I am on her defense team."

"Let's go for a walk," said Phil and put his arm around Cathy's shoulder. And holding her tight, they moved out of the room.

Phil tried to convince Cathy there would be no positive outcome from confronting Bill.

"He will say something stupid that will anger you even more, and as there is nothing much you can do, you will only become more frustrated and depressed. If you are going to confront him anyway, at least wait until Richard completely cuts his ties with Bill. Otherwise, he may put Richard in trouble."

Finally, Cathy agreed to wait to confront Bill.

CHAPTER EIGHTEEN

Andrew explained to Richard in the office the following morning that they intended to ask for a psychiatric evaluation of Gloria before proceeding with the case.

"Keep on reviewing the file as much as you can, and come up with a detailed approach to successfully argue a manslaughter plea. When we need information to file for a motion for a psychiatric evaluation, we will get resistance from the district attorney. You have to be ready to reply immediately; there is no time to go back and review the file. You should know everything that is there and what is being added, too, but you will have plenty of time before the trial. So, you can catch up on your studies for the bar exam."

Richard spent all day reviewing the file's contents, including witness interviews and the chronology of events. He checked the time—it was 5:00 p.m. He ran toward Andrew's office to catch him before he left for the day.

"There's a lack of any personal information about the accused," he told Andrew.

"It's a clear-cut case, and it doesn't matter if there is no personal information, but it won't harm the case if we get the necessary information. Go see Gloria and get the information," replied Andrew.

Richard thanked Andrew and spent a little more time on the file.

When he arrived home, everyone was there. He told them he would see Gloria to obtain necessary information and hopefully get answers to many of his questions.

"I am begging you, Richard, get out of Bill's law firm and forget about your dream forever," said Cathy.

"All my life, I've been waiting for this moment. There is no way I'll quit now and forget about my dream," replied Richard.

* * *

Richard was waiting in the prison's meeting room. A guard brought Gloria in. Richard stood up, greeted her, and introduced himself as Mr. Andrew Ramstone's assistant. He asked Gloria very politely and respectfully to have a seat.

For a couple of seconds, they surveyed each other without saying a word. It was like they were trying to remember where they had seen each other before. They both felt they had known one another for a long time but could not remember from where. Then, like waking up from a sweet dream, Richard started the conversation by apologizing to Gloria without giving any reason for apologizing and started explaining that he had some questions he needed to ask.

Before Richard started with his questions, Gloria said, "You look familiar. Have we met before?"

Richard was trying not to appear crazy by talking about his dream. He also didn't want to lose credibility with Gloria, and so, to act more professional, he merely replied, "Maybe in Bill's house?"

Gloria spoke in a very soft and friendly voice. "Maybe, but I think it was a long time ago. Have you been to Tijuana?"

"No, I haven't," replied Richard.

"I have been working for Bill for several years, but I was mostly working on the farm," Gloria explained. "Many times, I was asked to work as a maid or hostess in the mansion when there were parties."

Then she recalled the different times she was in the house, mostly during business parties for Acrebond's high-ranking employees and other corporate executives and politicians, but sometimes other parties, too.

"I think I saw you once, many years ago," replied Richard. "You were carrying a big tray, and one of your co-workers helped you. I think he is the staff manager now."

"You mean Gabriel," replied Gloria.

"You said that you came from Mexico several years ago. Which city in Mexico was it?" asked Richard.

"Tijuana," replied Gloria.

"I thought you were from Juarez?" asked Richard.

"No, I'm from Tijuana. Why did you think I was from Juarez?"

"I'm not sure," replied Richard. "Do you have relatives in Tijuana?"

"Yes, all my family are there, my parents, brother, and sister," replied Gloria.

"Can you give me their names?" asked Richard.

"Yes, Jose Luis and Maria Elena are my parents, and I have a brother, Jose Antonio, and a sister, Rosa Maria. I send them money every month. I hope Acabar, sorry, Mr. Bill will keep his promise and help them while I am in prison."

"Why would he promise you that he will look after your family?" asked Richard.

"He promised if I do as he says, he will look after them," replied Gloria.

"What did he ask you to do?" asked Richard.

"You know…saying that I killed that man," replied Gloria.

"You mean you didn't kill Earl?" asked Richard.

"Mr. Bill told me never to say that I didn't kill that man," replied Gloria. Then she asked Richard, "On what occasion did you see me in Bill's house many years ago?"

"Probably it was a Christmas party, I don't remember exactly," replied Richard.

"Is your dad working for him?" asked Gloria.

"Well, my mom is working for him . . ."

But before Richard finished his sentence, Gloria said, "That explains it."

Then Richard continued, "We were not invited because while my mom is working for him, he is also her brother."

"He's your uncle? Dios Mio! Now I am in trouble for sure, please don't tell him I called him Acabar or said I did not kill that man. It was a slip of the tongue!" Then she sat straight and became very formal and untrusting of Richard.

"And that was a slip of the tongue on my side when I said 'my uncle.' I promise I won't tell him anything about our conversation."

"Thank you," said Gloria.

But Richard realized the connection between them had ended, and he became more formal but still polite and caring and asked about her hometown and parents and if they were aware of what had happened.

Gloria said, "No, I did not have a chance to talk to them and explain the situation."

Richard told her he could arrange for her to call her parents.

Gloria became excited, and for a moment, let down her guard and acted friendly and innocent, asking Richard, "Can you really do that?"

But very soon, she remembered she was talking to Acabar's nephew and straightened herself and became more formal again.

"Yes, I'm sure that can be arranged," replied Richard. "Now, let's talk about the incident. I understand you had nothing to do with the murder, and when you entered the room, Mr. Murphy was already dead. Can you tell me where you were at the time of the murder, around 11:00 p.m.? Who were you working with, and what were you doing?"

Gloria became disappointed and hopeless. She was confident Acabar had sent Richard to find out whether or not she was cooperating and how soon and easily she would tell the truth. She thought the sincerity Richard was showing was only an act, and the talk about calling her parents and helping her was also to fool her. So, she repeated the story that she entered the room to clean, and then Mr. Murphy entered the room and tried to rape her. But then she remembered that the story had changed.

"I'm sorry, I haven't slept much since the incident. I forgot that the story has changed. I promise I won't make that mistake again. Earl and I were lovers, and Earl had promised—"

Richard interrupted and said, "Please stop. I am here to help you, and I'm trying to collect evidence to prove that you did not kill Earl."

She felt she might be in bigger trouble than she thought. She became quiet and looked desperate for a couple of seconds. She thought that Bill was breaking his promise and that she had been tricked into accepting that she committed the crime following Bill's blackmail and promises of help. Now she had to face the full force of the injustice all by herself.

She realized that even if Bill hadn't promised to help, she would still do as he had said. She wouldn't put her family in danger, and she calmed down a little. She made the sign of the cross and whispered a short prayer in Spanish, *"Dios, me entrego a ti, por favor protégenos a mi y a mi familia del mal. Te escucharé y haré lo que digas, enfrentaré a los demonios sin mostrar debilidad o duda porque se que estas conmigo y aceptaré lo que sea tu voluntad."* (God, I deliver myself to you, please protect my family and me from this evil. I will listen to you and do as you say and I will face the demons without showing any weakness or hesitation because I know you are with me and I will accept anything that is your will.)

Richard did not understand everything Gloria had said, but with his limited knowledge of the Spanish language from high school, Richard realized that Gloria did not trust him anymore. She was praying to God to protect her and her family from evil, including himself. By accepting responsibility for a crime, she did not commit; she was determined to face the consequences without hesitation, all for the safety of her family.

Then she turned to Richard very calm and indifferent, like talking to a stranger, and said, "As I said, Earl and I were lovers. Earl had promised me that—"

"Please stop."

And Gloria kept quiet. Richard realized that Gloria was talking to him like she was far away; her body was there, but her soul was in the heavens. She had surrendered herself to a higher power. Now Richard was very disappointed with himself. He came with all the intention of helping, giving hope, and trying to save her, but he had done the complete opposite. *How did this happen?*

Then he realized that while they were living in the same city, they were living in two completely different worlds. She was just a commodity in her world; his uncle had complete control over her life and destiny. They were talking the same language, but words had different meanings. As a result, a miscommunication had occurred, and he was about to lose her trust completely.

"The hell with Acabar," said Richard. "I am here to help you."

"But you are working for your uncle, aren't you?" asked Gloria.

"Yes, but I only took this job so I could help you," replied Richard, realizing how stupid it sounded.

"How long have you been working for your uncle?" asked Gloria.

Richard quietly replied, "Three years."

He wanted to explain the dream, Bill's photo, and why he accepted working for his uncle, but he thought he might make things worse, and also something did not match here. The girl in his dream had lost both her parents and her brother. Gloria's parents, her brother and sister were all alive. He thought that he had done enough damage for one day and was better off keeping quiet until he found out more.

They remained quiet for a few moments, Richard desperately trying to find a way to get out of the hole he had dug himself in, and Gloria not knowing what to think because Richard sounded both silly and truthful. There was something different about this guy that Gloria couldn't figure out.

"I am going to talk to your parents," said Richard. He started writing down: Jose Luis (father), Maria Elena (mother). "Sorry, what were your brother and sister's names?"

"My brother is Jose Antonio, and my sister is Rosa Maria."

Happy that he could get Gloria to talk to him again, he asked if he could have their address and phone number and handed her his pad and pen, and she wrote down the information.

Richard stood and told Gloria, "I will do everything I can to help you, and if I must, I will leave my uncle's law firm in order to help you."

"Just remember, no one can go against him. He has the police, judges and politicians in his pocket, and I will not do anything to put my family in danger," said Gloria.

Richard left Gloria feeling disappointed and confused. Gloria had the same birthmark at the exact location, but she was from a different city, and her parents were alive. He was happy that her parents were alive, but how could that be? He had managed to alienate her instead of gaining her trust. He wanted to call her parents right away from his car, but he thought, *what if I ruin this potential contact as well?* He felt he could not work in this state of mind, so instead of going to work, he drove home.

*   *   *

There was no one at home except Flore. He explained to Flore about Gloria's parents, her brother and sister, and that she was from Tijuana, not Juarez.

"I want to call Gloria's parents. Could you talk to them with me?" Richard asked.

"Calling them with all this news and information is not a good idea. We should go and meet them in person. It is just a one-day trip to Tijuana," said Flore.

Richard agreed and started locating their address and finding out any information he could about Gloria's family. Phil, Cathy, and Mary came home one by one, and Richard reported his findings to them.

Cathy was very happy and said, "I was right all along! Richard's dream was just that, a bad dream, and now he can forget about the whole thing and get out of Bill's law firm and get on with his life."

Richard reminded his mom that the girl in his dream had the exact birthmark as Gloria and in the same place.

"You remembered the birthmark after you saw it on Gloria. That is called imagination," replied his mother.

"It is just a one-day trip. Why don't you let them go so that he will have peace of mind one way or another?" said Phil.

"Can I go with you?" asked Mary.

"Let Richard and Flore go together," replied Phil. "It is better that way. You have to get their trust somehow so that you can get the correct information. Otherwise, it may backfire if they don't trust you and report your visit to Bill."

"We were not there, and we don't know the truth," said Cathy. "If she was innocent, then why did she confess to murder?"

"Because she was afraid that Bill would put her family in danger if she didn't confess," replied Richard. "When I asked Gloria about it today, she first said that Earl wanted to rape her, so she stabbed him, then she remembered this was the original story she was told to tell, but it was later changed to the love triangle. When I told her that I knew she did not kill Earl, she said that Bill asked her to take responsibility, and she knows that bad things will happen to her and her family otherwise."

"She must have a good reason for taking responsibility for the murder. So, what if she goes to prison for a couple of years? It is not like she would lose much or get behind in life. Either way, she won't be doing much," Cathy said.

"Mom, I can't believe you just said that," said Mary.

Cathy was caught off guard. She realized that she was thinking out loud. "I can't believe I just said that," said Cathy. She knew that while everyone thought like that, it was not nice to say it loud, especially in front of her Mexican maid.

Richard was speechless. He looked at his equally surprised father. Flore's eyes became teary, and she walked away to the kitchen. She started crying quietly while keeping busy washing some dishes. Cathy followed her to the kitchen, hugged her, and said, "I'm sorry, the words came out wrong. I didn't mean what I said. I'm worried about Richard getting involved in something that is over his head, and I'm afraid to find out more horrible things about my brother."

Flore accepted the apology as she had no other choice. She loved Richard and Mary like her own children. If she didn't accept Cathy's false apology, she would probably be cut off from the children. Flore apologized to Cathy for being selfish and inconsiderate of what Cathy was going through.

When they returned from the kitchen to change the subject, Cathy turned to Mary and said, "I don't think that you should go with Richard and Flore."

"Do you have the address and the phone number?" asked Phil.

"It is in an unnamed road branching from Teresa Garcia Street. I located the house on the map from the landmarks Gloria wrote for me," Richard replied.

CHAPTER NINETEEN

Early the next morning, Richard and Flore drove to Tijuana so they could return by the afternoon. On the way out, Cathy tried once again to change Richard's mind about going.

When she couldn't, she told him, "Be very careful and stay away from danger. As soon as you realize that it is useless, do not push for answers; just come back." Cathy then turned to Flore and said, "Please take care of my baby."

"I promise you that I will look after Richard. People in Mexico have heart. He will not be in danger," Flore said.

Richard messaged Andrew Ramstone, his boss, from his car and explained that he wouldn't be at work that day because of some family matters.

On the way to Tijuana, Richard and Flore talked about the different reasons why Gloria would think her parents were alive. Unlike Cathy, Flore believed that Gloria was the lost daughter of her childhood hero: the great Kiki Coto. She brought up different theories why Gloria would not be aware of that. But the most logical theory for both Richard and Flore was that Bill gave Gloria to this family, and when she grew up, he took her back to exploit her.

"I have to remember not to mention Bill is my uncle. His name sends shivers down people's spines," said Richard.

"Let's go to a coffee shop, get some rest and strategize our approach with Gloria's family," said Flore.

They exited the highway and went to a coffee shop. They ordered coffee and started talking.

"When we go to their house, if only the husband or the wife is present, we should not talk about the issue and instead wait until both of them are present," Flore suggested.

Richard agreed and added, "We should act like we are aware that Gloria is not their daughter and ask for an explanation for how they got her."

"We could even tell them that we know she is the daughter of the legendary Kiki Coto," said Flore.

Richard became a little worried and quiet.

Flore sensed his change of mood and asked, "What are you thinking?"

"What if Bill kills Gloria to keep her quiet?" said Richard. "But maybe killing her won't solve his problem. People want to see someone go down for killing a politician. Otherwise, he wouldn't hesitate for a second," continued Richard, trying to calm himself and give himself hope.

Flore didn't respond. It was what she had thought, and she was not sure why Gloria was still alive. She couldn't give an opinion and live with the consequences in case she was wrong. Richard looked at Flore and kept quiet. For a couple of minutes, there was a sad silence and mutual despair. They both felt it but did not want to actualize it by acknowledging it. Otherwise, it would mean turning around, going back, and capitulating. Flore broke the silence with a prayer in Spanish.

"Gloria said a prayer like this the other day," said Richard. "If I didn't know better, I would say you know each other."

"We all come from the same source and are connected through the same source," replied Flore.

After a short silence, Flore said to Richard, "Gloria's parents, or whoever they are, probably are simple people who will become afraid very easily. They won't trust strangers, so when we are in Gloria's house, we have to be careful that before we get their trust, one of them doesn't call Bill while the other one is talking to us. Otherwise, the minute they talk to Bill, they will stop talking to us."

"If we go to their house and only one of them is there, while we are waiting for the other parent, they may call Bill as soon as they find out where we are from. They may first call Gloria, and if they don't reach her, they will call Bill. After all, their main concern will be Gloria, and they cannot wait until the other spouse gets home for us to tell them why we are there. If they call Bill, all our plans will be neutralized," said Richard.

"Let's go and do some sightseeing and wait until 6:00 p.m. to make sure that when we get there, both of them will be home," said Flore.

Richard searched for interesting places to see in Tijuana and chose the Tijuana Cultural Centre, and they went there. After a couple of hours, they left and drove toward Gloria's house. They stopped on the side of the road close to Gloria's house to make sure they would arrive around six. Finally, they drove to the house and knocked on the door. A young man opened the door. Flore started talking in Spanish.

"Hi, are you José Antonio?"

The young man was surprised and said, "Yes."

"Are your parents home?" Flore asked.

He called his parents. Jose Luis, Maria Elena, and their daughter, Rosa Maria, came to the door.

"We are from California and want to talk about Gloria," Flore explained.

Gloria's mother got very upset and excited and asked fearfully, "What is happening with Gloria? Is she okay?"

Richard asked Flore, "Why is the mother so excited, and what is she saying?"

Maria Rosa answered in English, "My mother wants to know if Gloria is okay and why you are here."

Richard was happy to hear Maria talking in English and asked, "Do you all speak English?"

Jose Luis said, "Yes, we are working with Americans, and we travel to the United States often and had to learn English. I work in construction, and when there is no construction, my wife works in one of the hotels or on a farm."

Maria Elena interrupted the conversation and asked again, "Is my Gloria okay? Did something happen to her?"

"She is okay physically, but she is in jail," Richard replied. "We are trying to help her and need some information from you."

"Why is she in jail? What did she do?" asked the mother.

"She did not do anything, but she was forced to confess to a murder," explained Richard.

"Why did she take responsibility for something she did not do?" asked Jose Antonio.

"To protect you," answered Flore.

"I don't understand. What does it have to do with us?" asked Rosa Maria.

"Maybe your father can explain," answered Flore.

The father was surprised for a couple of seconds and then became sad. "It is Mr. Bill, isn't it?" he asked.

"Yes, it is. Gloria is taking responsibility for a murder that Bill or one of his men committed," said Richard.

"How can we help?" asked Jose Antonio.

"Yes, tell us now, how we can help?" asked Rosa Maria. "We will do anything to help our sister."

While everyone was listening attentively, Richard explained the murder scene and how Bill had asked Gloria to take responsibility. He said that Bill thought he could get Gloria off the hook by claiming self-defense, but his advisors informed him that it would not be acceptable, and someone had to go to jail. And so, Bill changed the strategy and was going to let Gloria go to jail.

"Why did Gloria accept to go along with Acabar's plan?" asked Rosa Maria.

"Because she is afraid if she doesn't, Bill will hurt you, her family."

"We will tell Gloria that we are not afraid of Acabar," said Jose Antonio. "We are not even afraid to die."

"Gloria will not accept it," said Richard. "Unless we tell her the truth, then she will know that you will not get hurt."

"What truth?" asked Rosa Maria.

Richard looked at Jose Luis and Maria Elena and asked, "Why don't you explain?"

Father and mother looked at each other and looked down for a couple of seconds.

Then, the father said, "The truth is that she is our daughter, and we love her like our daughter, and Bill is aware how much we love her and how much she loves us. But we are not afraid of Acabar, and we are ready to fight and even die for her. Tell her that she must tell the truth and should not take responsibility for something she didn't do."

"What do you mean, we love her like our daughter?" asked Rosa Maria.

Jose Luis took a deep breath and started explaining.

"Your mom and I were married for several years and could not have children. I was working for Mr. Robert, Bill's father, in his construction projects. When I was working north of the border, Abraham, Robert's partner and a friend, called me and told me he knew how much we wanted to have a child. He told me he had asked someone to take a little orphan girl to my house and asked me to take care of her as my own. When I called your mom, she was ecstatic and told me that God had answered our prayers and brought us a little angel. We decided to raise her as our own and not tell anyone she was adopted. For that reason, we moved far away from that neighborhood to this location."

Tears started running from Richard's eyes. Seeing Richard crying, Rosa Maria and Jose Antonio got teary-eyed as well.

Maria Elena started talking. "Gloria was the best thing that ever happened to us. She made us very happy and brought us good luck. A couple of months later, I became pregnant with Jose Antonio, then a couple of years later, Rosa Maria was born. Did Acabar tell you that Gloria was adopted?"

"What you have done is admirable. You have raised Gloria like your own," said Richard. "No, Bill didn't tell us that she was adopted."

"How did you know then? Abraham told us that no one knew about Gloria," said the father.

Realizing that once he started explaining, the whole subject would shift, Richard replied, "It is a long and tragic story. It was Bill who killed Gloria's father. But he couldn't possibly know that Gloria is Kiki's daughter, as he would never have let the children of his victims stay alive for fear of their retaliation. I will tell you another time."

"Poor Gloria," said Rosa Maria. "Why did Bill kill Gloria's father?"

"Is it the same Bill that Gloria is working for?" asked Jose Luis.

"Yes, the same Bill. But neither Gloria nor Bill is aware of this fact. Tell me, how did Gloria end up working for Bill?" asked Richard.

"I was working for Robert on different construction projects. After Robert died, I continued working for Bill. Some years ago, Bill asked me if any of my children would want to work on his farm. I asked Gloria, and she agreed," explained Jose Luis.

"I am sure you didn't know what kind of monster he is, and he is treating his workers like slaves, forcing them to do anything he wants by threatening to kill them and their families," asked Richard.

"No, we did not know. Who was Gloria's father?" asked Jose Luis.

"Perhaps you have heard of him. We believe that Gloria's father was Enrique Coto or Kiki Coto," said Flore.

"Yes, I have heard of him. But I did not know who killed him," replied Jose Luis.

"So, tell us, how can we help?" said the mother.

"I talked to Gloria yesterday. She doesn't trust me, and she would not listen to me," said Richard. "Maybe if you call her and tell her to trust me, she would listen to you. I can call you when I go and see her and give her the phone to talk to you."

"You appear to be a nice and trustworthy man, but we have only just met each other. How do we know that Acabar didn't send you to find out information on how we feel about his dirty plans? And even if you really want to help Gloria, how much chance do you have fighting Acabar?" asked the father.

"Maybe you should tell them about your dream," said Flore.

"I don't think they will be interested in my dream," said Richard.

"They will trust you after hearing about it," replied Flore.

"What dream? Please tell us about it," asked Rosa Maria.

Richard realized that it would not hurt, so he started from the beginning with every detail. Everyone was listening with intense fascination. But when Richard reached the part where he saw the heart-shaped birthmark on the little girl, everyone jumped and made a 'wow' noise and got goosebumps.

"So, you are the reincarnation of Kiki Coto," said Jose Antonio.

"Whenever someone is doing something courageous and noble, but very risky, that has almost no chance of succeeding, we tell him, 'Don't be a Kiki Coto,' said Jose Luis.

"It's interesting. Even my mother has never acknowledged that this could be true. I sometimes thought about it, but this is the first time someone is saying it out loud," said Richard.

"What happened after Acabar killed Kiki and left?" asked Jose Luis.

"I don't know. I never passed that moment in my dream. I always woke at the same moment," replied Richard.

"I have a thought. There is an American in the market selling different herbs and herbal medicine. I have heard he can make people see their dreams. Maybe we should go and see him," said Jose Luis.

"It's late. We have to go back," said Richard.

"It is already too late to go back," said Jose Luis. "Why don't you stay here for the night, and tomorrow morning we will go to the market and see this American. Then you can return."

Richard did not believe that anyone could make him see the end of his dream. He had tried for many years but could not.

He was looking for an excuse to decline the invitation when Rosa Maria, realizing his dilemma, asked him, "Why don't you want to see the rest of your dream?"

Richard smiled and replied, "How can a stranger make me see the dream when I cannot?"

"Unusual things happen in Mexico," replied Flore. "There is more faith and spirituality south of the border."

Richard agreed to stay. He thought that it wouldn't hurt.

"Richard, you sleep in Jose Antonio's room, and Flore, you will be in Rosa Maria's," said Maria Elena.

*   *   *

The next day, they drove to the market. They parked their car and walked through a maze of small streets full of merchants. You could find almost anything and everything there. Finally, they arrived at the herbal store.

Jose Luis pointed to a Native American talking to a customer and said, "This is the guy. His name is Wapi"

After a couple of minutes, Wapi became free, and Jose Luis, Richard, and the whole gang approached. Richard told him about his dream and explained he could not see the ending. Richard also described the present time troubles and the possibility of a connection to the dream.

Wapi asked Richard to sit on a chair, close his eyes and concentrate on the last part of the dream he could not see beyond.

Richard, following Wapi's suggestions, started visualizing the dream, and slowly, he fell into a deep sleep and was really dreaming. He reached the point where Kiki was shot several times by the gang leader and was left to die and the little girl to be burned alive.

After a few minutes, Richard opened his eyes and told everyone he saw an additional couple of seconds of the dream but not to the end. He explained that after Kiki was shot multiple times and was left dying, trying to save the little girl from burning alive, he lay down on his side, back to the fire with his knees bent, and placed the terrified little girl in between his knees and chest, away from the fire, whispering something in the little girl's ear before taking his last breath.

"It's interesting. I saw more of the dream, but only a couple of seconds more," said Richard.

"You have to see your troubles solved in your mind first. When something becomes completely real in your mind, it will become real outside your mind. The universe will summon all that is necessary to accomplish your wish. If you do ayahuasca, you will see your dream to the end and may find solutions to your problems as well," said Wapi.

"What is ayahuasca?" asked Richard.

"It is a spiritual journey customary to the indigenous people of the Amazon. You drink a spiritual medicine, and with the help of an ayahuasca master, you pass to the other side while you are still alive. There is a shaman outside of Cusco, Peru, called Joel. You can visit him," said Wapi, then opened a book and wrote the contact information on a piece of paper, handing it to Richard.

"I thought it could be done here, around the corner. Peru is far away. Who has the time?" said Richard.

"Just keep the contact info. You will make time when the time comes," replied Wapi.

They thanked Wapi and asked how much it would be, but he said there was no charge. Richard asked Flore to help him choose some herbs to buy as an indirect payment for Wapi's time, and they did so before leaving.

On the way to their cars, Jose Luis suggested it would not be necessary to tell Gloria the truth about her being adopted. Richard accepted this because there would be no benefit in telling the truth since it would cause more confusion for Gloria if she found out under the present circumstances.

Richard told Jose Luis, "I will visit Gloria tomorrow, and in her presence, I will call you and let Gloria talk to all of you. Please convince Gloria she can trust me."

Richard and Flore returned home and told the rest of the family everything they had learned about Gloria's family, how they came to have Gloria, and that Richard could see a little more of his dream.

Cathy was surprised and disappointed at the same time. She had hoped the trip would result in not finding anything and that Gloria was not the girl in Richard's dream. Phil suggested Richard quit his position at Bill's law firm, join him and represent Gloria through his law firm.

"There may be psychiatric evaluations for Gloria so we can postpone the court proceedings. Then, it will become an old story, and people will not seek vengeance as much. The longer I stay with Bill's law firm, the more information I will collect," Richard explained.

"I disagree," said Phil. "Gloria should change her confession immediately, and she cannot do that through Bill's law firm. And if you stay longer with Bill, you may not be able to part from Bill so easily. Bill may not let you leave."

CHAPTER TWENTY

Richard went to see Gloria again in the morning. As soon as Gloria walked into the meeting room, Richard told her that he had met her family and showed her some photos. Gloria was excited and asked about her family. Richard told her they were okay and started dialing her father's phone number.

While Gloria was talking to Jose Luis, she started crying. She explained that she was in prison. Her father told her that he had met Richard and trusted him completely and asked her to trust Richard, too, and consider him like family. He then explained that Wapi saw Richard and approved of him. After Jose Luis, Gloria talked to her mother and Jose Antonio and Rosa Maria. They all said prayers for her and told her they trusted Richard and asked Gloria to trust him.

Hearing that Richard had her family and Wapi's approval, Gloria calmed down. She felt relaxed and was much more friendly with Richard as she felt more trusting of him. After Gloria finished her conversation and hung up, Richard started explaining.

"After your family found out about the chain of events, the fact that you had nothing to do with the murder, and how you were called after the fact and asked to pose for incriminating photos, your family decided to fight Bill. They are not afraid of any harm Bill may inflict on them."

Before Gloria had the chance to reply, Richard continued, "I am also willing to fight alongside your family against Bill any way I can and at any cost."

"So, you really went and met my family and even Wapi? That is a lot to expect from a stranger, especially from Acabar's nephew. My father asked me to trust you like family, and I'm going to do that. I'm glad you are on my side, and my family likes and trusts you, but do you know who you are going against and the dangers you will face? So, there must be a reason for so much kindness and willingness to sacrifice. There is a saying, 'don't be a Kiki Coto' for situations like this. Can you now tell me the whole story, too?" asked Gloria.

"Let's say I don't like to see an innocent person go to jail because of an evil gangster. The details are not important and will not change anything. When you get out of here, which I hope will be very soon, I will tell you everything, but for now, let's concentrate on how we are going to fight this evil," replied Richard.

"That night, I was very shocked and confused when I saw that guy's body," Gloria said. "Acabar kept threatening my family and me. He kept promising that nothing would happen to me and forced me to pose for photos. I wish Abraham had been there; I am sure things would have gone differently. The way Acabar explained, it was supposed to be self-defense, and I would not go to prison. I'm not sure what I would have done if I had known I would end up in prison. I would probably do the same thing. In prison, I feel safer, and I know my family will be safe. The police, Sean Wilderson, and Andrew Ramstone tell me that if I cooperate, I will only go to jail for a couple of years. They are all together in this. They all work for Bill. You know that. For a couple of years in prison, I don't want to fight Bill and be on the receiving end of his evil side. I feel safer here than when I am out; that's why I decided to do as they told me."

"Why do you think the police and the district attorney are cooperating with Bill?" asked Richard.

"They told me themselves. When they came to see me and asked me to change my story from attempted rape to a so-called love triangle, they told me that this was what Bill had agreed on. They suggested I should go along. Besides, I see them at Bill's parties all the time. They are talking and strategizing about different cases while playing cards in Bill's basement. Of course, everyone is aware that if they tell anyone, even one word about these meetings and conversations, a family member will die. Only when high-ranking politicians come, we are not allowed to go in the room."

"But it is unfair. You had nothing to do with it. Why should you do time for a crime that someone else has committed?"

"You know how easy it is for Acabar to kill me in here if I don't do as they say? I have already received threats as warnings to cooperate. Besides, he can kill my family one by one. Why should I take a chance, fight him, only to cooperate with him after he has killed someone to prevent a second murder?" said Gloria.

"I hate to admit it, but from what you told me, it appears to be a good plan, a safe one," replied Richard while very saddened and feeling despair. Then asked Gloria, "Is the Abraham you mentioned the same Abraham who was friends with Bill's father?

"He is friends with my father and was friends with Bill's father, and he was one of the top managers of the company when Bill's father was running the company. But when Bill's father died, Bill forced him to step aside," replied Gloria. "He used to come and see me while I was still in Mexico and would bring me gifts. A couple of years ago, when Acabar asked me to work on the other side of the farm, where I was working up to now, I called him, and he stopped me from being transferred to that other side."

"Which side of the farm was that?" asked Richard.

"The drug processing side," answered Gloria.

"Can you elaborate?" asked Richard.

"If I hadn't talked to my dad just now, I would say you are testing me and that Acabar sent you to see how much information I would give out. But I realize now that you don't actually know anything, and you take everything at face value. The farm is a front for drug processing and storing. Planes drop off the drugs at the farm from a low altitude. While the farming part is very profitable, its profit is only a fraction of the drug side of the farm. The drug processing and storage part is under a separate deed owned by one of Acabar's assistants. Of course, he has many storage places around the state and even other states, but the main one is the farm. The side I was working on is a legitimate farm. We do farming; there are cattle, chickens, pigs and other animals. You have no idea who your uncle is, do you? Ever wondered why there are so many police officers in and around the farm? To protect the farm from other drug dealers and other police," Gloria said.

"I am getting to know him better," replied Richard.

"You should not get involved with him. Keep your distance. Otherwise, he will suck you into his dirty world, and you will never get out and be a free man again."

"The only reason I started working for him was to help you."

And so, they came to an unofficial conclusion to accept what was forced on them. Richard was not in any hurry to leave, and the guard had orders to be more lenient on Gloria. So, he stayed, and they chatted a little longer. Richard started talking about Phil, Cathy, and Mary and told Gloria that he considered her a family member. He also told Gloria how his parents used to fight over Uncle Bill until recently when Mary found out that Bill had cheated his mother out of her inheritance.

"But I am happy we did not know about it. Otherwise, I would not have found you," said Richard.

Gloria appeared to be relieved by hearing 'a family member.' Finally, they said goodbye, and Richard returned to the office.

When he arrived home, Richard spoke about his conversation with Gloria. He talked about the farm and what was actually going on there. Cathy did not question the authenticity of these findings like she used to.

"I don't know who he is anymore, and I'm afraid there are going to be worse findings," she said.

"You should not talk to Bill about any of this," Phil insisted. "And Mary, the same goes for you."

Again, Cathy asked Richard to get out of Bill's firm.

"I will only participate in Gloria's case and will not take any other case by using the excuse of studying for the bar exam," Richard said.

"I disagree," said Phil. "Why don't you quit Bill's law firm and go to court as an observer, just like news people and the general population?"

"No. I won't abandon Gloria," Richard said.

CHAPTER TWENTY-ONE

Pedro, Jack's assistant and his eyes and ears on the street, called Jack and asked for a meeting.

"There are usually random dealers on the street working solo for some extra income, but there appears to be an organized group trying to take over part of the city," Pedro said.

Pedro showed some photos and provided names of some of the dealers and samples of their products that he had purchased so that their labs could analyze and trace them to the source. Jack thanked Pedro for recognizing the group in formation and left.

Jack called Antonio Donatelli immediately and asked for a meeting. He explained his findings and provided all the photos, names, and samples. Antonio called Bill and asked for a meeting. He told Bill that Scott should also be present without describing the situation on the phone. Bill asked Antonio to call Scott and ask him to come over first thing tomorrow morning. The following morning, Antonio arrived before Scott and while describing the situation, Scott joined the meeting.

"Scott, you are getting sloppy. If we depended on you to keep the streets safe for our troops and help eliminate the competition, the competition would soon take over our streets. What are your officers doing all day? Why should our people have to find out there is a competition being organized and getting stronger every day? Isn't it your job to eliminate them before it is too late?" demanded Bill.

"Bill, I assure you we are scouting the streets like a war zone," Scott began to say, but Bill stopped him by throwing at him the photos, samples, and the list of names and where each individual was stationed.

Scott was speechless and started looking at the evidence.

"Well? What do you have to say? How did this happen? This time, we were lucky that our soldiers became aware of the situation before it was too late," said Bill.

"We will get all of them before noon," replied Scott.

"Are you stupid? These are just foot soldiers. You have to get their leaders if you want to stop them. Otherwise, the leaders will hire other soldiers and continue their operations. You should form a task force, identify their leaders, locate their headquarters, attack at once in all directions, and capture the leaders and their merchandise and cash. That's how you eliminate the competition," Bill said.

Scott formed the task force, and after four months of intense investigation with the help of Bill's people, the leaders and warehouses were located. In a synchronized operation that included task force members from other police stations, they captured them all: sixteen drug dealers, including the bosses, a couple of tons of drugs, and over twenty million dollars in cash. The warehouses where the drugs and cash were held were invaded by

Scott's people only. The officers from other police stations were assigned to capture the small dealers on the streets or at their houses.

The day before the police raid, Richard overheard a couple of partners in the law firm talking about the operation to eliminate Bill's competition but pretended not to hear, following his dad's advice to stay away from trouble. The morning after the drug raid, the headlines on all media said that police, with the expert and dedicated leadership of Chief of Police Scott Timmins, had captured sixteen drug dealers, over fifty kilos of drugs, and $185,000 in cash.

Scott announced there was only one minor, non-life-threatening injury to one of his officers, Henry, who was recovering in the hospital. Except for the three leaders, the rest of the gang, or soldiers, as Bill put it, were offered a deal: either go to prison for the rest of their life or change ranks and join Bill's group. All accepted the deal and through judges and district attorneys on Bill's payroll, were freed after several months of jail time and continued their employment with Acabar. The injured police officer was given a medal and assigned to desk duty as he had a small limp from his injured right foot.

A couple of months after the court proceedings and closing of all the cases, fifty kilos of drugs left the warehouse for the incinerator. On the way, the truck entered a warehouse, but a different truck with fifty kilos of sawdust continued its journey to the incinerator.

CHAPTER TWENTY-TWO

Bill called for a brainstorming meeting to find a solution for replacing Earl Murphy, an important contact and government official who helped obtain lucrative government contracts. All his top assistants, the police chief, Judge Éclair, Sean Wilderson, Andrew Ramstone, and many others were present. Bill opened the meeting by explaining that with Earl out of the race, they were worried that his replacement would not be as cooperative and they would most certainly lose the construction contract they were hoping to receive.

"Earl's opponent, Pastian Braxton, is well respected, has a strong character, and is famous for his honesty and transparency. One of the reasons he was not elected last time was because I helped Earl by publishing negative articles about Pastian and positive articles about Earl in the media owned by my friends and me. I had also made significant donations to Earl's campaign. This time, Earl's assistant, Dylan Jaref, is Pastian's opponent. Dylan is a weak character and a joker compared to Pastian. No amount of bad publicity for Pastian and good publicity for Dylan will work this time. We have tried many times to get Pastian to cooperate, but no matter what we offered him, he would not. So far, we could not even get viable blackmail material to force him to cooperate with us. The only person who is willing and eager to cooperate with us fully if elected is Dylan."

"He has no chance of being elected. Pastian will eat him alive," said the police chief. "He doesn't know how to debate. Heck, he doesn't even know how to talk."

"If Pastian Braxton is eliminated, I am sure Dylan Jaref will win," said Antonio Donatelli.

"You cannot kill another politician. We are still coping with one dead politician. If you kill Pastian Braxton, it will backfire," said Judge Éclair.

"What if we kill him professionally?" said Bill.

"How are you going to do that? We've tried everything to collect blackmail material on him, but we couldn't," said Andrew Ramstone.

"We can create one," replied Bill. "We will find an old girlfriend, a classmate, or an acquaintance who will claim that Pastian raped or groped her. That will be the end of Pastian Braxton without killing him."

"What a genius idea! Bravo," said the police chief.

"How are we going to do it?" asked Judge Éclair. "We have tried to pin something on him for years, but we couldn't."

"Well, desperate times call for desperate measures," replied Bill. "We have to assign an investigative journalist to Pastian, to locate all his classmates, girlfriends, colleagues, and anyone Pastian has come into contact with in his life. We will find someone who is willing to cooperate or is desperate enough for cash to testify that Pastian raped her."

"What if people don't believe our story?" replied Sean Wilderson. "In that case, it will blow up in our face, and Pastian will gain more popularity."

"People are addicted to gossip; they thrive on gossip. You broadcast the news and watch how people devour it, then regurgitate it and chew on it repeatedly. That is how the general population spend their time, constantly gossiping and feeling important by kicking a down and out individual," remarked Bill.

Everyone agreed with Bill's plan and promised to investigate to their utmost ability and find as many old friends of Pastian Braxton as possible.

Bill called Barbara, one of his contacts in the newsroom, for a meeting. After greetings, Bill reminded her of the different news leads he had provided and explained that this one he was working on would be very big news. All she had to do was to create it. Bill went on to explain the situation and the necessity of helping Dylan Jaref win the election.

Hearing the name of Dylan Jaref, Barbara started laughing and asked Bill, "Are you serious?"

"I am dead serious," Bill confirmed.

"How is Dylan going to win the election having Pastian Braxton as an opponent?" she asked.

"That's where you come in," replied Bill. "You should find all of Pastian's old girlfriends, colleagues or classmates he has dated and locate the one who has a grudge against him. Pastian was young one day. He has certainly done something we can use against him."

Barbara promised to find what Bill was looking for, then said goodbye and left.

CHAPTER TWENTY-THREE

A couple of weeks later, Andrew Ramstone and Richard visited Gloria in prison. Andrew explained that as part of their defense strategy, they would ask the court for a psychiatric evaluation. Andrew usually talked freely and without any pretense to Gloria, but while Richard was present, he pretended this was a real case, and Gloria was not being forced to accept responsibility for someone else committing murder. Gloria played along and did not let Andrew know she and Richard communicated freely and honestly. She agreed to what Andrew said, and they left.

The next day, they prepared and filed the documents to commence the psychiatric evaluation. Meanwhile, Judge Éclair was talking unofficially to different officers in the court to get the case. A week later, Judge Éclair called Bill.

"I asked to be assigned to this case, but the case has been assigned to Judge George Razien."

Bill got mad and yelled, "You imbecile, you were asked one simple thing, and you could not do it!? If Razien gets the case, we are in trouble. I have been working on him for many years, and I could not buy him. He is uncooperative like hell, and he will find the facts and expose us all immediately. You screwed it up big. You fix it!"

"Bill, if I insist I want the case, not only will I not get it, but it may raise suspicion, too. There is due process on who gets what case," replied Éclair.

"What do you expect me to do?" asked Bill.

"Call Jarred Trendad. He can arrange it," replied Thomas Éclair.

"It will cost me, and I will deduct it from your next pay," replied Bill.

Bill called Jarred Trendad and explained the predicament that the incompetent and clumsy Éclair had created for him and asked him to take care of it.

"But it is not that easy," replied Trendad. "There are procedures and regulations for assigning a judge to a case."

"Don't tell me about procedures and regulations. I am the creator of these regulations. Don't worry, you will be well-compensated, and it is coming out of Éclair's pocket," replied Bill.

"Well, I don't promise you anything, but I will try my best and let you know," said Jarred Trendad.

"It is very important. Don't try; just do it. Promise me you will take care of it. You can assign George Razien another case that starts on or around the same time as our case. Or, we will delay our case until he is unavailable, then assign it to Thomas Éclair. Couldn't you come up with something like this?" yelled Bill.

"Okay, I will find a way and let you know," replied Jarred Trendad.

A couple of weeks later, Jarred Trendad called Bill and informed Bill that he had rearranged all the cases, and all they had to do was postpone their case for three weeks so Éclair would get the case.

The court date for psychiatric evaluation was set in about six weeks as part of a delaying tactic. Andrew Ramstone asked for another three weeks postponement so that Jarred Trendad could assign Thomas Éclair to the case.

A couple of days before the court date, a limousine picked up all parties, including Andrew Ramstone, Sean Wilderson, Thomas Éclair, and the psychiatrist, James Calmad. It brought them to Bill's mansion for a preparatory meeting. As customary, the limousine entered a covered area so nobody would see who was coming in and out. There was food and booze in the conference room. After greetings and eating, they started brainstorming different strategies for the court as there would be many reporters, and anything they said in court might be broadcast in media.

Bill interrupted them and said, "This is a simple procedure, and you should keep your energy for the actual trial." Then he said to Andrew Ramstone, "Call James to the stand. After letting him describe his credentials, including his Ph.D. and how he is the author of several books and a professor at the university, ask him his opinion about Gloria's mental state. He will say he has to run some tests. Sean will tell him that during his conversations and interactions with Gloria, she appeared to be alert and in a sound, mental state, and James will very politely tell him to shut up as he is not an expert. With this conversation and exchanges, the media, and in turn, the public, will be convinced that justice is being done and individual rights are being protected."

They continued reviewing the details again and finalized the strategy.

The court date came and was adjourned until after the psychiatric evaluations and the report from James Calmad, which they knew would take approximately one year as had been planned.

CHAPTER TWENTY-FOUR

Barbara reviewed Pastian's school yearbooks, and his social media accounts, trying to locate his contacts to be interviewed. Except for a few, she found most of them and contacted them one by one with the excuse that she was preparing an article about Pastian Braxton. She interviewed them but could not find any dirt on him.

She finally called Pastian himself, pretending that she was a fan, and asked for an interview. Pastian happily agreed to the interview, thinking every little bit of promotion would help. During the interview, Barbara asked for the names of all his past girlfriends.

"I didn't have many girlfriends," Pastian replied. "After brief friendships with a couple of classmates, I found the love of my life, and after several years of friendship, we married and are still happily married." He did not provide any name.

Disappointed and hopeless, Barbara met Bill and explained that she could not find even a small amount of dirt on Pastian. On the contrary, everyone talked about Pastian with adoration.

Bill got angry and started yelling at Barbara. "You are getting sidetracked! You should stay focused on the bull's eye instead! Did you interview all the people who Pastian knew his entire adult life?"

"I had interviews with all his past girlfriends. There weren't many. I couldn't locate some girls in the yearbook. But they are not important because Pastian didn't date them."

"They are the most important people. They have no affection toward him. Find one in some financial need, and for the right amount of money, they will sing any song you ask them to," said Bill. "Give me their names and any information you have about them, and my people will find them."

Bill provided the names to the police chief and asked him to assign the best investigators to locate them. A week later, the police chief returned with all the contact information of the people on the list. He also provided details of any arrests or files that they had in the past. Bill and the police chief reviewed the individuals one by one until they reached one of Pastian's grade twelve classmates, a woman named Susan, who had been arrested a couple of times for possession.

Bill called Barbara and asked her to call Susan to her studio in her house and interview her. Susan was the single mother of a twenty-one-year-old son. She could not hold down a job because she was drinking and using drugs.

"I didn't date Pastian. As far as I remember, I danced with him at one of the school parties, but only one time," Susan explained.

After hearing that Susan had danced with Pastian, Barbara became interested in Susan. "Did anything inappropriate happen to you while dancing with Pastian?" she asked.

"No, he didn't do anything inappropriate. What do you mean?" asked Susan.

"Like kissing you against your will or touching you inappropriately, that's what I mean," replied Barbara.

"I was hoping that he would kiss me, but he didn't," replied Susan.

Barbara became very disappointed. She was worried about Bill's reaction and his disappointment when she told him that his last hope had ended without any positive results. Barbara thanked Susan for going to the studio and having the interview and said goodbye.

Susan, with a shameful face, asked, "Am I going to get paid for the interview? The only reason I'm asking is that I'm having financial difficulty. Otherwise, I wouldn't bring it up."

All of a sudden, a big bright light turned on in Barbara's mischievous brain. Instead of saying no to Susan and explaining that there were no fees paid, she said, "There are usually no fees, but because you are a nice person and in need, I may be able to arrange for a fee. I will call you in a couple of days. Don't talk to anyone about this meeting. Otherwise, there won't be any fee."

Very excited, Barbara called Bill and arranged a meeting.

"Susan only had good things to say about Pastian, but she is desperate for cash. I think for a fee, Susan will be willing to testify that Pastian groped her."

"Money is no issue. We need her to testify that Pastian raped her. That will ensure that Pastian will never be able to be in politics for the rest of his life," said Bill.

"I am not sure about Susan agreeing to accuse him of rape because she adores Pastian, but maybe I can convince her to admit in front of the camera that he groped her," said Barbara.

"For the right amount of cash, she will admit to anything. Just increase the amount until she agrees," said Bill.

Barbara called Susan immediately, told her that she had good news, and asked for another meeting. The studio in her house was decorated like a TV studio with mirrors all around and hidden cameras behind each mirror. When Susan arrived, Barbara treated her like a friend.

She gave her a drink and asked, "Is there any possibility that Pastian could have raped you while you were at the high school dance?"

"Oh no, he was a gentleman; he would never do such a thing. Besides, all he had to do was ask. I would go out with him gladly; he was so handsome," replied Susan.

"That's too bad. Because if indeed he had raped you, you would get paid very well," replied Barbara.

"But how could I say he raped me when he didn't?" replied Susan.

"You see, I make my money by making news. If I make money, I can pay you. Otherwise, if I don't make any money, how can I pay you?" asked Barbara. "A politician raping a classmate in high school is big news, and there is big money in it."

Susan did not want anything to do with this kind of accusation toward Pastian, but she could not resist asking, "How much money are we talking about?" Even if it was just to satisfy her curiosity.

"How much money would it take for you to admit Pastian raped you?" asked Barbara.

"But he didn't rape me," replied Susan.

"What do you think will happen to Pastian if you said he raped you? Nothing," said Barbara. "He is filthy rich, and nothing will ever happen to him. He will go on with his life as though nothing happened. Except, I will have a job because I would have discovered good news, and you will become wealthier by saying one short sentence."

"But it will ruin his career," replied Susan.

"Pastian is a millionaire. He will retire to his multimillion-dollar villa and enjoy the rest of his life instead of the hustle and bustle of politics. You would be doing him a favor. He has so much money that he does not have to worry about it for the rest of his life. Did he ever think about giving some to the needy, like you?" asked Barbara. "I am sure if you received a fraction of his wealth, it would solve all your money problems forever. Now is your chance."

Susan was very tempted. On the one hand, she did not even want to consider the possibility of claiming that Pastian raped her, but on the other hand, she could not resist finding out how much money was involved. She struggled to control herself and do the right thing and get out of there before doing something stupid that she would regret for the rest of her life.

Barbara saw the struggle in her face and continued. "What did Pastian mean to you any way that you are protecting him with your life? Do you think he is going to thank you for sacrificing for him? Because that is exactly what you are doing, you are denying yourself a happy life without worrying about money anymore, and for what? You don't owe him anything. Just one sentence, and all your money worries will go away. You owe it to yourself to have a good life and be able to help your son, too."

"Exactly how much money are we talking about?" asked Susan unintentionally, and then realizing the inappropriateness of her question, she continued that she couldn't do it regardless of the amount.

"How much money would solve all your financial problems?" asked Barbara.

Thinking that the amount involved was probably small, Susan replied, "$100,000." She was thinking there was no way she could get paid that much for saying one short sentence, and this way, she could end the uncomfortable conversation.

Surprised that she had a breakthrough finally for such a small amount, Barbara thought that if she accepted Susan's offer, she would only increase the amount, so she replied, "How about $50,000?"

Susan was flabbergasted with the acceptance of even half the amount. Trying very hard to control her enthusiasm, she said, "No, fifty is too little."

"Okay, seventy," counter-offered Barbara.

Not believing her ears, Susan said, "No, I won't do it for less than one hundred."

"You know, it has been a while since I had worthwhile news. You are driving a hard bargain, and I need the news. I accept. Let's do it," said Barbara.

"Oh my God, what am I doing?" said Susan.

"$100,000 for one short sentence," said Barbara.

"I need my money first," replied Susan.

"Let's practice first. As you can see, there are no recording devices around. I want to make sure you are relaxed and convincing enough. If you do well, then I will pay you, and we will record the conversation. I still have to go to the bank and withdraw the cash. I don't have $100,000 sitting around. Let's start," said Barbara.

*   *   *

"We have Ms. Susan Walkertin in the studio. Hello, Susan, welcome to our show. You have —"

"You said you would not record the conversation. This feels real," said Susan.

"We are not recording," replied Barbara. "But we have to practice like the real thing, so when we do it for real, we will know what to say and do. Do you see any cameras in here? We are just practicing to make sure you know what to say when you come tomorrow. Let's start over. Try to be convincing, serious and real."

"Okay, I will try my best," replied Susan.

"We have Ms. Susan Walkertin in the studio. Hello, Susan, welcome to our show. You mentioned that you attended the same high school as Mr. Pastian Braxton, is that true?" asked Barbara.

"Yes, it is true. We attended the same high school."

"You mentioned that there was an incident involving Pastian. Can you elaborate on that?"

"Yes, he raped me," replied Susan with reservation and shame.

"This is why I wanted to practice. The way you said, 'he raped me.' It is obvious that you don't believe it, that you are lying. You must be very convincing, angry and hurt. You should describe the mental pain you went through and are still living to this day. Say, 'We did not date, but sometimes we were at the same parties. At one of the parties at a classmate's house, after Pastian and I danced, he took me to a room. I thought we were only going to kiss, but he raped me. I asked him to stop. I screamed. I tried to get out from under him, but I could not.' Can you say it with a sad voice, feeling pain and show that you have been agonizing about it all your life? Then say that because of that incident, you could not study, you could never hold a job, and you became an addict."

"I am not going to say that I am an addict on TV," said Susan.

"We are not on TV. It is just a practice. Say it for practice, and tomorrow, if you decide not to say it, it's okay," replied Barbara.

"No, I don't like the word addict. I'm not going to say it," replied Susan.

"Okay, we will call it substance abuse. How is that?" replied Barbara.

"Well, it sounds a little better, although it is the same thing."

"Okay then, let's start from the beginning," said Barbara.

They repeated the process again and again, all day long, until at the end, Susan became so tired and annoyed that she said everything Barbara asked her to say without even thinking about what she was saying. Her tired voice made her appear sad, angry, and depressed from talking about the incident. Barbara thanked Susan and told her she would call her tomorrow morning and that she could leave.

As Susan was getting ready to leave, Barbara realized it might be better to let her stay in her house, in case she changed her mind by tomorrow. If she talked to Pastian and he asked her to publish a denial before her recording was broadcast, it would not have the same effect.

"Susan, you must be very tired as we have been practicing all day. Why don't you stay at my place tonight? We will have dinner and watch TV," asked Barbara.

"Okay, if it is not a burden. I am kind of tired and depressed about what I'm going to say tomorrow. I could use the company," replied Susan.

Barbara led Susan to her guest house and showed her around. Then she excused herself and called Antonio Donatelli.

"I have exciting news!" she told him. "I have a perfect clip for broadcasting where Susan is accusing Pastian of raping her. Susan is in my house now and is asking for her money. I think she should get paid, so she won't deny everything after it is broadcasted."

"I will call you back shortly," replied Antonio.

After a couple of hours, Jack, Antonio's assistant, knocked on Barbara's door. After having dinner, Barbara and Susan were watching TV while drinking wine. Susan was half asleep. Barbara excused herself and went to the door. Barbara took Jack to a room in the basement. Jack gave her the envelope with the money.

"The boss thinks it is better to give her the money in installments rather than all at once. This way, Susan will have an incentive to keep her mouth shut and cooperate, and in addition, she won't go on a shopping spree or deposit it all in the bank and raise suspicions," Jack explained.

"I am not sure if she will accept installments," replied Barbara.

"She has no other choice. You said you have the clip. You will broadcast it tomorrow morning. What choice does she have? If she denies it, she won't get the rest of the money, and no one will believe her denial. Once the news hits the street, it doesn't even matter if she denies it. That will be the end of Pastian Braxton. That brings us to our next issue. It's been decided that she should go on a vacation to a villa in Mexico and stay there until the election is over," continued Jack.

"Who is going to take her there? I can't. I'm busy. I have to be in the studio to broadcast the recording," said Barbara.

"I have someone in the car who can take care of it. Just introduce me as your boyfriend and him as my brother, and he will take care of the rest," explained Jack.

"Oh, I don't know if it will work. How can you ask her to leave everything and go to a villa in Mexico?"

"She does not have much going for her around here. Besides, the guy I brought with me is a professional, just trust me," replied Jack.

"I am already nervous about what I'm going to do tomorrow. I don't want things to blow up," replied Barbara. "What if they connect the villa to Bill and find out it was a setup?"

"You know that nothing will be connected to Bill. The villa is registered under someone who is completely clean. Let me get the guy. His name is Rodrigues; we call him Rod. You introduce him to Susan and let him take care of the rest. He will even tell her about the installment payment," replied Jack.

"Rod? I like the name," said Barbara.

"I am your boyfriend, not Rod, don't get confused," replied Jack.

Jack made a phone call, and Rod appeared at the door.

Jack introduced him to Barbara and reminded her again, "I am your boyfriend, and Rod is my brother."

Barbara looked at Rod with adoration and said jokingly, "Can't Rod be my boyfriend, and you be his brother?"

"No, Rod will spend the next month with Susan. I don't have that kind of time," replied Jack.

"I was just joking," replied Barbara.

Barbara introduced Rod to Susan, who fell in love with him immediately, especially after hearing that he was single. She was excited, and her mood changed completely. She was not tired, depressed, and sleepy anymore.

Rod said to Barbara, "If I knew she was so beautiful, I would have worn a nicer outfit!"

Susan said, "Everything is perfect."

She excused herself to go to the bathroom. She put on some makeup, fixed her hair, and came back. Barbara went to the kitchen to prepare some snacks.

Susan followed her to the kitchen, and as though she was Barbara's friend, like a schoolgirl, she asked, "Is Rod really available? Would you mind if I hit on him?"

"Of course not. I saw the spark between you two; go for it!" Barbara said.

They had some snacks and drinks, and Rod got on with the business.

"Jack and I are helping Barbara with the payment to you. Barbara told me that you have agreed on $100,000. Is that correct?"

"Yes, it is," replied Susan.

"We think it may raise suspicions if you deposit the whole amount in the bank at once. We think it will be better for everyone if we pay you in installments. However, rest assured you will get paid the whole amount. What do you say?"

Susan wanted to say no, but Barbara continued, "Before you say anything, let me explain. I don't want to withdraw $100,000 at once and raise suspicions. And you don't want to deposit $100,000 for the same reason. I promise you that I will give you the full amount but in installments. Here is the first installment," said Barbara, handing Susan the envelope.

"We are your witnesses," said Rod. "Jack and I promise that you will receive the full amount you were promised."

Susan had a lot to drink and was mesmerized by Rod. She did not want to upset him. She flipped open the envelope slightly, and with the sight of a bunch of hundred-dollar bills, she tried very hard to act casual.

"It is okay," she said.

"Very well then. I am going to my villa south of the border tomorrow morning for a couple of weeks. Who is coming with me?" asked Rod.

Susan started blushing.

"Why don't you take Susan?" replied Barbara. Then she asked Susan, "How about it?"

"It would make me very happy to have such beautiful and attractive company," said Rod.

Trying to curb her enthusiasm, Susan replied cautiously not to reject the idea but also not immediately accept it. She wanted to show she needed some persuasion.

"I barely know Rod. How can I go on a trip with someone I just met?"

"We will get to know each other over there," replied Rod.

"It is a big villa with many rooms. You can have any room you want. When the news comes out, everyone will chase you if you are in the city. It will be much better if nobody knows where you are."

"Well, my son lives on his own, close to the university. Sometimes, I don't see him for weeks. He won't miss me. Besides, my mother is here. If he needs anything, my mom will help him. But wait a minute, if we are going south of the border tomorrow, when are we going to make the recording?" asked Susan.

"Don't worry about it," replied Barbara. "When we were practicing, I recorded the last one on my phone. That will do it."

"What a relief," replied Susan. "I thought we would have to start all over again tomorrow."

"No, you can enjoy life at the beach. I will take care of the rest," said Barbara. "I was going to suggest that you don't show up in public until the election is over, but now that you have decided to go with Rod, that issue will be taken care of too."

Something clicked in Susan's head, and while she was trying to put two and two together, Barbara said, "You have a win-win situation. You get your money, you get to go on a fully paid vacation, and on top of it all, you get the most handsome stud to spend your time with. Don't tell me that you're not happy?"

"I guess it is okay," replied Susan.

"When do you want to go?" asked Rod.

"I thought we were going tomorrow morning," replied Susan.

"We can leave tonight," said Rod. "You can sleep in the car, and we will get there early in the morning."

"I have to go to my apartment and get some stuff," replied Susan.

"We can make a stop at your apartment," replied Rod. "Take the necessary stuff, but don't worry about anything else. You can find everything over there."

Susan and Rod left, and Jack also left after a short conversation with Barbara to discuss the payment manner and timing.

"Tomorrow is a big day. We are going to turn the tables on Pastian Braxton," said Jack and wished Barbara good luck.

*   *   *

The next morning at 7:30 a.m., Barbara talked about an old classmate of Mr. Pastian Braxton and explained that she had come forward and informed the news agency that Mr. Braxton raped her in the last year of high school. She played the video.

For days, all the TV and radio stations, newspapers, and magazines talked about this shocking revelation. Pastian Braxton appeared on many TV and radio shows and explained these were all lies. He even took ads on TV and radio, denying the allegation and explaining that he is from a religious family with high moral values and would never do anything like that. He begged Susan to come forward and explain why she was making these accusations. But every time he denied the allegation, he was confronted with a simple question. "Do you know Susan? Was she in your class? Why would she make up something as horrible as this? There must be some truth behind the story."

Now, all of a sudden, Dylan Jaref, an old-time alcoholic and drug addict with only half a brain, who looked more like a comedian and a puppet than a politician, appeared to be a good choice as a candidate. Pastian Braxton lost the election with only 0.3 % of the votes. People lost a good politician, and Bill got a puppet for a politician and his government contracts.

In his losing speech, Pastian Braxton blamed the gangs that created and nurtured the untrue sex scandal and constantly fed the population with lies.

One of the reporters connected to Bill said, "This is a free country, and people are free to elect whomever they want."

Pastian replied, "In this election, some gangsters won the election, not the people."

Rod was instructed not to let Susan watch any of the TV programs that showed speeches made by Pastian Braxton. Rod wasn't to allow her to see Pastian's pleas for her to come forward and tell the truth, that this was a lie and nothing like this had happened. After Braxton lost the election, Rod was also instructed to show her many TV programs and shows that broadcasted her interview and bogus claim. Bill's advisors wanted to know what her reaction would be. Would she become upset about what happened to Pastian or not care at all? As Rod showed her interviews and Pastian's pleas to her, Susan was devastated by what she had done.

She started crying, drinking, and saying, "I am sorry, Pastian. I'm going to set the record straight."

Rod reported the situation to Jack. Jack consulted with his boss, Antonio Donatelli, who consulted with Andrew Ramstone, Sean Wilderson, and Judge Éclair. They all confirmed that the consequences of her talking and telling the truth were severe, and she had to be terminated. Rod and Susan left Mexico, and Rod brought her back to her apartment. He gave her a lot of booze and drugs. Then he went to the other side of the city and sat in a bar while Jack entered Susan's apartment with a hoody and gave her drugs with pentanol. A couple of days later, Susan's son came home and found her body. The coroner concluded that it was an overdose with a bad batch of drugs.

Barbara, in her commentary the next day, announced that after many years of living with the bad memories and pain of what Pastian Braxton had done to her, Susan found refuge in alcohol and drugs and had overdosed.

CHAPTER TWENTY-FIVE

Cathy was struggling with severe depression. She had lost her brother. She was essentially an orphan now as both her parents had passed away long ago. Her kind and honest brother had turned out to be a murderer and a gangster who had cheated her out of her inheritance.

All her life, she was very thankful to her brother, thinking the job Bill had given her was out of kindness, and she was always working very hard to reciprocate his good deeds.

Several times, she had mentioned to Phil if they had received their fair share of the inheritance, not only would they not have had to work as hard as they had all their lives, but they could have built a real estate investment company of their own and managed their assets. For over twenty years, Phil tried to convince Cathy that her brother had cheated her, and now he was trying to calm her down, so she would not do something stupid like confronting Bill.

"Bill is not going to give you a penny," Phil would explain again and again. "By confronting him, not only will you put Richard in danger, but you will also put everyone else in danger, and all for nothing. You will not get a penny from Bill, so why tell him that you know what he has done? The opportunity may appear in the future. When and if the time comes, you will use your knowledge to your advantage. But if you confront him now, you may lose the opportunity forever."

Cathy would always consider it a joke and would laugh and tell Phil, "I am not in a mood to laugh at your jokes." She didn't realize that Phil was very serious about it.

Cathy had seen several shrinks and received various prescriptions for depression, but Phil would always advise against pills.

"Once you go on depression pills, not only will you have to keep using them all the time, but you will not be yourself anymore, and you will not be able to live a regular life," he advised her.

Phil believed that depression pills were for people with more serious chemical imbalances in their brains than Cathy.

Phil convinced Cathy to go for walks in the park and practice tai chi, yoga and meditation. He would go with Cathy to all her classes for yoga, meditation and tai chi, and he would take Cathy for a walk in his favorite park almost every day. Not only were these activities very helpful for Cathy, but they also made her happy that Phil was spending so much time with her and cared so much for her.

Sometimes, she would wonder whether or not she was over the depression. She would wonder if she was subconsciously pretending to be still depressed so Phil would continue to spend more quality time with her.

She would feel guilty about it. She even once confessed to Phil that it might be possible she was pretending to be depressed because she liked Phil's company and attention. Of course, Phil laughed about it and replied that he was enjoying it, too. But Phil knew that Cathy was not over her depression.

Once, Cathy commented to Mary that one good thing that had come out of this was how close she and Phil had become. Cathy's change of character would worry Mary and Richard, who would often ask Phil about her. Phil would tell them everything was going well and ask the children not to argue with her. He said they should be nice to her, but not too nice that she would feel they considered her mentally ill.

They had both reduced their working hours significantly. Phil was seeing fewer clients, and Cathy explained to her supervisors, Hector and Fabrizio, that she had migraine headaches after working more than a certain number of hours. Hector wanted to let Cathy go.

"Even with fewer hours, Cathy is not the same as before. She is not acting like a manager; she is acting more like an employee. She only orders supply and prepares the employee charts," he said to Fabrizio.

But Fabrizio, the Director of Operations for the hotels and restaurants, reminded him that Cathy was not just another employee as she was their boss's sister.

"Even if Bill agrees to let his sister go now, six months later, he will regret his decision and blame us. So, while we can mention to Bill that Cathy is having a hard time coping with migraine headaches, we should do it out of concern for Bill's sister, not to complain about an employee not doing her job as expected. We will let him decide what to do about it."

One day, Richard came home very happy and informed his family that his accident lawyer had settled the case for a very large amount, such that if he did not work for the rest of his life, he would be okay. He proposed to buy properties and let his mom manage them instead of working for Bill.

"Now you will have a good excuse to quit working for Bill!" said Richard.

And so, Cathy quit her job with Bill.

CHAPTER TWENTY-SIX

Knowing that in approximately nine months to a year, Gloria's trial would begin, Richard was determined to pass the bar exam so he could officially be a lawyer, in case he found it necessary to represent Gloria by himself.

While he was working in Bill's law firm against his parents' wishes, he was studying very hard for the bar exam. The first bar exam was in two months. Perhaps there was not enough time for studying. Richard knew the chances that he would pass were not great, but he wanted to go through the experience anyway. He did not pass the first time by a relatively small margin.

In the beginning, he visited Gloria often. They would chat like two relatives about everything from childhood memories to politics and current news topics. It was during one of these visits that Richard felt compelled to tell Gloria that her present parents were her adopted parents. He told her who her real father was and how he was murdered. And then, one day, Gloria told him that she was sure Bill had some contacts at the prison, and if he kept on visiting, Bill would become suspicious and cause problems for them.

Richard visited less often, not knowing that for every move Gloria made and every visitor she got, a report went to Andrew Ramstone, who reported it to Bill in a summarized form.

Gloria was aware that Richard was studying for the bar exam. Richard was not sure if Gloria asked him to visit less often for fear of Bill or if she just wanted him to study harder. Finally, the exam day came, and this time Richard passed with high marks.

CHAPTER TWENTY-SEVEN

Phil liked to organize BBQ parties in his backyard and invite friends and some clients, so when Richard passed the bar exam, he took the opportunity to officially introduce Richard to his clients as a lawyer who would be taking over his practice soon. And for this reason, he invited more clients than usual.

Among this year's guests were: Phil's assistant, Voski, and her husband Davit; Rancho and his wife, who were longtime clients and owned and operated a very successful online travel agency; Ugo, who owned an advertising and marketing business; Tom and Alice, Phil's clients and friends who Phil had been helping with different legal issues free of charge; Jasper and his wife, who operated a drugstore chain; Richard's old friends, including Mike; and many other close friends, colleagues, relatives, neighbors and some other clients.

For these parties, Phil usually hired bartenders, cooks and servers. It allowed Phil and Cathy to mingle with their guests. Phil and Cathy greeted the guests, talked to each group for a couple of minutes, and moved on to the next group. They reached a group where Rancho, Ugo, and Jasper were present. They congratulated Phil and Cathy for Richard's passing of the bar exam. Cathy realized that the wives were standing near the bar waiting for their turn, excused herself, and approached them.

Rancho told Phil, "I know that your brother-in-law is not coming to your parties because of a lack of security for him, but George would usually come to your parties and socialize with regular people like us. I don't see George today, either. Such a nice guy, how can such an evil man have such a good kid?"

"Maybe George takes after his aunt rather than his father," Ugo replied, and they laughed.

"It is not for lack of security; it is because he thinks he is a big shot and does not want to waste his time with regular people like us," said Ugo.

"Bill is one of the worst criminals and one of the biggest gangsters, but he presents himself as a philanthropist, and you know what is even worst, the media buys it all," said Jasper.

"Of course, the media buys what he says. Bill owns the media," said Rancho.

"If the media doesn't buy what he says, he will buy the media," added Ugo, and they all laughed.

Kim and Larry, Phil's clients, approached Phil and started complimenting him. "You were always very helpful to us. You are such a real nice guy, someone we could trust all the time, more like a friend than a lawyer." Larry continued, "When I had a workplace accident, you spent so much time on my case. Without your help, my employer would not give me anything, and we would have gone bankrupt. Phil, you are the reason that we can live with a little dignity. I hope one day I can reciprocate your kindness."

"Thank you for inviting us, Phil," said Rancho. "When something good happens to such deserving people like you and your family, I become very happy like it has happened to myself. I appreciate you and your family so much."

Jasper and Ugo confirmed Rancho's praises and raised their glasses for a toast.

Usually, Phil would invite Bill, too. Of course, Bill would never go with the excuse of being busy, but this time, he did not ask him in case he decided to attend. Phil did not want Bill to know they were aware he had cheated his sister out of her inheritance. Phil was not sure if Cathy could control her anger and act sisterly as before. He was not sure how Bill would react if he found out that they knew his cheating. He was worried for Richard as he was still working for Bill. And knowing what Bill was capable of, even with his limited knowledge of his capabilities, he was worried for the whole family. Another reason Phil did not invite Bill was Phil thought it would be awkward to introduce Richard to his clients as their future lawyer in the presence of Bill while Richard was still working for him.

"I find the situation somewhat amusing," Phil told Richard. "In the past, I was inviting Bill so Cathy would not be mad at me. Now I am not inviting Bill, so Cathy will not be mad at me, among other reasons."

Mike, Richard's childhood friend, was also invited. Richard had not seen Mike and some other friends for a while. Because of the life-changing experiences he'd had with the accidents, studying law, and meeting Gloria, it appeared to him that his world had changed, and he was a different individual. He envied Mike for being the same old Mike—hardworking but relaxed, very friendly, and a simple lifestyle. Mike realized that while Richard was acting happy, knowing him from childhood, he actually seemed distracted and unhappy. He was surprised that with all the achievements and with everyone celebrating his achievements, Richard was unhappy. Mike was aware of Richard's involvement in Earl's case and his weekly visits with the alleged murderer. He asked Richard about it. Richard was surprised and a little worried by Mike's information about the case and asked him how he had obtained the information.

"I've been following the murder case of Earl Murphy on the news. I'm aware that you are one of the assistants in that case. How's the case going?"

Richard confirmed that he was on the defense side. "It is not going well," he admitted. "How do you know about my visits to Gloria in prison? The visits aren't reported in any media."

"You know that I am doing home renovations," replied Mike. "One of my clients is the warden of the prison where Gloria is being kept. I worked many times at his house, and we became friends. I told him that my friend was on the defense team. And he told me that you are visiting her more often than usual."

"Wow, what a coincidence!" exclaimed Richard.

"Everyone, including the warden, knows that the girl did not kill Earl Murphy. Why is it so difficult to prove this in court?" asked Mike

Richard then asked Mike, "Do you remember the dream I saw when I was younger?"

"Of course, how could I forget such a crazy thing?" said Mike. "You were talking about it all the time."

"Well, the girl I see every week in prison is the girl in my dreams," replied Richard.

"Oh my God, it is unbelievable. I would have never guessed that it was real or would become real. Tell me, who is she and why were you seeing her in your dreams?" asked Mike.

Richard told Mike about Kiki Coto and how Bill killed him and all his family except Gloria. He explained the evidence he had that would prove her innocence and how he was afraid that Bill might kill her in prison.

"I wish there were a way I could help," replied Mike.

"There may be," replied Richard.

"Anything," replied Mike.

"I will let you know when the times come," replied Richard.

After everyone had arrived and had had a chance to enjoy some appetizers and a couple of drinks, Phil called for everyone's attention. He officially announced Richard's passing of the bar exam. Phil thanked everyone for being loyal clients and invited them to accept Richard as their lawyer in the near future.

After everyone took a sip and before they sat, Larry reciprocated Phil's gratitude by thanking him for being there for him and anyone else who needed his services in good times and bad and called Phil an important member of their family, more like a brother. Then other guests, one by one, came to Phil, congratulated him, and wished Richard success and happiness.

Miguel Hormanzo, a travel agent working for Rancho, thanked Phil for helping him during the difficult times of his divorce. Theodore, the president of a charitable organization, thanked Phil for providing his legal services for the last thirty years for free whenever they needed him. Kim and Larry, both laborers, thanked Phil for always considering their financial difficulties when helping them buy a house or negotiate a mortgage. One by one, guests thanked Phil and Cathy and started leaving.

CHAPTER TWENTY-EIGHT

Richard was not happy with Gloria's manslaughter plea. Still, he somehow convinced himself to respect Gloria's wishes and accept them, especially with the recent knowledge he had acquired from different sources regarding his uncle. Richard was expecting there would not be any trial as Gloria would plead guilty to manslaughter and receive a short jail sentence. And with the time she had already served, she would be out in a couple of years.

When the time came for the result of the psychiatric evaluation to be announced, a high-ranking politician visited Bill.

"The manslaughter charge will not be acceptable to people in general, and Earl's family in particular. It will be an embarrassment for the present elected politicians. It will indicate that Earl was partly responsible for his own demise, which will hurt anyone associated with him. People want to see blood for Earl's blood," he said. "One hundred percent fault on the murderer and no-fault or contribution on Earl's part. No rape claims, no love triangle, just attempted robbery and murder."

Bill answered casually, "If this is so important, then I will ask Sean Wilderson, the district attorney, to change the charges to murder. Why didn't you call instead of coming all the way here?"

"I thought you would be reluctant to change the manslaughter charge," replied the politician. "And it is more secure in person."

"Not at all," replied Bill. "There are thousands more like her where she came from. For me, family and friends are more important. I am sure she will have a better life in an American jail than where she came from."

"You are referring to your so-called farm or somewhere else?" asked the politician rhetorically. "Thank you for your understanding and cooperation, Bill."

Then he left the same way he had entered, climbed into the limousine from a covered yard, and left Bill's mansion. After the politician left, Bill called Andrew for a meeting and explained the new developments. Andrew told Bill about Richard's visits to the prison and meetings with Gloria.

"Richard has no experience in litigation, and he cannot pose any problem," Bill said. "It will be a short trial, and before Richard comprehends what is going on, it will be over. Gloria will get life in prison, and Richard will forget about her. I need Richard for my operations, and I think this is an important case for him. It makes him very proud to be on this case, and he will do anything for me after the case is over, even if the outcome is not to his liking. Let his father dream about Richard joining his firm. Who will leave a firm like Acrebond to join a small and unknown firm like his? Not even his son."

While they had plans to extend the psychiatric evaluations for another couple of months, they instead wrapped it up and went to court. In the court, instead of the plea of manslaughter by Gloria's lawyer, Andrew Ramstone, and the district attorney accepting it uneventfully, Sean Wilderson stood and informed the court they intended to try the case as a murder rather than manslaughter. Even though a couple of days ago, Judge Thomas Éclair, Sean Wilderson, and Andrew Ramstone were in Bill's mansion, playing poker, drinking, and practicing their parts, they acted very seriously, as they always did in court.

"What are the reasons for elevating the charge to murder?" Judge Éclair asked.

"We could not find any trace of a relationship between the victim and the accused. We think this was a story made up by the accused to mitigate the charges. All evidence points to attempted robbery and murder," Sean explained.

Richard was baffled and furious. He wanted to stand up and yell that it was all lies and someone else had murdered Earl. He looked at Gloria and saw her sitting very calmly. Andrew realized Richard's turmoil and tapped his knee to calm him down. Then he stood and told the judge he needed to see all the prosecutor's evidence.

"We could not find any shred of evidence that there was any relationship between the victim and the accused. And we have witnesses indicating that Earl entered the room first, and the accused followed him for the purpose of seducing and killing him in order to rob him," replied Sean. "We ask the defense to produce evidence to prove otherwise."

At this time, Richard yelled, "These are all lies!"

Judge Éclair immediately called for order in the courtroom and asked Andrew to control his colleague. Andrew again tapped on Richard's knee and signaled for him to stay calm. Richard looked at Gloria. This time, Gloria also looked surprised but kept her calm.

Judge Éclair adjourned the court for a future date for jury selection and court proceedings. Gloria was taken to prison. Judge Éclair left the court, and the prosecution team also left immediately. Andrew sat down with his head in his hands, shaking his head in disbelief while the reporters were taking photos and videos and asking all kinds of questions. On the way out, Andrew told Richard that he was exhausted and they should have a meeting the following morning.

Richard called his father very angry and reported the situation. Phil told him that he had already heard it on the news and asked Richard to go to his office for a chat. Phil and Richard went to the park, walked a little, and talked.

"Richard, don't show anger in front of your mom. It is funny. For the last twenty-five years, she has been getting angry at me for saying bad things about her brother. Now she is getting angry at me for not saying enough bad things about him," said Phil. "I had a gut feeling Bill cheated his sister big time and while it was annoying to see your mom not realizing it and idolizing him, I did not want to crystallize his cheating by investigating the timing of that big contract like Mary did recently. Knowing Bill, I knew the more we found out about him, the worse the situation would get because we could not do anything and it would be more awkward every time we met. If he becomes aware we know what he has done, the little civility he pretends to have will not be there anymore. I'm afraid we're going to find out far worse things about him. You said that you had reviewed the file thoroughly?" asked Phil.

"Yes, I have," replied Richard.

"It will be months before the trial begins. From tomorrow, any spare time you get, go and meet the people involved and interview them. Try to record the conversations if they allow it, and if not, take complete notes. I have a feeling the decision to change the charges to murder is a recent one, and they may not have had the chance to align their strategies yet. No matter how insignificant a witness may appear to be, talk to them. You will be surprised by the evidence you can find," said Phil. "Start from lower positioned individuals. If you are talking to police officers, start with the rookies. If you start with the chief, he will order the others not to cooperate—the same thing with the coroner's office. Talk to the assistant instead of the coroner. The chances that the top positions are cooperating with Bill are much higher than the lower positions. Just remember, don't reveal any of your findings to anyone, especially not to Andrew. Let's review and analyze your findings among ourselves first."

They went home. As agreed, Richard tried to cap his anger, but he realized that Flore was worried about him and was about to burst. They talked briefly about the case at the dinner table while trying very hard not to mention Bill's name. But it was obvious that Cathy was in turmoil, and with every opportunity, she would ask Richard to leave Bill's firm.

"Why do you want to put yourself in danger for a…" She wanted to say a Mexican girl, but she hesitated and continued, ". . . for a girl?"

After dinner, Richard went to his room and started reviewing his notes and the copies of the documents he had.

Flore knocked on the door and came in. "What do you intend to do now?" she asked. Before Richard replied, Flore continued, "I think Gloria should tell the truth that she was not involved at all, and she was set up. If she was afraid of Bill's retaliation, nothing could be worse than this. I would rather die than go to jail for life. I am sure her family thinks the same way."

"Yes, that is what I have decided to do," said Richard. "I will meet with Gloria tomorrow and tell her that. The bad thing is that she has confessed to murder already, thinking it would be manslaughter and only a couple of years in jail. Now, based on the same confession and evidence, they have changed it to murder."

"I will be praying for you constantly," said Flore. "That is all I can do. Don't underestimate the power of prayer. When you pray from deep in your heart, the universe aligns itself to accommodate and provide you with what is best for you."

The next day, Richard visited Gloria and suggested she change her plea to not guilty.

"Does Acabar know about it? Did he agree with it?" asked Gloria.

"I have not talked to him yet. But I am sure he knew about it before it was presented to the court."

"So, he has not agreed to change the plea," replied Gloria.

"It is your decision. After you agree, I will inform both Andrew and Bill."

"I am not afraid to change my plea. Not for my life which he can take any time he wishes, especially in here. But I am afraid for my family. He will kill my family one by one until I do as he says. That is why I asked you not to visit very often. If he thinks that you matter to me, he will kill you, too. The truth is, I am surprised he has not had me killed already. Probably killing me will create more of a headache for him and more controversy than this Mickey Mouse court."

"But your family is all behind you one hundred percent, whatever you decide," said Richard.

"I know that. But I cannot live with myself knowing that my decision has cost them their lives," said Gloria.

"You see, Gloria, there is a lot of work ahead of us—lots of preparation before the court date and not enough time. If we hesitate, the time and opportunities will pass. I have to start collecting evidence immediately. If we spend time hesitating, we may lose the opportunity to collect evidence," said Richard.

"Do you think it was my decision to take responsibility for the murder or even work for Acabar in the first place?" asked Gloria. "I would not work for him if I were to die of hunger. Anything he wants, he asks very politely. If you don't do as he says, he will either kill you or kill your loved ones. Acabar decided that I should work on his farm, so I did. He decided I should pose for incriminating photos with Earl's body, so I did. I was lucky that when he wanted me to work in the drug processing section of the farm, I told Abraham and he kept me in the farm part, which is a front for the drug business. I was praying all the time that God would somehow get me out of that prison without harming any of my family. I don't know why I got into a worse situation. But I don't question God. I am sure He has very good reasons. I may find out soon; I may never find out, but I accept it and am not about to put my family in danger now. There is not much difference between the two prisons, inside here or out there," said Gloria.

"Oh my God," said Richard, remembering what Cathy had said earlier.

"Why are you so surprised?" asked Gloria.

"Nothing, it is not important," replied Richard. "Okay, let me think about it. I will see you soon."

Richard said goodbye to Gloria and went to meet his father. Phil was with a client. Voski offered him a piece of homemade cake and coffee until the client left, and Richard explained the predicament he was in.

"This Gloria of yours is getting to be a very interesting individual," said Phil. "She has more guts and soul in her than a whole city block. You could ask Bill about changing the plea. He may agree, thinking it is a done deal, and Gloria will only make things worse for herself by changing the plea after confessing to murder to the police. The coroner, the police and guards are lined up to testify against her as eyewitnesses. Of course, if you get any closer to exonerating Gloria, which for now appears to be impossible, it will shift the direction to his men or even himself. Then he will consider it as crossing him and will retaliate."

"But that will buy us some time," said Richard.

"That is what I thought," replied Phil. "You should also ask Gloria's parents to talk to her and convince her to go along with you."

"They are determined to help Gloria any way they can, even if it means putting themselves in danger," said Richard. "It is Gloria who will not accept to put her family's lives in danger. She explained that if she opposes Bill, he will start killing her family one by one until she accepts whatever Bill says after losing a couple of members of her family."

Richard went to see Bill at his mansion. Bill's secretary told Richard that Bill was in a meeting and asked him to wait in the reception. Bill was usually operating from home as it was more private, and the visitors came and went without anyone seeing them or knowing who was coming and going. Richard sat.

After ten to fifteen minutes, an older man came out while telling Bill, "This is not right. You have to make it right."

The receptionist said goodbye respectfully while the older man looked at Richard curiously but kindly like he knew him. Richard said hello, and the older man said hello back.

Richard entered Bill's office, and after greetings, Bill said, "I've heard about the prosecutor elevating the manslaughter charge to murder. That son of a bitch did it without warning and without any valid evidence."

"That is why I have come to see you. What if we change the plea to innocent?" said Richard.

"I don't see how you could do that without embarrassing yourself and making things worse for Gloria. There are many witnesses and evidence of her confession. Just try to help her with reducing the time she will be behind bars," said Bill.

Richard tried to convince Bill to change the plea to not guilty.

On a couple of occasions, he hinted that he did not think Gloria had done it, but Bill got irritated and said, "You're being illogical and wasting my time. I don't know why everyone is interested in this case."

Finally, Richard left.

CHAPTER TWENTY-NINE

Richard had prepared a long list of the names of the police officers, security guards, and other people at Bill's house on the night of the murder, including the coroner and his assistant. There were two groups of officers. One group was dispatched by 911, and the second was called by Bill's buddy, Chief Scott Timmins.

He called the police station and asked for one of the officers. The officer was not there, so he left a message. He called again and asked for a different officer, who was there. Richard introduced himself and asked for a meeting. The officer refused and told Richard that he had his report in the file and there was nothing more to talk about. Richard called again and asked for yet another officer. He was not there, either, so he left another message. Then he called the coroner's office and asked for the assistant by the name of Addis Olizar. He was told that Addis was no longer working in that office.

"Which office is he working at now?" asked Richard.

"I'm not sure, but I think he's at the Houston office now," replied the secretary.

Richard found the phone number for the Houston office and called and asked for Mr. Addis Olizar. After several wrong extensions, the person who answered the phone told Richard that Olizar was on a different extension, but he could connect him. After a short wait, Addis Olizar picked up the phone. Richard introduced himself and explained that he was calling about the Earl Murphy murder case and asked for a meeting.

"I left the Los Angeles office right after that case started and before their report was completed," Mr. Olizar told him. "I suggest you talk to the coroner there."

"I will meet with the coroner," Richard replied. "But since the charge has been elevated to murder, and I am trying to prevent an innocent person from spending the rest of her life in prison, I want to interview every witness, everyone who was present at the scene and see if there is any information that might have been omitted from the report. Could we meet tomorrow? Say at 1:00 p.m. in a restaurant of your choice?"

There was silence on the other end for a couple of seconds, and Richard thought he'd been cut off.

He started saying, "Hello, hello?"

He was about to hang up and dial again when Addis started talking. "But Martin assured me she wouldn't be charged with first-degree murder."

"Well, they changed it last week, and unless you want an innocent woman to go to prison for the rest of her life, let's meet so you can tell me what you know," replied Richard.

"I'm sorry. I can't. I left that office before the autopsy was done, and I don't have any more information," said Addis.

"Sometimes, there is information you think is not important but is possibly lifesaving. Let's meet for lunch tomorrow and talk."

"I think you are wasting your time coming here, but I have to go to lunch anyway. I will text you the name and address of the restaurant," replied Addis.

"Please keep this conversation and our meeting confidential. You don't know who you are dealing with. Not a word to anyone, okay?" asked Richard.

Richard heard Addis say in a very low voice, "Yes, I do know who I'm dealing with . . . Okay, we will keep it between us."

Richard did not ask about the first comment as it was in a very low voice, and he realized that Addis was just thinking out loud and he was not supposed to hear. He thanked Addis, told him that he would see him tomorrow, and hung up.

Richard described his experience and conversation with Addis to Phil that evening.

"Specifically, there are two issues. First, Addis said Martin had promised him that Gloria would not be charged with first-degree murder. And second, when I said, 'You don't know who you are dealing with,' he said, 'Yes, I do,' in a very low voice as though he was talking to himself."

"Maybe this is the break you are looking for. He knows more than he's saying. Make sure that he doesn't get scared. Treat him like a friend and promise him whatever he tells you will stay between you two. And describe Gloria's position, talk about her hero father. This may encourage him to cooperate. If you don't get his complete cooperation, at least you will know if he knows more than he is telling you, "said Phil.

Richard flew to Houston the following morning and went directly to the place of their meeting. Addis arrived, and they started talking.

"Why did you move to Houston?" Richard asked him.

"A better job opportunity became available with higher pay, and I grabbed it," Addis explained.

"I guess you are not married. That's why you could relocate easily?" asked Richard.

"No, I am not," replied Addis.

Richard asked Addis if he could record the conversation, but Addis refused, and so Richard took out his notebook.

"Can you explain the whole series of events from the time you entered the murder scene?"

Addis explained step-by-step the events, and Richard realized that everything he said was in the damning report—there was nothing new.

"I told you that you are wasting your time," added Addis.

"There must be something that will prove Gloria did not commit this murder. Poor girl lost all her family to a gangster when she was three, and now she will be spending all her life in prison for a murder she did not commit," replied Richard.

"That is not true. Her family is alive in Tijuana," replied Addis.

"No, they are not. That is her adopted family," replied Richard. "She was born in Juarez. Her father was a police chief, and his name was—"

But before Richard said Gloria's father's name, Addis asked, "Is it Kiki Coto?"

Richard nodded.

"Oh my God, I did not know she is that Gloria. Everyone thought she was killed like the rest of her family. Is Bill the same as Acabar?" asked Addis with fear and shame for what he had done.

"Yes," replied Richard. "How do you know all this?" asked Richard, but then he realized that Addis was far away, deep in his thoughts.

"So, Gloria was not killed. We were living in the same neighborhood. Sometimes, we would play together. Her father would give us rides on his shoulders, Gloria on one shoulder and me on the other. Of course, Gloria did not kill anyone," continued Addis.

Richard showed the birthmark on Gloria's shoulder and asked Addis, "Do you remember this birthmark?"

"This is one hundred percent her; I remember it vividly," replied Addis.

"The same man that killed Gloria's father and her entire family killed Earl and asked Gloria to take responsibility for the murder," replied Richard.

"Why did Gloria agree?" asked Addis.

"After her family was murdered, Gloria was given to another family in Tijuana for adoption. When Gloria was sixteen, Bill asked for Gloria to work for him on his farm . . ."

"Oh my God, so Bill is the same as Acabar…" said Addis.

"You still think that Gloria killed Earl?" asked Richard.

"God, no," replied Addis. "There were many people there who had the strength to kill Earl the way he was killed, but this was not the job of a delicate woman like Gloria."

"Why are you saying that? How was he killed that needed that much strength?" asked Richard. "I thought a knife was driven into his chest."

"Yes, but it had to shatter his rib before puncturing his lung and heart. It needed a tremendous amount of force. Unless she was a boxer or a bodybuilder, and we did not know, she could not have done it."

"But this information is not in the report. I reviewed the report many times. I'm sure it's not in there. How can such important information be missing?" asked Richard.

"I didn't complete the report. I was working on the body when Martin called me and asked me to stop working and take the rest of the day off. When we met the next day, he explained that we were dealing with very powerful people who could make anyone disappear. Martin explained my life was in danger unless I did exactly as he said. By chance, I was assigned a case, and at no fault of my own, a hit order was on my head. Martin told me to delete my report and all the photos I had taken, as though I had not yet examined the body, and to go to Houston where his friend gave me this job. The only reason I agreed with him was that he assured me Gloria would not go to prison for more than a couple of years. Otherwise, I would not agree, even though I did not know this was the same Gloria. But had I not agreed, I would have been taken out. I thought everybody had come to an agreement, including Gloria. I thought she was being paid big time for her sacrifice. But had I known she was my childhood friend and the daughter of Kiki Coto, my childhood hero, I would not have agreed to cooperate. I would have stayed put and testified against Acabar and made Gloria change her mind," continued Addis.

"Maybe it was a good thing that you didn't know. Otherwise, you would be dead, and all the evidence you thought would exonerate Gloria would be dead with you. Now, regarding the evidence, what do you have?" asked Richard.

"The reason Martin asked me to delete my findings and told me I would get killed was that the individual who killed Earl must have been a very strong and big man. Not a delicate woman like Gloria."

"Do you have any evidence regarding the shattered rib?" asked Richard.

"Other than Earl's body lying under the ground, no other evidence. But I assume that the body will be enough. You can exhume the body by court order," said Addis. "However, while I deleted all the images on the official evidence camera, I had downloaded them to my device in case I wanted to continue working from home. When Martin asked me to delete the photos, I deleted them from the office camera but forgot I had downloaded them to my device. Later, when I remembered, I was going to delete them, too. But I was curious. I thought there must be something in the photos that Martin wanted me to delete. Otherwise, he wouldn't go to the trouble of trying to collect photos from third parties and download them into the camera and then the office device."

"Did you find something?" asked Richard.

"Indeed, I found something very interesting," replied Addis. "The time of death was around 11:00 p.m. Both Martin and I came to the same conclusion after examining the body. There were other factors as well. The time that Earl's driver entered the room and saw the body while talking to Earl's wife. Some witnesses saw Earl and Bill moving away from the crowd around 10:30 p.m. while Gloria was on the floor serving food and beverages to guests."

"Yes, that's what the report said," replied Richard.

"Except in some of the damning photos where Gloria is standing over Earl's body with the so-called knife in her hand, there is a wall clock showing the time at 11:48 p.m.," replied Addis. "The witnesses, all Acabar's associates and employees, indicated that when they heard a commotion and entered, they saw Gloria standing there right after the murder, which was 11:01 p.m.," replied Addis.

"But police also took some photos. Was there any clock in their photos?" asked Richard.

"I am sure there was, but I'm not aware. I have my own photos," replied Addis. "With these two pieces of evidence, you can exonerate Gloria. I will email them to you this evening."

"I hope so, and I will do my best. But Bill, or Acabar as you call him, has contacts everywhere and is very powerful and determined. He will do everything in his power to quash the evidence, but it is my life's mission to save that girl," said Richard. "As soon as the evidence is presented and Bill's people connect it to you, especially when it comes time for you to go to court as a witness, they will try to kill you," Richard explained. "Start getting ready to vanish at short notice, and when the time comes to present the evidence, I will let you know. That means possibly losing your job. Are you prepared to do that?"

"Yes, I will do anything for Kiki Coto's daughter and my childhood friend," replied Addis.

They said goodbye, and Richard left for the airport to go home. So far, he had two ironclad pieces of evidence that would exonerate Gloria immediately when presented to the court. Richard became very calm and hopeful and was full of positive thoughts. He thought that there was law and order after all, and the truth would eventually surface. He thought how wrong Wapi, the Native American medicine man, had been when he told him that heaven's intervention was the only way out of this predicament.

Richard was very excited when he arrived home that night. He told his father about the conversation with Mr. Addis Olizar and was surprised that while Phil appeared happy, he did not share the same enthusiasm as Richard. Phil told him not to talk to anyone about his findings until interviewing everyone else on his list. Richard was sure the moment the court received the documents, the government would withdraw all the charges. He was just not sure how Andrew and Bill would react to the new evidence.

Richard and Cathy, and to a certain extent Mary and Flore, agreed that Richard should show the evidence to Andrew Ramstone, and if he refused to take action on the evidence, then he should ask Gloria to change lawyers and choose Phil as her lawyer. But Phil was not so sure this was the best strategy. Phil's specialty was not criminal law, but he was hoping that when the evidence was presented to the court, the charges against Gloria would be dropped, and there would not be any court proceedings at all.

However, deep down, Phil was worried that if the evidence was presented to Andrew too early, Bill would come up with different strategies to neutralize and quash all the evidence. He couldn't think of any way the court could undermine such solid evidence. He did not allow Richard to see his fear, but Richard realized that Phil was not as enthusiastic about the new evidence as he should have been.

"Don't jump the gun and give all the evidence to Andrew now," Phil advised. "They should not be given the time to come up with ideas to counter the evidence."

"You should take over the case and present the evidence to court yourself," Richard suggested.

"I agree that Gloria needs to change lawyers," Phil said. "But I am not a criminal lawyer, and even if Gloria changes her lawyer and the new lawyer presents the evidence, Bill will either force Gloria to admit to the murder despite all the evidence by threatening her family, or he will kill Gloria. For now, Gloria is not in danger as it is more beneficial for Bill that Gloria stays alive. There is still a long time before the trial. Keep quiet about the evidence you have so far discovered and continue interviewing witnesses for more evidence."

Richard did as Phil suggested. He did not show the new evidence to anyone. He visited Gloria once a week and Gloria's family once every couple of months.

CHAPTER THIRTY

Richard kept calling the police officers who were present at the murder investigation. As usual, the officers either were not available, or they refused to talk to Richard and referred him to the official report that they had provided at the time.

Henry, one of the officers dispatched by the 911 call to Bill's house when Earl was murdered, now had desk duties due to injuries sustained on duty. He would always refuse to talk to Richard but finally accepted Richard's invitation for lunch. However, he warned Richard there was nothing to be added to his official report. It appeared to Richard that he agreed to meet him simply to put an end to his calls and because Richard told him the lunch was on him.

During the meeting, Richard asked him to describe the murder scene and talk about anything unusual that he might have seen. Henry's answers were always the same as his report on file.

"Word on the street is that Gloria did not kill Earl. What is your opinion?" asked Richard.

"As a police officer, I will never go against other officers, especially when other officers saved my life and I have received a bravery medal for operations during which I was injured," replied Henry.

Richard became suspicious when he heard, "I will never go against other officers." He thought there must be something he was hiding and that if he were to reveal it, he would be going against other officers. Richard changed the subject and asked personal questions about where he was born, his family, children, and accident. Henry proudly described the sting operation and how he was part of the officers helping the police chief and his group arrest the whole gang of drug dealers. Richard realized that Henry was talking about the operation that eliminated Bill's competition. He explained the situation to Henry and told him that the reason why all the gang members, except the leaders, only got a couple of months of jail time was that they agreed to testify against their leaders and work for Bill.

"The only thing the police accomplished was to eliminate competition for Bill and make his operation stronger by adding to his territory and distribution team," Richard explained. "While I was not present when you were injured, I suspect the reason you were injured was that you were put in front of the fire as you are not a member of the chief's gang."

As though he had hit a raw nerve, Henry became very angry and started saying profanities to Richard and left. Richard was now sure that Henry had more information than he was willing to share. He was hoping that being a police officer, Henry would investigate the operation that injured him.

Henry went to his office, but he was very angry and too anxious to work. He told his superior that he did not feel well and went home. He began to replay the events in his mind that ended in his injury. He slowly realized that none of the chief's gang were on the front line. He remembered receiving the order to attack, which put him in a very vulnerable position. He kept seeing the events vividly like a video, all night and day. Finally, Henry decided to investigate the issue himself and find out the truth to put an end to all these thoughts and doubts.

Every day after work, he would scout the downtown streets and bars to locate some of the gang members arrested that day. He finally located one. He parked far enough away to see the gang member, but the gang member could not see him. He could see that the guy was dealing drugs. He called his chief and reported the situation, and asked for a cruiser to arrest the drug dealer. His chief refused Henry's request and explained that this was Chief Scott's jurisdiction and he had no business investigating it.

Henry didn't listen to his chief. He approached the drug dealer, showed his badge, and arrested him. He realized that one of the guys who came forward from the commotion of the arrest made a phone call, and before he could drive away, a police cruiser approached and cut him off. Two officers came out and asked Henry to release the drug dealer and told him to mind his own business. Henry showed the drugs he had taken from the dealer as evidence. The other officers grabbed the evidence from him and told him to go away. Otherwise, they would arrest him.

"You are touring around all day. You know he is selling drugs. Why don't you arrest him?" said Henry.

"This is a sting operation. We were working on it for months; now you ruined it," answered one of the officers.

The next morning, his boss called him to his office.

"I'm giving you a warning to mind your own business. For your bravery and injury, I will not report you this time, and I have asked Chief Scott not to report you, either. Next time, though, you will be tossed out to the street."

Henry's world was turned upside down. All his life, he had believed in justice. He thought that he sacrificed for justice, and he was happy and proud of his injuries. Now, he realized he was only eliminating the competition for the worst gangster. All his life was a waste. He became depressed and started drinking heavily, but it did not cause any problem with his employment. He realized he was just a decoration in the police force.

One night while very drunk, he called Richard and asked him to meet at the bar where he was drinking.

When Richard arrived, the first thing he said to him was, "Don't tell me I told you so," and he started swearing at him.

Realizing that he was too drunk, Richard acted very casually and pretended not to hear all the swearing. "What is the purpose of this meeting?" he asked Henry.

Henry put his hand in his pocket, and after searching for a while, he pulled out a memory stick.

He gave it to Richard and said, "Use this wisely as a life will be sacrificed for it. When I arrived at Bill's mansion the night Earl was murdered, my superior asked me to set up the recording equipment in the interviewing room. While setting up, I accidentally left the audio recorder on while I left the room to get more equipment. When I returned, Scott had arrived and ordered his people to set up another room for interviews. I went to collect my equipment, and I realized that it was on. I did not pay much attention as I thought it had probably recorded some casual chats between people. The next day at the station, when I listened to it, I realized that some of Bill's associates and guards were talking about the murder. They said it was Doug, Bill's assistant, who had killed Earl. I took this copy before I presented the original to my chief. He took the original and told me that for some very highly classified and national security reasons, I should never discuss this conversation with anyone."

"You were not kidding when you said a life will be sacrificed for it," said Richard. "But an innocent life will be saved because of it."

"Just call me a couple of days before you are going to present the evidence. I want to have a nice meal."

"Be ready to vanish for a couple of weeks," Richard told Henry. "And I promise that before the recordings go public, I will call you. Will you need money to go away and hide for a couple of weeks?"

Henry replied that he did not. Then Richard thanked Henry and asked him to call if he needed anything and left. Richard drove home very content, calm and happy. This time, he was sure justice would be served, at least for Gloria. He had three ironclad pieces of evidence. He thought, even if they did not work individually, the synergy created by the combined evidence would exonerate Gloria one hundred percent. This time, his father, too, would share his enthusiasm.

Everyone was asleep when he arrived home. He went quietly to his room. First, he made a couple of copies of the evidence, and then he started listening. He could not believe his ears. Bill's associates and guards were describing the killing in detail and very clearly. Richard thought he could not sleep from the excitement. He could not wait to play the audio to everyone, especially his father. Early in the morning, he woke to the sound of footsteps and his family's conversation. He ran downstairs with his device to catch his father before he left. He played the audio Henry had given him.

Phil was in awe. "How did you get it?" asked Phil. But before Richard could answer, he continued. "With this evidence, on top of the others, I think you may have a chance to force Bill to change his strategy and drop the charges against Gloria!"

"What do you mean, I may have a chance? What else do I need to clear poor Gloria of a murder charge?"

"The law works in funny ways. It is not what evidence you have that counts. It is what connections you have. And in this case, Bill has all the connections he needs," said Phil.

"How can he discredit all this evidence?" asked Richard.

"I don't want to speculate. Let's hope it will work," replied Phil. "We will talk in the evening. I have to go now. I have an appointment."

"There is the blood-stained shoe, too," continued Richard.

"We will talk in the evening," repeated Phil.

CHAPTER THIRTY-ONE

They spoke again that evening.

"Bill is the enemy. He is the one who has created all these problems and asked Gloria to take responsibility for a murder she did not commit. Still, I think that if you circumvent him and change lawyers without telling Bill first or present the documents without first showing them to Bill, he will lock heads with you and have a direct and open confrontation. Let it flow smoothly as long as it can. Let Bill think you don't know the truth," said Phil. "Maybe when he realizes there is overwhelming evidence that Gloria did not commit this crime, he will come up with an alternate solution. Instead, show the documents to Bill and pretend that you are not aware of the truth, to mitigate his backlash and avoid direct confrontation, hoping that Bill will voluntarily change his strategy, which will result in Gloria's freedom."

"I'm concerned for the safety of everyone involved, especially Gloria, her family in Tijuana, Addis, and now Henry. Thank God with the insurance settlement, I can provide for all expenses for Gloria's family, Addis, and Henry, while they are hiding from Bill. But I have to find a way to arrange protective custody for Gloria. Otherwise, Acabar will kill her," said Richard.

"How are you going to do that?" asked Phil.

"At my graduation party, Mike—by the way, thanks for inviting him—mentioned he has done a lot of work for the warden of the prison, where Gloria is kept, and they have become friends. I am planning to see what he can do," replied Richard.

"I doubt he can ask the warden for such a big favor," replied Phil.

"We will find out," replied Richard. "It is just that I have not been in touch with Mike for a long time, and now I am embarrassed to meet him just to ask for a favor."

"Mike is different from all your other friends. I am sure he will understand all your past troubles and won't mind, and he will be happy to help you if he can. Let's hope he can pull this off," said Phil.

Richard called Mike the same night, apologized for calling late, and asked Mike for a meeting at his earliest availability.

"How is tomorrow evening after work at our favorite place?" Mike replied.

Richard thanked him and said goodbye.

*   *   *

Richard arrived before Mike. He ordered a beer and tried very hard to act as casually as possible and not show his anxiety over this life and death situation.

Mike arrived and, after catching up, asked Richard, "What was the issue you wanted to discuss?"

"Last time we met, you mentioned you did some work for the prison warden where Gloria is being kept and have friendly relations with him," replied Richard. "I have evidence to exonerate Gloria, and I am planning to present it to Bill and probably to the court soon, right after I secure Gloria, her family's, and other related individuals' safety. Gloria's family and the other individuals' safety is easy. All they have to do is go into hiding until things calm down, but Gloria is in prison and very vulnerable, like a sitting duck. Only the warden can keep her safe by putting her in protective custody. Do you think he will do it if you asked?"

"Do you want me to set up a meeting with the warden?" asked Mike.

"He may accept our request; he may not. The important thing is that I don't want him to keep Bill's gang informed. How much do you trust this guy" asked Richard?

"I'm not sure if he can arrange and guarantee her safety, but I am sure he will keep this between us and not let Bill's gang find out. I trust him completely, he is a straight-up guy," replied Mike.

Mike talked to the warden. He asked the warden to promise not to tell anyone what they were going to discuss.

The warden accepted Mike's request for discretion.

"Okay, there is new evidence that will exonerate Gloria. But Richard is afraid that Gloria will be murdered before her name is cleared," Mike said.

"Well, if the prison administration has suspicions about a prisoner's safety, the prisoner can be placed in protective custody," the warden said. "And as of now, I have suspicions that Gloria's life is in danger. When do you want me to put her in protective custody?"

Mike thanked the warden, told him that he would let him know, and left. As soon as Mike left the warden's home, the warden called Antonio Donatelli. He explained the conversation with Mike and sent his regards to Bill. He asked Antonio to talk to Bill and let him know what Bill wanted him to do. Antonio thanked him and told him that he thought Bill would not want to eliminate Gloria, but to make sure, he would talk to Bill and let the warden know. A half-hour later, Antonio called the warden and told him that Gloria and Richard didn't pose any threat, and everything was set up for a smooth court proceeding.

"Just in case the situation changes, I will let you know and set up for a hit. But for now, eliminating Gloria will cause more problems than it solves. Bill appreciates your loyalty, as usual."

Antonio then called Andrew and informed him that Richard would be providing new evidence to him.

"Praise Richard for a good job, and don't let Richard suspect anything."

Mike met with Richard and described his conversation with the warden. Richard told Mike that when he had everyone involved in hiding, he would let Mike know to ask the warden to put Gloria in protective custody. Richard called Jose Luis and said that he was going to see them the next day.

He went to Tijuana with Flore in the early morning the following day. He explained the situation to Gloria's family and asked them to go into hiding. He gave them enough cash to provide for their whole year's expenses. A couple of days later, he met Addis and asked him to hide, too. He offered money to pay for his expenses, but Addis explained that he had enough savings.

Richard then met Henry and informed him that he should hide for a while. But Henry was very depressed and defiant and refused to hide.

"I am willing to testify in court, and I'm ready to meet my creator," Henry said.

"If you do not hide, you will meet your creator before you can even testify," Richard explained, but Henry was too depressed to understand.

After everything was arranged and Gloria was in protective custody, Richard presented all the new evidence to Andrew. To his surprise, Andrew praised him for the excellent job and told Richard that he would talk to Bill for the necessary course of action.

"Can you help me to prepare the documents to present the new evidence to the court?" Richard asked.

"It is not difficult, and I'm confident that you can do it on your own. You'll obtain experience while doing it, too. Just wait until I talk to Bill."

While Richard started searching to find out what documents he needed to complete to present the new evidence to the court, Andrew left the room in a hurry to call Bill and explain Richard's new findings.

"What was your reaction when Richard presented the evidence?" Bill asked.

"I was very convincing, don't worry. I did not want Richard to go to another law firm and present his findings.

I think if Richard presents his findings with me, the issues will be more manageable as he has no experience."

Bill was aware of all the evidence. After all, he was the one who suppressed it by collecting and destroying what he thought were all the photos with the wall clock in them, and by asking the chief coroner to get rid of his assistant and not mentioning the broken rib in his report, and the recording with his guards and assistants' confession about the true murderer. Now, he was a little worried and told Andrew that he would arrange a meeting with Judge Éclair, the coroner, the police chief and the district attorney at his place tomorrow evening to discuss the issues.

"There is also the shoe problem to be taken care of," he reminded Andrew.

Another clandestine meeting took place in Bill's mansion. Bill presented the three pieces of evidence and added that there was the shoe issue too, but fortunately, Scott had taken care of it already.

"The photos with the clock and the recordings with Bill's associates and guards talking about the murder," Judge Éclair immediately explained, "I will not allow them as evidence. I will label them as forgeries because they were obtained from outside sources, but the broken rib is a tough one."

Bill became a little worried regarding Éclair's last comment. He looked at the coroner angrily, then asked Judge Éclair to elaborate on his comments.

"Well," said the judge, "If there is no wall clock in any of the photos registered as evidence, we will consider the new photos as edited and forged. The same goes for the recordings."

At this point, Bill interrupted the judge. "No, elaborate on your comment regarding the broken rib."

Before Judge Éclair had a chance to reply, the district attorney jumped in. "Maybe it will be better if instead of the photos and the recordings being dismissed by Judge Éclair at the time of presentation, we have them examined by our experts and dismiss them as forgeries after their testimony."

Andrew agreed with the district attorney and confirmed that to dismiss the evidence with an expert's testimony would validate their case more.

"The expert's testimony can be arranged," Bill said. "Let's get experts on those two pieces of evidence, but what about the broken rib? Why did you say it is a tough one?" he asked, looking at Judge Éclair.

"Can't you say the rib was broken during the autopsy?" asked Scott, the police chief.

"I don't think so," replied the coroner. "There was only one stab mark on the body, and that stabbing resulted in Earl's death. My report, which everyone has, indicates that one stab punctured the victim's lung and heart and resulted in the victim's death. I did not mention the knife went through the rib, shattered the rib, and then continued through the lung to the heart. If the broken rib is brought up, whether our nice judge dismisses it or not, Earl's family will want the body exhumed and examined again. Besides, my previous assistant was the one who started the autopsy and saw it."

"You assured me your assistant would not be a problem. Otherwise, I would have gotten rid of him, and we would not have a problem," Bill said.

"Don't worry. I got rid of him. I sent him to the Houston office," replied the coroner.

"Well, if you had not promised that he would not talk, I would have sent his corpse to Houston, not given him a better position in Houston. This is all your fault, and you will pay for your mistakes."

"It is too late for that," replied the coroner. "Even if you get rid of him, Earl's body is still there and can be exhumed at any time."

"What if we get rid of Gloria? That will end all our problems," replied Bill.

"That will make things very complicated. It will look bad, and the problem of the broken rib will persist. Besides, from what I hear from my informants in prison, Gloria is in protective custody," said Scott.

"I would not worry about her being in protective custody," replied Bill. "I could do it in a day. But since you think it will make things worse, we will let her be."

"Can't you say your assistant broke the rib during the autopsy?" asked Scott.

"No. As I said, it is very clear it happened during the stabbing, and besides, what if my assistant comes to testify?" replied the coroner.

"You can confidently assume that your previous assistant will not testify. Can you think of something?" asked Bill.

"As I explained, it is very obvious it was broken as a result of the stabbing and that there was only one stabbing," replied the coroner.

"What if we exhume the body first?" said Bill. "Can you think of something to solve our problem?"

"Maybe we can break all his ribs. In that case, the evidence will be lost.

"In that case, we have nothing to worry about," said Judge Éclair.

"Okay, I will take care of your previous assistant and the additional stabbings," said Bill. "I will need your help in exhuming the body," Bill told Scott. Before Scott agreed and asked what kind of help, Bill continued. "I will need the cemetery perimeters cleared and guarded by police cruisers for a couple of hours until the job is done."

"Consider it done. Just tell me when," replied Scott Timmins, the police chief.

"I am sure my previous assistant will not go against us," said the coroner. "But let me talk to him first."

"It is too late for that. He has revealed confidential information," said Bill. "If we were in the business of assuming things, we would be dead long ago."

"If you are going to take care of the corpse, and Addis Olizar will be blamed for it, then why kill him?" asked the coroner.

"No, I don't like uncertainty," replied Bill, "I want peace of mind, and I don't want anything to keep me awake at night. That is how I operate."

Before leaving, the coroner asked Antonio Donatelli to let him know a couple of days ahead of time when they would need him at the cemetery.

*   *   *

That Sunday night, several police cruisers encircled the cemetery and blocked the entrances while Bill's people erected a large tent over Murphy's gravesite. The casket was brought up and the coroner did his job of messing up the body, so if it was exhumed, no one could say for sure if the original wound broke the rib.

In the meantime, Richard started getting worried that there was no news from Andrew or Bill regarding the new evidence. To calm down, he sometimes went to his sanctuary—the park—trying to meditate and relax.

Andrew came to Richard's office on Monday morning and asked him if he had prepared the documents to file with the court to present the new evidence. While excited, Richard replied that he was waiting for Bill's approval.

"Of course, he approves. This is crucial evidence that must be presented to the court," replied Andrew and directed Richard to a couple of precedents so that Richard could get the right forms.

Richard was surprised by Andrew's change of heart and started doubting himself and his father that they may have misjudged Bill after all. On the way home, he became worried again. The facts did not add up. It was Bill's man who killed Earl. If Gloria were exonerated, the law would be looking in Bill's direction.

At home, he discussed the situation with his father and shared his confusion with him. Phil's position was that they must have a plan, and most probably, it involved rejecting some of the evidence. But he suggested not to get excited and be prepared for different outcomes and have a plan for each situation.

A couple of weeks later, it was time to present the evidence to the court. Andrew stood up and informed the judge that they had collected new evidence that would exonerate their client, Gloria. Judge Éclair asked for the evidence, and Andrew presented them one by one. Sean Wilderson, the district attorney, called experts regarding each piece of evidence who testified that the images were edited and the clock was added during editing. In other words, it was a forgery. Another expert testified that the recording was a forgery, too.

Before the judge announced his decision, Richard asked for a recess to call his own witnesses and cross-examine the experts. Judge Éclair looked at both Andrew and Sean. They both nodded yes, and Judge Éclair granted a recess, announcing that the court would resume the following morning.

"Who do you want to call?" asked Andrew.

"I will try to find the police officer who recorded the conversation and someone who can testify that the clock was on that wall all the time," replied Richard.

"Good luck with that," replied Andrew. Then, realizing that his tone of voice was not appropriate, he continued. "I hope you can find the officer for the recording and someone who can testify for the clock."

Richard asked Gloria if any of the maids or other workers in Bill's house would testify that the clock was in the room and on the wall all the time. Gloria replied that everyone would testify, but they would be murdered, and for that reason, she would not ask anyone to testify.

Richard called the staff manager in Bill's house, explained the situation, and asked him if he would testify or knew anyone who would. The staff manager refused to talk to Richard. He told him he did not understand what Richard was talking about and asked him not to call again. Richard called the officer and explained that the district attorney had challenged the recordings as forgeries and asked if he could go to court and testify. The officer got offended and told Richard that he would be in court at 9:00 a.m. tomorrow morning.

In the meantime, Andrew and Sean were in Judge Éclair's office discussing the issues. Andrew called Bill and described the situation. He informed him that the police officer who recorded the conversation was on his way and asked Bill if he could get rid of him.

"That will look very bad," Bill said. "Thomas should take care of his testimony."

"Okay. Also, Richard is trying to call one of the employees to testify regarding the clock," Andrew said.

"Richard has already tried to do that, but don't worry because no one will testify."

*   *   *

The next morning, Gloria was sitting quietly and listening to the court proceedings. She was very calm, not letting herself be affected by the proceedings. The police officer was sitting outside the courthouse, waiting to be summoned.

"What is your job, and why do you think the recording is a forgery?" Andrew asked Sean's witness during the cross-examination.

"I'm a DJ," the witness answered. "The reason I think the recording is a forgery is that there are some tapping sounds in the recording, and the recording was stopped and started again, which indicates it is a collection of some sentences out of context made into a conversation."

"I have no further questions," Andrew said, but before he sat down, Richard asked the witness a question.

"Do you know that the recording equipment was set up on a table, and the tapping sound is people's feet hitting the table legs?"

"No, in my professional opinion, they don't sound like feet hitting the table legs," replied the witness.

Andrew called on the police officer.

"Did you set up the recording equipment?" he asked.

"Yes," the officer answered. "By mistake, the recording equipment was turned on and left on, until I was ordered to remove them by my sergeant.

"Why didn't you come forward with the evidence at the time of the murder?" asked Sean Wilderson.

"I gave the tape to my sergeant, and I was under the impression that he provided it to the court," replied the officer.

"May I ask what is the cause of your limping?"

"I was wounded in a drug raid."

"You presented the recordings after you were wounded. Why is that?

"I thought it was a drug raid, but then I realized that we were only eliminating the competition for another drug lord."

"Were you upset when you were wounded and could not carry out your police duties and were confined to desk duties instead?"

"In the beginning, I was proud of myself to be a part of the officers that stopped a drug-dealing gang. But when I realized later that I was only helping a bigger gangster eliminate his competition, of course, I was upset."

"May I suggest that you forged the recordings because you were mad you were wounded and confined to desk duties?" asked Sean Wilderson.

"No, that is not true," replied the officer.

"No further questions," said Sean Wilderson.

"It appears to this court that the officer became angry and upset about being wounded in the raid, had an incorrect understanding about the raid, and made up these recordings by putting together pieces of conversations to incriminate an innocent man. The officer lied about the recording. Therefore, this court dismisses the evidence," announced Judge Éclair.

The officer was very upset. He tried to convince the court that he was not lying, but the judge ordered him to step down and keep quiet. Otherwise, the court would find him in contempt.

Regarding the broken rib, the judge asked Andrew to get permission from Earl's family to exhume the body.

"Only then, if it is proven that Earl's rib was broken during the stabbing, will I allow the evidence."

The coroner called Addis again several times but could not reach him. He talked to his colleagues and found out Addis had not gone to work for a week, and no one knew his whereabouts. Andrew asked Richard to get permission from Earl's family to exhume the body. They strongly objected, but when Richard explained how the murderer might escape justice if the body was not exhumed, they agreed. They exhumed the body and found out that Earl's body had been violated and stabbed multiple times.

That evening, Richard was sitting at the dinner table with a grim face. It was as though he was far away. He was not eating anything or talking to anyone. Everyone else was hushed, trying to keep busy by pretending they were eating. Instead, they were playing with their food and sometimes forcing a bite into their mouths.

Phil broke the silence. "Today's events were not in our favor, but we still have other evidence that has not yet been presented."

"I'm sure they will think of something about that evidence, too," said Richard.

"Let's be hopeful," said Phil.

"Usually, Richard is the hopeful one, and you, Dad, think negatively about this case. Now, it is the opposite. If Richard thinks there is no chance, it indicates that there is really no chance of winning the case," said Mary.

"I know we will eventually win the case, just maybe not this time. And I don't know when and how. But I know we will win, and Gloria will be exonerated," said Richard.

"That is a very good approach," said Phil with a grim face. He wanted to continue his speech but forced himself to stop.

"But don't get your hopes up," said Mary.

"Why do you say that?" asked Phil.

"I just finished what you were going to say, but you bit your tongue," replied Mary.

"I agree with Mary," replied Richard. "We don't have any way of winning this case."

"But you said you are confident that you will win?" asked Flore.

"That is my feeling. But when I think about it logically, I realize that the whole justice system is corrupt and controlled by Bill or other gangsters like him. He would not agree to present the evidence if he thought they would pose a threat. And the same goes with the blood-stained shoe," said Richard.

CHAPTER THIRTY-TWO

The police officer who confiscated the blood-stained shoe was sitting on a bench outside the courthouse. He had been subpoenaed to testify, and he was very nervous. He was confident he would be shot before reaching the courthouse and was surprised he was still alive.

On the bench, on the other side of the courthouse door, was the guy wearing the shoe. He looked at him. He was relaxed and confident. He looked back at the officer with a smirk. He remembered the last time he testified regarding the recordings. He was called a liar and told that he had fabricated the evidence and forged the conversation by putting together unrelated conversations out of context.

He was confident that this time, too, he would be called a liar and would be ridiculed. He was not sure whether to be sad or happy about it. If his testimony were accepted and Gloria went free, he would not be alive to testify. He would have been murdered long ago, or he would be murdered soon. He thought he would probably be charged with perjury for his previous testimony and this one would be added. Then he thought there was no way Acabar would let him live to be charged. Deep inside, he was sure he would be murdered. His evidence would be quashed in court; no one testified against Acabar and lived, no matter if the testimony was accepted or not.

The court officer called his name. He stood up, entered the courtroom, and started walking toward the witness stand. He thought he would not get shot in the courtroom. If they wanted to kill him, they had had plenty of opportunities. He knew when he left the court, after testifying against Acabar, he could and would be killed at any time. He reached the witness stand and sat nervously.

"Please stand and swear that you will tell the truth," the court officer said.

Andrew Ramstone stood up, greeted him, and asked him to introduce himself by stating his full name and occupation. Then he asked the officer to describe his rank in the police force, years of experience, and his present job. He picked up a plastic bag containing a pair of shoes and asked the officer to describe the evidence.

"While investigating Earl's murder, an individual walked in. When I asked him if he had witnessed the murder, the man answered no because he had just walked in. But I realized there was a bloodstain on the bottom and side of his shoe," Henry explained. "So, I asked him to remove his shoes and kept it as evidence. I confronted him about the bloodstain on his shoes and the ones on the carpet, but he insisted he had just walked in. I collected his information and, along with the shoes, gave it to my captain."

"Based on your experience as a police officer, can you explain what is significant about this evidence?" asked Andrew Ramstone.

"The photos taken from the crime scene indicate that while the accused was standing beside the body with the knife in her hand —"

The district attorney jumped up from his seat and said, "Objection, Your Honor! Earl was killed with a letter opener, not a knife."

"Sustained," said Judge Éclair.

The officer continued. "There were no bloodstains on the carpet from the accused's shoes, while there were bloodstains from these shoes. It indicates that the accused did not kill the victim. She was called to the scene after the victim was murdered. Someone else killed the victim."

The audience and jury were surprised and made an 'Ahhh' noise.

"No more questions, Your Honor," Andrew Ramstone said to the judge.

"Your witness," the judge said to Sean Wilderson.

"When you removed his shoes, did you find any bloodstains on his clothes? Did you remove his clothes, too?"

"No, there were no bloodstains on his clothes."

"Are you telling this court that the man committed murder, but there was not even one drop of blood on his clothes? How do you explain that?"

"He probably was not the killer either, but he probably asked the accused to stand beside the bloodied body for photos, and when he left, his shoes left blood marks on the carpet. There were no bloodstains on the accused, either."

"Your Honor, please direct the witness to answer the questions and refrain from speculation."

"The witness will only answer questions. The jury will not consider the witness's last statement," said the judge.

"If the killer should have bloodstains on his or her clothes, as you mentioned, then according to you, the accused is innocent," continued the officer.

"You are in contempt of the court. One more comment and I will hold you in contempt," said Judge Eclair.

The district attorney picked up the plastic bag containing the shoes and asked the officer, "Are you sure you removed these shoes from Mr. Evan Fontaine?"

"Yes, I did."

"In your opinion, what is the size of these shoes?" asked Sean Wilderson.

"I don't know. I didn't check the size," replied the officer.

"So, what you are saying is that you did not do your job accurately? Otherwise, you would know that these shoes are size nine, and Evan wears size ten, and you would not lie about it."

"I removed these shoes from Evan, and I even took photos showing he was wearing them with stains on them," said the officer angrily.

"What happened to the photos?"

"I gave them to my captain," replied the officer.

"There are absolutely no photos of Evan with the stained shoes," replied Sean Wilderson. "These shoes do not belong to Evan. How could you have photos of him wearing these shoes? Or maybe you are lying again like before."

"Objection," said Richard to Andrew Ramstone. "He is badgering the witness."

Andrew did not move.

Richard stood up and said, "He is badgering the witness, Your Honor!"

"No more questions, Your Honor," said Sean Wilderson.

"The witness may step down," said the judge. Then he saw that Richard was still standing and told him to sit down very rudely.

"We call Mr. Evan Fontaine to the stand," said Sean Wilderson.

Evan came to the witness stand.

Sean asked if the shoes belonged to Evan while holding the bag with the shoes.

Evan asked to hold the shoes and examine them closely. Then replied, "I don't think so."

"Can you explain why you don't think these are your shoes?"

"These shoes are too small. The officer must be mistaking me for someone else. He never asked me to remove my shoes," replied Evan.

"With your permission, Your Honor, may I remove the shoes from the bag so Evan can try them on and see if they fit?" asked Sean Wilderson.

"Yes, go ahead," replied the judge.

The district attorney removed the shoes from the evidence bag. He asked Evan to step down from the witness stand and come around so that the jury could see him clearly and to try on the shoes. Evan removed one of his shoes and tried very hard to put the evidence shoe on, but his foot did not fit.

"I would have to cut a couple of my toes to fit in this shoe," said Evan.

Everyone in the court, including the jury, laughed.

"Can you put the evidence shoe side by side with your shoe?" asked Sean Wilderson.

"Of course," said Evan and put them side by side, and started laughing.

"Your Honor, it is clear that the evidence shoe is much smaller than the witness's shoe size. This evidence is clearly a forgery. I have no further questions for this witness, Your Honor," said Sean Wilderson.

"Your witness," said the judge to Andrew Ramstone.

"No questions, Your Honor," replied the council.

"You may step down," said the judge to the witness.

"Why didn't you ask any questions?" asked Richard, very angry and upset.

"What could I ask? I did not want to make things worse."

Both the counsel and the district attorney gave their closing arguments. The jury came back after a couple of hours with a guilty verdict. Richard left the courtroom without talking to anyone, not even Gloria. He drove around for several hours, and as Flore was telling Phil that she was getting worried about Richard, he walked into the house.

Flore, who had heard the news on the radio, hugged Richard and said, "I am sorry for the injustice that just happened. Please don't give up, Richard."

Without saying anything, Richard looked at Flore, Phil, Cathy, and Mary and went upstairs. Phil wanted to say something. He even moved his lips, but the words didn't come out. He bowed his head in sorrow.

Flore called from the bottom of the stairs. "Kiki, darling! Dinner is ready! We are waiting." She was trying very hard to hold back her anger and sorrow as if nothing had happened. She was afraid that Richard might not go down for dinner and isolate himself.

Cathy didn't like Flore calling Richard Kiki, but she gestured her confirmation by nodding at Flore, approving her efforts to persuade Richard to join them by any means. Cathy was afraid that Richard would slip into depression again, and this time, there would be no prospects of getting out of it.

Richard came downstairs, and everyone breathed a sigh of relief and started passing him different foods. But Richard would take the plate and pass it to the next person without taking any food.

"You know, son, I am thinking of writing a letter describing all the injustice that happened. I will collect as many signatures as I can from people who know Bill very well and are aware that he is the murderer and not Gloria and send it to the head of the justice department," said Phil.

"Do you remember when we were visiting Tijuana? Wapi suggested you should go to Cusco and do ayahuasca?" said Flore.

Without acknowledging what Phil or Flore said, Richard, in a desperate, low voice as though he was thinking out loud, said, "A bunch of gangsters without even a vestige of humanity within them, and with police and dirty judges on their payroll, make a mockery of the judicial system, enslave people, imprison and waste innocent people's lives and even kill people, and nobody can do anything. A despicable, filthy judge like Éclair is given the power to suppress evidence, manipulate the law, lie about evidence, twist the truth, and send innocent people to jail so that the real criminals will walk free. And the public will be happy someone is paying for the crime, not knowing the truth. All my life, I was convinced the day would come when I would have a second chance to save that little girl. Now, any way I look at the situation, I realize the more helpful I try to be, the more harmful I become."

"Not if God is with you," replied Flore. "Give yourself and your problems to God. Tell Him that it is beyond your abilities and ask Him for help and guidance." Then Flore started praying. When she finished praying, she made the sign of the cross while saying, "In the name of God, Jesus Christ, Mother Mary, and the Holy Spirit, Amen."

Cathy remembered hearing this prayer before. She wanted to ask Flore why her prayer was different from everyone else's. She turned to Flore, opened her mouth to ask, but she didn't want to change the subject and the dynamics of the moment, so she kept quiet.

Realizing Cathy's reaction, Flore said, "This is my version of the prayer. I always include Mother Mary in my prayers to ask for her help." Then Flore turned to Richard and said, "You didn't hear what I said, do you remember Wapi . . .?"

"Yes, I heard what you said, and I heard what you said, too, Dad. What would a letter to the chief justice do, or what can Wapi do?" said Richard.

"I don't know what the letter will do, but I believe in Wapi. If he said that you could find a solution while doing ayahuasca, I am sure you will. Sorry, Mr. Phil, I am sure your letter will help, too," said Flore.

"What is ayahuasca?" asked Mary.

"Wapi explained that when you do ayahuasca, you enter the spirit world and find answers to your questions and problems. And he said it would be a different experience for different people depending on what their problems are and what they are fighting for," said Flore.

Cathy, who was strongly against anything unfamiliar and unusual, struggled to keep her mouth shut. She could not come up with a solution, but she thought Richard needed time to forget this horrible experience, and maybe a trip would help. However, she did not comment.

"That is interesting," said Mary. "Maybe I will do it with you."

Cathy could not keep quiet and said, "Don't you see your brother is hurting!? Instead of helping, you are squeezing yourself in. Do you think this is a game!?"

"I am trying to help," replied Mary. "I want to keep him company and experience ayahuasca with him."

Richard excused himself and said he was not hungry and wanted to go out for a walk.

Phil asked Flore, "Is there any danger in doing ayahuasca?"

"According to Wapi, if an authentic shaman performs it, and I'm sure Wapi's referral is one, there should not be any danger," said Flore.

"That may keep him busy and give him time to heal," said Cathy. "I don't believe in these things, but I don't want him to go through another depression. It is fine with me if he decides to do it."

"And I will start working on an appeal and my petition," said Phil.

CHAPTER THIRTY-THREE

Phil went to his home office and called his lawyer friend, Alexander Parvello. Before Phil could explain why he had called, Alexander told him, "I'm sorry for the gross injustice. How is Richard taking it?"

Without going through the details of Richard's connection to Gloria, Phil answered, "Well, it has become personal for Richard."

"I understand," replied Alexander. "When I started practicing criminal law, I used to get personally attached to the cases. What can I do for you?"

"The case must be appealed. And we cannot let Bill's law firm do it for obvious reasons. Can you take the case?"

"Actually, I know just the right lawyer for this case. One of my colleagues, Martin Ryden. He had similar cases before and was quite successful. I will send you his contact info," said Alexander.

"I know Martin, and I have his contact info," replied Phil. "But tell me, why do you think he is better than you? You had similar cases too, didn't you?"

"Yes, but his practice is more concentrated on murder cases," replied Alexander.

"I will tell him that you recommended him," replied Phil and said goodbye.

Alexander's wife was present in the room during the conversation.

After he hung up, she asked Alexander, "Why didn't you take such a widely publicized case and try to help a friend? He has referred many big cases in the past and you are not that busy these days, so why didn't you take the case?"

"I was sure they would lose the case, and I was afraid he would call me. I have not lost my mind. I'm not going against Bill and making an enemy of him and a mockery of myself. Besides, Phil has referred many cases to me. I could not charge him my regular fee."

"Why did you think Bill's law firm would purposely lose the case?" asked his wife.

"There were many guards and employees in the mansion when Earl was murdered. In addition, many police officers examined the murder scene.

They were all aware that one of Bill's assistants called Doug killed Earl. These people talk freely with their relatives and friends, and the news spread fast that the girl did not kill Earl. In one of the interviews with Bill set up for damage control, when Bill was asked about the word on the street that the girl didn't kill Earl, he branded it as a "Conspiracy Theory." Some people only believe what they hear in the official news media and reject any information branded as a conspiracy theory, not considering the fact that the official news media cannot broadcast the truth, as they will be sued by Bill and may even lose their license."

"Earl was murdered in Bill's mansion. Had he won the case for that innocent girl, Bill would be implicated in Earl's murder," replied Alexander. "From what I hear, that poor girl was asked by Bill to pose with Earl's body so they could take photos. The case against the girl had so many holes in it that her conviction was a joke on the street. Bill himself is not shy talking about it with his friends. I think he considers it a demonstration of power and a warning to other criminals not to mess with him."

Phil, on the other hand, realizing why Alexander must have refused the case, became very sad. He thought about how for years, he had referred clients to Alexander and never asked for anything in return. He would take the case if he thought there was a chance to win, or maybe he did not want to fight against Bill.

He started calling his friends and clients and asked them to go to his office the next day. The next day, around noon, twenty-five people gathered in Phil's office in his small conference room. Voski was making coffee and preparing trays of cookies for the people, and her husband, Davit, was serving them. Phil, sitting at the head of the table, started explaining the situation.

"Ladies and gentlemen, you are all aware that a gross injustice has been inflicted on our society. You all know that a murderer got away with a murder, and an innocent young lady has to go to jail for a crime someone else committed."

Everyone nodded and said 'yes' in confirmation.

Jasper, the owner of a large drug manufacturing company, said, "It was a sham, not a court. Everyone is aware who killed Earl, but that psychopath, the so-called

Judge Éclair, who is nothing more than a puppet for Bill, dismissed all the evidence and found an innocent girl guilty of murder."

"Over 3500 years ago, one of Hammurabi's codes regarding the justice system said that if a judge incorrectly fined someone, that judge would not only have to pay twelve times the amount of the fine but would also be removed from office," said Michael, a law professor at the local university. "Dirty judges are not something new. They have existed throughout history. Not only have we not advanced in our justice system in the last 3500 years, but we are even worse off."

"I was very disappointed when I heard the news on TV. The more civilized humans become, the more crooked, dishonest, and fraudulent the justice system is," said Alice, while her husband, Tom, confirmed his wife's opinion by saying, "Indeed."

"What can we do?" asked Rancho, the owner of a large travel agency. "Do you have a plan? I will do anything to help."

"Yes, I was getting there," said Phil. "I set up a petition letter addressed to our head of the justice system and congressmen, explaining the whole shoddy court proceedings and how Judge Éclair dismissed valid evidence to protect his buddy, Bill. We have to get as many signatures as possible for it to be effective. You can go to the website and enter your information and email the link to all your friends and relatives so that they can add their names, too."

Everyone was excited and promised to collect as many signatures as possible. After getting all the information, one by one, they said goodbye and left. While walking toward their cars in separate groups, people started talking to each other.

Theodore said to Jasper, "Do you believe this stupid Phil? He expects us to side with him and go against Bill?"

"He is a very naïve small-town boy. He does not know the rules of the game in big cities," said Jasper.

Rancho said, "I can't believe this guy. Bill will destroy him, and he expects us to join him and get crushed by Bill alongside him. I thought he was smarter."

"But he is very kind and helpful," replied Tom.

"Yes, he is kind but stupid. Doesn't he know that with one phone call, Bill will take away my travel agency license, my livelihood, and even worse?" Rancho replied.

Tom and Alice became very scared and uncomfortable.

Tom started mumbling, "I am sure Bill will know who was present in this meeting and may want to retaliate."

"Don't worry, as long as your name is not on the petition, nothing will happen to you. Besides, I am good friends with Bill. I will tell him that you are on his side," said Rancho.

Tom and Alice thanked him and said goodbye, but Tom worried all day.

Finally, at night, he told Alice, "I'm not sure if Rancho will mention our loyalty to Bill when he is talking to him. I'm going to call Bill myself and assure him that I'm on his side."

"Bill doesn't know you, and I'm sure he doesn't care if you exist or not. Why would Bill care that we are on his side? We are nobodies. By calling him, you may even aggravate him," said Alice.

"But if I don't and he hears about us, who knows what he'll do? Besides, this is a good opportunity to introduce ourselves to Bill. When we talk to our friends, we can say we are friends with Bill," replied Tom.

"Why do you want to pretend that you are friends with Bill? You said so many bad things about him. As long as you don't sign the petition, nothing will happen to us," said Alice.

"Then Phil will be disappointed with us. How can we confront him?" continued Alice.

"Don't answer his calls and don't show up to future meetings that he sets up. If later on, he asks why you didn't sign the petition, tell him you were sick and forgot about it," replied Tom.

Jasper checked the website periodically to see how many had signed. After several days, when there were some signatures, he went to Phil's office.

"I had a heated argument with a congressman once, and I think the congressman may have a grudge against me. If I add my signature, it will backfire on your case," Jasper explained. "However, I asked many other people to participate."

Phil sensed great anxiety and fear in Jasper toward Bill, and he felt terrible for putting Jasper in this awkward position. Phil also realized that Jasper did not collect any signatures and was just taking credit for other people's work but pretended he believed Jasper anyway. He thanked him and acted as if he agreed with Jasper that putting his name on the petition may negatively affect him. He didn't want to embarrass Jasper any further. Phil was counting on Jasper and his acquaintances and was very disappointed by Jasper's refusal to help. Jasper was a prominent member of society, and his voice would have gone a long way. Phil felt hopeless against Bill. *If Jasper, being the bravest of all, is so afraid of Bill, no one is going to help,* he thought.

Rancho, on the other hand, called Bill's office and talked to Antonio Donatelli and described his meeting with Phil in detail, and asked for directions. At first, Antonio was offended that Rancho had attended a meeting to mobilize the attendees to fight against Bill.

"You can attend as many meetings as you want, and Bill will not get offended because Bill is a philanthropist and honest men are not afraid of anything," Antonio arrogantly spoke.

Rancho, realizing that Antonio did not trust him, explained that the only reason he attended the meeting was to find out what was going on and pass it on to him.

"I idolize Bill, and I think that Bill is a very successful businessman and indeed a philanthropist. I will do anything I can to help Bill. I will never side with Phil against him."

Antonio calmed down a little and, with a friendlier voice, thanked Rancho. "Bill has no connection to Judge Éclair except for having some cases through his law firm where Judge Éclair was the presiding judge," Antonio explained. "I find Judge Éclair to be very impartial and respectful of the justice system. He never makes a biased judgment."

"Yes, sir. I have great respect for Judge Éclair, too," said Rancho.

Without listening to what Rancho was saying and before he finished his sentence, Antonio continued. "Bill's mistake was letting Richard get involved in this case. He is Bill's nephew, and he thought it would be a good experience for him. We didn't know that he would become personally attached to the case. Now that you have offered to help, can you find out why he is so attached to this case? Is he in love with that girl?"

"Of course, I will find out," replied Rancho.

"You know what," continued Antonio. "I don't want Phil to waste his time with his futile gatherings. After all, he is Bill's brother-in-law."

"Yes, I was surprised that he is trying to fight Bill. Not only is he a nobody compared to Bill, but he is also Bill's brother-in-law," replied Rancho.

"Yes, Bill's sister's husband," repeated Antonio. "You can actually help Phil by deterring him from pursuing his useless meetings."

"How can I help?" asked Rancho.

"Next time you attend a meeting with Phil, take some of your friends with you, who, while pretending to help Phil's cause, will explain to Phil that Judge Éclair is a respected judge and no appeal court will go against his judgment and listen to any argument. I'll send one of my lawyer friends to join this meeting, too."

Rancho called Phil the next day.

"Several of my influential acquaintances would like to sign the petition, but they want to get to know the case better and would like to participate in the next meeting you organize," he told Phil.

Phil set up the meeting in his office that Friday evening and invited other people who could not participate in the first meeting.

Phil briefly explained the case and added, "I am sure everyone is familiar with the case through the media and is aware of the injustice that occurred in the court at the hands of the Acrebond organization and with Éclair's help, too."

One of the individuals accompanying Rancho asked Phil to elaborate on the details as not everyone knew the complete story.

"Judge Éclair struck out key evidence, including photos taken immediately after the murder that shows a wall clock with a time that conflicts with the coroner's report. This should have proven that Gloria did not kill Earl Murphy," Phil explained.

The individual interrupted Phil and asked, "Weren't the photos tampered with? A police officer introduced the photos several months after the incident. I think Judge Éclair was right not to accept the photos as evidence."

Phil was a little taken aback by the comments made by someone who pretended to be helping his cause but continued his explanation about the voice recording.

Another individual who had come with Rancho questioned the evidence as tampered with and explained, "I am a lawyer, and I've been in Judge Éclair's court before. I have complete confidence in him, and that justice has been served."

Phil realized the setup Rancho had arranged and brought up the shoe that had been replaced in the evidence room.

The same person who had responded to the voice recording laughed and said, "Are you suggesting the shoe was removed from the evidence room and replaced by a similar but smaller one? You must be joking because if it gets to the point that people can remove evidence and replace it, it means there is no justice system. Is this what you are saying?"

"When the lawyers, district attorneys, and the judges are paid by criminals and are working for the criminals, you are right; there is no justice," Phil responded.

"You are being ridiculous with your conspiracy theories. I'm not going to waste my time," said the lawyer and left the meeting.

After that, the negativity took over, and people started doubting Phil. If a lawyer thought that justice was served, who were they to think otherwise? After some more discussion, the meeting ended with disappointment for Phil.

That night, at the dinner table, Phil was quiet and deep in his thoughts.

Cathy usually wouldn't get involved with anything that had to do with her brother, but seeing Phil so depressed, she asked him, "How was the meeting?"

Richard, Flore, and Mary, guessing the meeting didn't go well, stopped eating and were all ears to hear what Phil had to say.

"It didn't go well. Let's leave it at that," said Phil. "I don't have too much hope on the appeal or the petition to the head of the justice department or the congressmen."

"I remember that Wapi told me this problem can only be solved by ayahuasca," said Richard. "Maybe he is right."

"I remember you talked about it before, but I forgot and don't remember who Wapi is, and what is ayahuasca?" asked Phil.

Richard reminded his dad that when they were in Mexico, Gloria's parents took them to an American indigenous medicine man who told him that he could solve this problem by doing ayahuasca. Phil didn't take it seriously and did not comment about it. But later, when Cathy and Phil were alone, Cathy brought up the issue and asked Phil why he didn't comment about it.

Phil replied, "There are real issues at hand like our appeal being rejected by the appeal's court."

"But do you agree that Richard should try ayahuasca?"

"Richard is grown-up, and he can do anything he wants," replied Phil.

"But what is your opinion?" asked Cathy.

Phil thought about it for a minute and said, "I think if this ayahuasca will keep Richard busy and occupied, he should do it because he is going to be very disappointed very soon."

Martin Ryden prepared the appeal documents and filed them with the appeal court. Sean Wilderson, the district attorney, called and informed Andrew Ramstone about the appeal filing.

"Does Bill know we are not on the case anymore?"

"Yes," replied Andrew. "Everything is going according to plan. We are out and detached from the case. No more connection."

The petition result was very disappointing—less than two thousand signatures were collected. Rancho informed Phil that there were not enough signatures for the congressmen to reply.

CHAPTER THIRTY-FOUR

Two of the three appeal judges were in Bill's mansion. Also present was Bill, Antonio Donatelli, Andrew Ramstone, Sean Wilderson, Judge Eclair, and Martin Ryden. Bill thanked everyone for attending the meeting and welcomed their new member, Martin Ryden. Everyone congratulated and welcomed him.

They discussed the appeal issues one by one and how they could dismiss them.

In the end, one of the appeal judges said, "In our view, the judgment by Judge Éclair stands, and there is no need to waste any time on an appeal, but I'm not sure how our colleague, Judge Coher, will vote?"

"He is not a member of our organization," replied Bill. "But we are working on it. At least, I think we can convince him to cooperate."

The next morning, there was an article regarding Judge Coher. The article talked about a murder suspect freed on bail by Judge Coher, who subsequently got into an accident while drunk, killing the other driver The article blamed the death on Judge Coher for releasing the murder suspect, but did not mention that the murder suspect was later exonerated of the murder charge.

The next day, a reporter contacted Judge Coher's office and asked for an interview. During the interview, the reporter asked about the accident and the death of the driver.

"This death occurred as a result of your mistake in freeing a murder suspect on bail. How do you feel about it now, knowing that the accident victim's wife and children are still grieving after so many years? What are the chances of you making the same mistake again?"

A couple of days later, the three judges had a meeting to discuss Gloria's case. It was obvious to Judge Coher that the defendant had a strong case and should be granted the appeal. But the other two judges referred to the case many years ago and asked Coher not to make the same mistake again and cause another innocent person to die. Coher tried to separate the two cases, but the other two judges insisted that if they granted the appeal, the defendant would probably be freed on bail and kill again. They presented Gloria as a monster and a cold-blooded killer and told Coher that the media would be all over the case if an appeal was granted, and it would make a mockery of the justice system. Judge Coher argued that Judge Éclair made a mockery of the justice system in his pseudo court by convicting Gloria of murder. But the other two judges kept warning and threatening Judge Coher of the consequences of granting an appeal. Finally, under pressure, Coher joined the other two in denying the appeal.

Hearing the news, Richard became hopeless and depressed. That evening at the dinner table, he did not eat anything and did not talk.

Phil, trying to start a conversation and change the atmosphere, asked Richard, "What did you decide about ayahuasca"?

Richard replied that he was thinking about it.

"I think you should do it," replied Phil.

Flore was surprised about Phil's change of heart and confirmed Phil's suggestion excitedly.

"Why don't you go with Richard?" asked Cathy.

"Can I go with you?" asked Mary.

"I should go alone. I need some alone time," replied Richard.

CHAPTER THIRTY-FIVE

Richard started looking for the ayahuasca contact information that Wapi had provided and finally found it. He first made a reservation for a session with master ayahuasca shaman Joel, then reserved the flight.

Richard was on the plane heading toward Cusco. The plane reached altitude, the seat belt sign turned off, and Richard took a nap. When he opened his eyes, he realized the aircraft was flying very close to the mountains, and he remembered that Cusco was located at a very high altitude.

At the Cusco airport, someone was waiting for him to give him a ride. When they arrived at their destination, he was greeted by Joel, the ayahuasca master, who led him to his room and asked Richard why he wanted to do ayahuasca.

After listening to Richard's story, Joel suggested doing individual ayahuasca rather than with a group. Joel instructed Richard not to eat anything for three full days, not to talk to anyone for three days, and only to drink coca leaf tea which was always available. He could meditate, walk in nature slowly but should not walk fast or climb hills as they were at a very high altitude and he would become exhausted easily.

The ayahuasca was scheduled to be done on the evening of the third day. A nurse took Richard's blood pressure and indicated to Richard and Joel that his blood pressure was too high and suggested trying again in the morning. Joel asked Richard to meditate, sleep and avoid walking. The next morning, his blood pressure was a little lower, and Joel led Richard to his sanctum and began preparing ayahuasca.

After an agonizing and long period of physical cleansing, Richard's body lay still, and Richard found himself surrounded by light and staring into a very bright light. He started thinking about Gloria and the injustice that had happened to her. After all, this was the reason he was there. After a while, he felt his problems were solved or would be solved shortly. It was a very good feeling as though everything made sense and there was a reason for everything, good and bad. Then he felt that there was neither good nor bad; it just *was*. He looked down and saw himself lying down while Joel was praying and raising smoke by burning different herbs and anointing his body with nice-smelling ointments.

Richard was mesmerized by the bright light; he tried to go toward the light but couldn't. While nothing was blocking him from the light, it was like he was pushing against a wall. He tried harder, and while his energy body was still, his physical body started struggling and moving. Joel realized the movements and went into a deep meditative state, and joined Richard on the other side. As a master shaman, Joel often moved between the two worlds.

Richard suddenly realized that Joel was talking to him. First, he thought the session had ended, but he realized he was standing instead of lying down. Joel was talking to him, but his mouth was not moving. He was not using words or any specific language, but Richard understood him.

"Using language is for the physical body only," Joel explained. "Humans use words and sounds to communicate with each other. In the spirit world, you communicate through intent. The more sins you commit, the less positive energy you will have and the less you can communicate with the Great Spirit. Follow me."

They went through a light shower made of white light rays. Joel explained that this was to purify the soul. When they stepped out on the other side, Richard found himself in the same light that he was looking at from the other side of the light shower. Richard wanted to move forward, but Joel asked him to wait. Again, they were talking with their mouths closed and without using any language.

A light jolted in front of Richard. It turned into a human form and introduced itself as Richard's spirit guide. "Why did it take you so long to connect? How can I help?"

Richard introduced himself, but he realized that he was one with the spirit guide and did not need an introduction. The guide told him that it was familiar with both Richard and his situation and asked Richard to follow him. All the conversations were done with closed mouths, without any words or language.

"Twenty-five years ago in Earth's time, or a split second ago in spirit's time, you appeared on Earth with one goal only: to fight evil and spread kindness. You decided to do this by saving your daughter in your past physical appearance and ending atrocities committed by some lost and sinful souls. You lost your way several times by disconnecting from light and getting attached to physical values, but every time, you eventually found your way back. Of course, you have many supportive souls who look after you and help you all the time.

If you are not evil and do not belong to evil organizations, the members of those organizations will exploit, harass, and torment you persistently. They will launch continuous smear attacks and defamation campaigns against you and try to force you into their organization. But it is better not to join the evil organizations, even if it means receiving insults all the time, than to join them, stop the attacks and become popular among criminals.

Evil thinking will lead to evil words, and evil words will lead to evil actions. You connect to the universe by kindness and positive energy. Kindness is God's gift. If you harm others, you invite evil into your life. To keep your connection to the universe, you must completely stop your mind and stop thinking at least a couple of times a day, every day. And only kind thoughts the rest of the time.

One million miracles occur every second to keep a pile of earth in the form of a living physical body. The mind provides the physical body with the ability to survive long enough so that the heart can spread kindness by not committing sins but by doing kind deeds, saying kind things, and thinking kind thoughts.

The universe is held together by kindness energy. Every time a kind act is done, a trickle of positive energy is added to this energy web, and the universal bond gets stronger. Every time a sin is committed, the universal bond gets weaker. This kindness bond helps the universe stay intact and prevents it from disintegrating and dismantling. The universe is now disintegrating rapidly.

Every kind word, thought, and action creates positive energy. Even the smallest kind act performed in quiet isolation without anyone knowing, like a sacrificing parent, a caring teacher, an honest judge or police officer, and other kind actions performed by all kind souls, creates a virtuous circle and promotes more kindness. A dirty judge or religious leader creates a vicious circle and spreads evil.

The eternal truth, universal wisdom, and God are in your heart. You should not join criminal organizations and follow the rules and regulations set by them that allow its members to commit crime against nonmembers. These individuals form evil organizations by controlling other physical bodies. They give their organizations fancy names to appear benevolent and reverent, and then spread evil. They control people both inside and outside their organization.

People who are in these organizations gain some materialistic benefits, like accumulating wealth, in exchange for them abandoning their souls and spiritual goals. And then, they end up here."

Suddenly, Richard found himself on the edge of a deep vortex that circled around and got deeper until it was completely dark. He was frightened and took a couple of steps back. The spirit guide told Richard not to worry. He could not get in the vortex even if he tried.

"There is a special karma magnetism in each level of the vortex, and in every one of the billions of compartments in each level," the guide explained. "The souls that have committed sin, depending on how sinful they were, find their place in the vortex by karma magnetism without having control where in the vortex they go. When they get into the specific compartment in the vortex, the karma in that compartment attaches to the sinner's soul, and they are reborn in the place and time according to the karma attached to them.

Karma is created in the spirit world, and most often, it is modified and changed in the spirit world. But that does not mean that karma cannot be changed while the physical body is still on Earth during a lifetime. Karma is a dynamic phenomenon, and human beings are a work in progress. Contrary to what most people on Earth think, karma changes and develops all the time depending on the actions the individual takes, and how much good or evil the individual commits.

Even during the same lifetime, if you are remorseful of the evil you have committed and truly repent your sins and do not commit sins anymore, change your lifestyle and strengthen your connection to the great spirit, you can visit the light and just by thinking about the things you want to change, they will change.

It takes a while in Earth's time for the changes to manifest, but you should keep connected because when you disconnect, the changes you desire will stop. Even after the changes you wanted have happened, if you stay disconnected for a long time, the changes will disappear, and the karma will regress to its original state.

Only the good and the evil attached to the soul stay with the soul and go to the spirit world and determine the karma for the next lifetime. Your karma chooses all the details of your new physical life, including mental, physical and personality traits, abilities and disabilities, which country, city and family you are born into, the neighborhood, friends and everything else, hoping that this time, your soul will not pursue mirages on Earth, and instead will stay connected to the Great Spirit and pursue the soul's purposes.

You have to know your karma, own your karma, and master your karma. Only then can you gradually let it go. Otherwise, if you blame others or your environment for your problems and unpleasant experiences, you will become a slave to your karma. Not only will you keep repeating the same karma in this lifetime, but it will also follow you to your future lifetimes and into eternity. You will be born with the same conditions and the same problems and obstacles all the time and experience the same undesirable and unpleasant situations and keep repeating the same mistakes over and over. If you live a conscious life and accept your personality traits and character flaws embedded in your karma, you can manage life's situations much more comfortably and easily, and specific components of your karma will change or disappear, and they will not follow you into your future lifetimes.

The sinners, who consider themselves gods on Earth, the more control they thought they had as physical beings, the less control they will have as spiritual beings. The souls of sinners return to Earth in such situations and conditions that the sole purpose of the physical being becomes doing kind acts with no opportunity to commit sins anymore.

A sinful soul enters the vortex, and with each additional sin, descends deeper into the vortex. The worst sinners are at the bottom. They exit from the bottom of the vortex and are reincarnated as different creatures other than human beings, such that they will have no other choice but to do good deeds. This may continue thousands of times before they can reappear on Earth as human beings again.

Religious leaders who live a life of blasphemy and sacrilege while preaching asceticism, precision, and the word of God on the altar, are the main promoters of atheism. A dirty religious leader and a dirty judge promote crime and apostasy more than a gangster. People follow religious leaders and judges thinking if they are doing something, regardless of how sinful it is, it should not be that bad, and it must be okay for them to do it, too. When religious leaders, judges, or other individuals in positions of authority commit crime, they sink lower in the vortex than other individuals who commit similar crimes.

Don't let any other human being be a middleman between you and the Great Spirit. If a human being tells you that your way to salvation and God is through them, he is a sinner, and you should stay far away from him as God is in your heart.

On the contrary, those who live selfless and spiritual lives, sacrificing their physical lives and spreading kindness, choose their own karma and choose to go to Earth as a physical being when they want and where on the Earth they want.

For most individuals, the minute they die and the mind and all the illusions created by it disappear, they realize they wasted a whole lifetime by choosing to amass wealth and power and have feelings like regret, hatred and fear instead of eternal love.

Humans are provided with minds and hearts. You have to control your mind with your heart. If the opposite happens and the mind takes control of the heart, the mind will completely silence the heart.

It is okay to have temptations on the mental level. It is part of the physical experience. The important thing is to have control over temptations by keeping a strong soul connection.

At birth, the physical body is completely connected to the soul and the great spirit. Over time, as the child grows and is introduced to the material world, the connection weakens. By committing sin to achieve material goals, the connection further weakens, and the temptations increase until the mind completely controls the physical body.

When the physical body keeps on exclusively thinking with its mind and ignoring the heart, it considers itself immortal and becomes evil and gains control over other physical bodies. And by misconception and self-deceit, considers itself a God, and starts committing more serious crimes and enslaves more physical bodies.

For the mind, there is only one purpose in life: to accumulate wealth, power, and other material things as much as possible. The mind does not realize that life on Earth is but a split second.

Your heart is connected to the universal wisdom, and only good exists in your heart. If you don't control your mind with your heart and instead let your mind control your heart, evil will penetrate you and you will become a lost soul. A lifetime on Earth is a split second in universal time. You should not exchange a split second of fallacious fun in exchange for eternal suffering.

When the physical body dies, all the wealth, joy and suffering you have accumulated and experienced and all other physical achievements die with it. It does not matter how wealthy or poor you were or how much you enjoyed life or suffered on Earth. It is like the physical body, all the pleasures and pains it has experienced and all the wealth and fame it accumulated never existed. Your physical body is only your soul's house and a vessel to accomplish your spiritual missions. The physical body is so insignificant even your soul does not remember the different physical bodies it has occupied before. For the soul, only the spiritual experiences are important: how kind or sinful the individual was. In absolute time, each lifetime is very short, like a split second, and the soul occupies one physical body after another. The only thing that remains and is passed on to the future lives is the soul and the good and the bad you have done when occupying each physical body.

"Now, tell me, what can I do for you?" asked the spirit guide.

"Can I see my dream in full?" asked Richard.

Yes, you can. In the spirit world, all you have to do is desire, and you will see. Of course, when you return to the physical world, you will remember very little of the spirit world experiences. We are communicating in spirit language which is completely different from the languages of the physical world. You will remember the ending of your dream because it happened in the physical world and some bits and pieces of everything else, but mostly what you will remember is the intense light and everything will come to you as knowledge and epiphany.

"You can take knowledge to the physical world, but not information. Even if you could remember certain things, the first thing you will know is that you cannot reveal any information from the spirit world in the physical world."

"It is the same as every visit you make when you meditate. First, you get access to infinite knowledge. Then you get help in achieving your spiritual goals."

"What do you mean, like every visit? Have I been in here before?" asked Richard.

"Very often. Every time you silence your mind through meditation, walking in nature, or just keeping quiet, you strengthen your connection to the spirit world."

Richard remembered he had asked to see the dream in its entirety. Before he asked again, the events unfolded in front of his eyes.

The arresting of Bill by Kiki Coto played in front of Richard in a fast-forward mode in different frames. Then he shifted his head and saw Bill escaping from prison. He shifted a little more and saw Bill and his gang surrounding the houses of the officers who had participated in his arrest, killing their families and burning down their houses.

After they left one of the houses, a man called Emanuel; an employee of Richard's grandfather, and Abraham's assistant, entered and grabbed a three-year-old boy, ran to the neighbor, and asked them to hold on to the child. Then he saw Bill and his gang chasing Kiki Coto. He saw them burning the cornfield, the last moments of Kiki's life, and Bill leaving Gloria with Kiki's dying body while the fire was approaching fast. He saw Kiki lying on his side, knees bent, his back to the fire, and placing the little girl between his knees and chest, away from the fire, hoping that his body would protect the little girl from burning, and whispering in the little girl's ear, "I will always be with you and protect you," and then taking his last breath.

Emanuel appeared from the cornstalks into the fiery field and took the little girl from Kiki's body. He called Abraham and reported the events. He told Abraham about the little girl and boy. Abraham instructed Emanuel to take both children to Tijuana and give the girl to Jose Louis and his wife and the little boy to another family. Abraham told Robert, Richard's grandfather, what had happened, and Robert got ready to go to Tijuana. Abraham asked Emanuel to keep an eye on Robert.

Then Richard observed another episode: a gathering with Bill, his men, and Bill's father, Robert. Robert was very angry at Bill and ordered Bill to stop murdering people and manufacturing and distributing drugs. He threatened Bill, saying he would disown him and fire him from his company. A little later, Emanuel realized that Bill and a couple of his friends were having secret conversations. He became suspicious and called Abraham while recording them from behind the bushes. Two of the men were preparing drinks. One of the men took a small container from his pocket and poured several drops of liquid into one of the glasses.

As the man approached Robert and gave the glass to him, Emanuel started running toward him while yelling, "Do not drink it!"

Before Robert could hear him, he took a large sip. At the same time, Bill's people drew their guns and started chasing Emanuel. Emanuel ran back toward the bushes. He found a tree trunk with a crack in it. He told Abraham that he was hiding his phone in the tree trunk crack. He slid his phone into the crack and kept on running. Bill's men caught up to him and shot him dead.

Meanwhile, Abraham called Bill and said that Emanuel had emailed him the recording of the plot to kill Robert and warned Bill not to harm Robert. Bill told him that he was bluffing as Emanuel could not have sent the recording to Abraham because Emanuel did not have his phone or any recording equipment with him. Abraham described Bill's secret conversation and planning with his men and how they poisoned Robert's drink. Bill believed him but said he was too late because both Robert and Emanuel were dead. Bill threatened Abraham, saying that if he gave the recording to the police, he would kill Abraham and his family.

Richard observed Abraham on many occasions, asking Bill not to murder Cathy and her family and not to kill Renzo and his family or Gloria and many others, too.

Richard observed Judge Éclair gambling and constantly losing money in different private gambling establishments, including Bill's mansion. Bill's people were lending him money. The amount he owed Bill was rapidly increasing. Bill was asking for his money, but Éclair was not able to repay Bill. One of Bill's assistants told Éclair that if he helped Bill with one of his cases, Bill might forgive his debt. The assistant provided information regarding the case and asked Éclair to call one of Bill's assistants and discuss how the case could be won. Éclair was asked not to mention Bill's name during any conversation.

Éclair studied the case thoroughly and made an appointment with Bill's assistant. He explained to Bill's assistant that he could dismiss the murder weapon as obtained unconstitutionally, and Bill's firm would win the case. He asked for his entire debt to be forgiven, and Bill's assistant agreed. The meeting was recorded from different angles. After that day, Éclair became 'Bill's bitch.'

Bill's assistant called a lawyer who was representing a client who a criminal had cheated. He asked the lawyer to cooperate with the criminal's lawyer to exonerate the criminal. The lawyer argued that his client was innocent and lost all his life savings to this criminal. The lawyer believed he could recover his client's life savings. Bill's assistant explained that the criminal was a member of Acrebond group, as was the lawyer, but the lawyer's client was not. The lawyer agreed to fold the case for the criminal's benefit.

They arrived at a light dome. The spirit guide asked Richard to enter the dome to meet other souls. The spirit guide looked on while several light bodies entered the dome. Abraham, Renzo, Gabriel, and Gloria were some of the souls that entered the dome and had conversations with Richard.

"I'm anxiously waiting to help you bring down Bill," Abraham said. "But my physical body is too old and too ill, and I'm deteriorating rapidly. I'm staying alive to help you, but I may not last very long. Please hurry and come see me, so I can tell you what to do."

"I'm waiting for an opportunity to take revenge against Bill for killing my parents," said Gabriel.

"Come see me in prison, and I will help you connect the dots," said Renzo.

"We are all in this together," Gabriel said. "We will hopefully succeed. Surrender to God, Richard."

Then the spirit guide spoke again.

"There are many advancements on Earth for the physical body to live more comfortably, but all these advancements on a physical level have made humans more materialistic and brought them further away from their true spiritual nature. As the number of sinners increases with each generation, more souls come to Earth in human form to repel their sins and become free spirits. Still, the vicious cycle continues, and they return as worse sinners than before. They return to Earth and increase the world's population and pollute the Earth to the point of destruction.

There are many free spirits on Earth trying to reduce pollution and reduce the world population by spreading kindness and preventing the universe from disintegration and destruction. So far, it has not worked. More drastic measures may be necessary to achieve favorable results."

Then the spirit guide showed some fast-forward scenes from the Earth: world conquerors, killing and enslaving others, individuals amassing money and gold, lying and using all kinds of tricks to advance materially. Individuals who accepted positions for serving others, like politicians, judges, religious leaders, teachers, and many others, and instead of doing their job, abusing their power and exploiting those whom they should have served, all for material gains."

"In the bottom of the vortex are the judges who follow orders from the leaders of the criminal organizations in which they belong. They receive bribes, free the murderers and instead put the innocent in jail. Politicians, who, instead of serving people and making their lives better, steal people's money and destroy the same country they were elected to lead. Murderers cut lives short and destroy the lives of the victims' relatives. Then there are religious leaders stealing from their congregation, and teachers who, instead of teaching, waste the innocent children's time just to get a paycheck, and parents who instead of taking care of their children, follow their personal pleasures. Then there are the gossipers who by spreading gossip, sentence their victims to a lifelong suffering and lapidation. After dying, all these sinners go straight to the depth of the vortex and reincarnate as creatures or vegetations that can't help but serve the universe in a positive way."

And then the spirit guide showed Richard honest politicians, parents who devote their lives to their children, teachers who actually care for the well-being and education of their pupils. Religious leaders who do not steal but stay hungry so they can feed others, honest judges who refuse to take orders from criminal organizations and follow justice and the law in their decisions, and ethical lawyers who work hard to defend the innocent.

"The minute the physical body dies and the soul leaves the body, all the life's events and experiences run before its eyes. If the individual was a sinner, he realizes that he wasted a whole lifetime by choosing to amass wealth and power by joining criminal organizations and inflicting pain on others. He then realizes that time is one of many limitations of the mind. It is the mind's default state and only exists while the soul occupies a physical body. There are no time limitations in the spirit world.

A lifetime, no matter how long it feels on Earth, is like a split second in the spirit world. The soul realizes it was only a split second ago that he left his cubicle in the vortex, determined not to commit sins anymore in order to stop going back to the vortex. But each time, he gets deeper and deeper in the vortex."

Joel, who was near Richard and his spirit guide the whole time, indicated it was time for them to leave the spirit world. The spirit guide said goodbye and disappeared. Richard and Joel went toward the light gate to wash off the energies that did not belong to Earth and returned to their physical bodies. After a couple of minutes, Richard opened his eyes. Joel asked him to wait a while before standing up.

There was a calm feeling surrounding Richard. He was completely aware that life on Earth was just a split second, regardless of how long it appeared or was perceived to be. He was aware that the purpose of life was to spread kindness, no matter how insignificant. He was sure that everything would work out for the best. He did not know why he thought that as he did not remember all the events in the spirit world, but he was confident that everything would be okay. He was surprised that he felt everything would be okay because logically, it was a closed case, and there was nothing that he or anyone else could do to change the results. Gloria had been convicted of murder by a dirty judge, and other dirty judges had decided that no one could judge a dirty judge. A judge could become as corrupt as he wanted, and there was nothing anyone could do about it. So, why did he think everything would be okay? But he was still sure that certain events would occur and Gloria would be free.

He knew that he had to meet and seek help from different people, although he did not yet know who. On the way home, Richard was calm and confident that Gloria would somehow be exonerated. When he arrived home, everyone was happy to see him and asked him about the ayahuasca experience.

Without going into too much detail, Richard said, "It was unlike anything I have experienced before."

"Did you see the whole dream?" Cathy asked.

"Indeed, I did see the whole event. It was Bill who killed Kiki Coto." Then he had a feeling that Bill even killed Robert, his grandfather. He started the sentence by saying, "He even killed . . ." but then he looked in his mother's eyes and did not continue.

"He even killed who?" asked Cathy.

"Nothing, I don't know what I was saying," replied Richard.

Flore and Phil realized right away who Richard was referring to and tried to change the subject. Flore asked Richard if he was able to find a lead in Gloria's case.

"Leave him alone," said Phil. "Richard, you must be tired. Why don't you get some rest?"

"Actually, I feel fine," replied Richard.

"You really look fine, and you have lost a lot of weight," said Mary. "Maybe I should do ayahuasca too."

"Did he kill Robert? Is he who you meant?" asked Cathy.

"I'm sorry, Mom. I don't know why I said that. It is not like I saw something. It's just a feeling that I have," said Richard.

"You mean intuition," said Mary.

"When Robert died, Terza kept saying that my brother killed her son, and she did not want to talk to me," replied Cathy.

"Oh, that Robert!" exclaimed Richard.

"Oh my God!" screamed Cathy. "You mean Robert, my father?" Cathy started crying and saying, "I am sorry, Dad, that I wasn't there to stop him from killing you."

"I'm sorry, Mom," said Richard. "Maybe I am wrong. I hope I am."

"How would you know about it? And how about freeing Gloria? Did you find any leads?" asked Mary.

"I don't know how; it just came to me. And regarding Gloria, I have the feeling new evidence will surface, and she will become free. I just have to follow my intuition," replied Richard.

"Mom, what was Robert's father's name?" asked Richard.

Hearing the words "evidence will surface" and "I have to follow my intuition," Mary was a little disappointed. Not that she expected anything helpful would come out of the trip besides a change of scenery for Richard, but now she was sure that nothing would change. She tried very hard not to show her disappointment.

"It is Renzo," replied Phil while Cathy was crying.

"I need to see him," said Richard.

"He's in jail in Chicago. Why do you want to see him?" asked Phil.

"I don't know yet, but I have a feeling that he will be very useful in Gloria's case."

Mary searched for the prison where Renzo was serving his time and sent the information to Richard. Richard reserved his trip and went to Chicago to meet Renzo.

CHAPTER THIRTY-SIX

Richard was sitting in a meeting room waiting for Renzo. When Renzo came in, he looked at Richard curiously as if he was trying to remember him. Then he sat down, picked up the phone, and waited for Richard to talk.

Very nervously, so as not to say anything to make Renzo mad, Richard told him, "I have come to tell you something important. Please don't hang up the phone."

Before continuing to introduce himself, Renzo replied, "You have not yet provided me a reason to hang up, but I have a feeling you will very soon."

"Please listen to me to the end before you decide to hang up," asked Richard.

"If you don't start talking, I will hang up the phone and leave right now," replied Renzo.

"I am Richard, Phil and Cathy's son," Richard said.

"Now I remember you. What do you want?" asked Renzo.

"Please don't hang up," said Richard.

"Why do you keep telling me not to hang up?" asked Renzo.

"Because your wife thinks my uncle killed your son, Robert. God bless his soul," replied Richard.

"I think that, too. That dirty criminal destroyed my son's life. Bill made Robert a drug dealer, an addict, and a gambler. Robert was a good student with a bright future. He was not used to the criminal lifestyle. He died of an overdose, but we don't know if he overdosed or was murdered by forceful overdose. In any case, it was Bill that forced him into his gang and drug dealing, so Bill killed him. Of course, my wife thinks that Bill killed him directly, and she does not talk to me because she thinks I introduced Robert to Bill. She does not believe that I would never have introduced my son to that animal. What do you want from me?" asked Renzo.

"An innocent girl is convicted of murder. I am . . ."

Before Richard finished his sentence, Renzo cut him off and said, "I'm aware of the situation. Doug killed Earl, and they framed that innocent Gloria. What do you want from me?" asked Renzo again.

"I want to know if there is any information that you may have that will exonerate Gloria," said Richard.

"Sorry, I cannot help you with this. When Abraham asked Bill to spare my life, Bill accepted it with one condition: I will not backstab him."

"That name is familiar, Abraham," said Richard while trying to remember who he was.

"Abraham is the reason you exist. He asked Bill not to kill your parents before you were born."

"Bill? Kill his sister?" asked Richard.

"Bill is a psychopath. He has no feelings of compassion, sympathy or mercy. After he killed his father, he wanted to kill Cathy and Phil, thinking that Phil, being a lawyer, would find out that Bill had inherited a fortune and ask for Cathy's share. But Abraham found out and stopped it. Of course, Phil never suspected," said Renzo.

"Yes, he suspected. But how do you know all this, and why would Bill listen to Abraham?" asked Richard.

"I heard from here and there that Abraham has something on Bill that makes Bill listen to him. It was Abraham who asked Bill not to kill Gloria, too. Otherwise, the warden is on Bill's payroll. And you think that the warden is keeping her isolated and preventing Bill from killing her?"

"How do you know all this?"

"In my world, this is common knowledge. But try to say that to someone in law enforcement, and they will dismiss it as a conspiracy theory," replied Renzo.

"I have to talk to this Abraham. How can I find him?" asked Richard.

"He was Robert's partner and friend. From what I hear, he is very sick. I am not sure if he is in any condition to help. But if there is anyone who can help you, it is him."

"I saw him a while ago coming out of Bill's office, very kind man," said Richard.

Then Renzo gave Richard Abraham's address and wished him good luck. Richard thanked Renzo for the information, said goodbye, and went straight to the airport to return home.

As Richard was scheduled to arrive home at midnight, he called Phil and asked him to stay up and wait for him so they could have a conversation. Phil was worried. He was curious about the information Richard got in Chicago. At night, just before their usual bedtime, he chose a movie and started watching.

"Why have you started watching a two-hour movie when it's your bedtime?" Cathy asked, very surprised.

"I can't sleep, but I will go to bed shortly," Phil replied.

As Cathy left, Phil closed his eyes and slept on the sofa while the movie was still playing. At the sound of the door opening, Phil woke and greeted Richard.

He impatiently asked, "What do you want to talk about that cannot wait until morning?"

"I didn't want Mom to hear. Do you remember the warden who put Gloria in isolation so Bill could not kill her?" Before Phil could answer, Richard continued. "Well, it turns out the warden is on Bill's payroll, and if Bill had told him to kill her, he would have," said Richard.

"Did Renzo tell you that? Do you trust him?" asked Phil.

"Bill also wanted to kill Mom and you, and he would have if he hadn't been asked by the same person not to," said Richard.

"Who is this person with so much power over Bill?" asked Phil.

"His name is Abraham, one of Grandpa's old friends. Apparently, he has something incriminating on Bill, so Bill listens to him," replied Richard. "I have his address. I am going to see him in the morning. He is ill, and if he dies before I talk to him, I will never know if he could be of help or what he has on Bill."

"My God, if he dies, nothing will stop Bill!" exclaimed Phil.

CHAPTER THIRTY-SEVEN

Richard woke early in the morning after a couple of hours of sleep. He checked Abraham's address while sipping his coffee.

As he was ready to leave, his father called and asked him, "How far is Abraham's house?"

"Around three-quarters of an hour drive if I leave now," replied Richard.

"Did you call him?"

"I could not find his number, so I am going there," Richard said.

"It is too early, especially for a sick man."

"If I go later, the streets will be too busy."

"Leave such that you will get there no earlier than 9:00 a.m. or even later," Phil suggested.

"Okay, I will leave in an hour."

Richard sat in front of the TV and anxiously watched the news. Phil left for work half an hour later. As soon as his father left, Richard went to see Abraham.

Richard was in front of Abraham's house. He was surprised as it was a very modest house, almost rundown. He was not expecting a mansion like Bill's house, but certainly not this house. He parked his car, trying very hard to wait until 9:00 a.m., but saw a lady in the house and decided it was okay to knock on the door.

A lady opened the door and said, "Hola."

Richard replied, "Hola. I am here to see Abraham."

"Please wait here," replied the lady. She went back into the house and said in Spanish, "Mr. Abraham, someone has come to see you."

An old voice asked in Spanish, "Who is it?"

"I don't know. He didn't tell me."

"You asked, and he didn't tell you?" asked Abraham.

Before the lady answered, Richard went in and said, "I am Richard, Robert's grandson."

For a minute, there was complete silence. Abraham and the lady looked at each other happily but also appeared to be cautiously surprised. Then, like coming out of a shock, Abraham asked Richard to sit and told him he was happy to see him. He asked the lady to bring a cup of coffee. Richard and Abraham looked at each other, not sure where and how to open the conversation.

Then Abraham told Richard again, "I'm happy to see you. Robert was a good friend."

Richard thanked him but still couldn't say anything. He didn't know where to begin.

"You know, I am sick, so if you have anything to say, say it now while I am still alive."

"Sorry, I had a feeling of déjà vu. I don't know why."

"There are lots of things that we don't know. Please go ahead," replied Abraham.

"First of all, I guess I have to thank you for my existence. If you hadn't stopped Bill from killing my parents, I wouldn't be born."

"You were talking to Renzo, that big mouth. But there is a reason for everything. You are welcome. Now, you didn't come all the way for that. Tell me what I can do for you."

Richard talked about Gloria's unfortunate situation at length and how Bill killed her father, the police chief in Juarez. He explained all the obstacles and collusion between the corrupt judges, lawyers and district attorneys. Then Richard realized he was boring Abraham. It seemed he was repeating what Abraham already knew, like teaching grade one math to a mathematician.

He said, "Sorry for boring you." Now Richard went straight to the point. "I have come to seek your help for freeing Gloria, and if in the process, I can put an end to Bill's and Acabar's atrocities, that would be a bonus."

"I was not bored," replied Abraham. "I wanted to make sure that Bill did not send you to see if I will keep our promise not to reveal anything. I was just curious to see how much you know. Okay, maybe a little bored. But, regarding your question about freeing Gloria and maybe defeating Acabar, well, you can't do one without the other. As long as Bill and the Acabar gang are in power, they will not let you cross them. Tell me, how did you find out that Gloria is Kiki's daughter?" asked Abraham.

Richard replied, "Since I was very young, I have had a very frightening dream almost every night." After describing the dream in detail, Richard said, "It wasn't until Gloria was arrested that I knew she was the little girl from my dream. I saw the birthmark on Gloria's shoulder, the same birthmark the little girl in my dream had, and so I decided to help her."

Richard also talked about their trip to Tijuana, meeting Gloria's family, and how they found out that she was adopted. He explained the photo he saw in Bill's office, his trip to Cusco, and the ayahuasca experience.

"I did the ayahuasca so I could find a way to defeat Bill and free Gloria. I think that our meeting today is also a result of the ayahuasca, though I am not sure how it will help Gloria's case. I would appreciate any suggestion from you. How did Gloria end up with Jose Luis and Maria Elena?"

"My assistant, Emanuel, took her from Kiki's dead body. I asked him to take her to Tijuana to Jose Luis and Maria Elena. He also saved Gabriel and gave him to another family."

"Isn't Gabriel Bill's staff manager?" asked Richard.

"Yes, that Gabriel," replied Abraham. "I was following your moves: meeting Gloria in prison and asking the warden to put her in protective custody, how you were unaware the warden is on Bill's payroll, meeting her family and hiding them from Bill, thinking that Bill could not find them. Not only did I need to be certain you were not working for Bill, but I also had to make sure that you are capable of pulling it off," said Abraham. "Everything aside, if you went all the way to Peru to drink that shit just to find out how you can help Gloria, it indicates dedication. I also like how you never revealed to Bill who Gloria was. Otherwise, he would have killed all those I asked him not to, regardless of the consequences to him. The child of an individual he has killed is more of a threat to him than I could ever be. So, you think you are Kiki Coto, huh? I can't say if I believe in what you are saying or not. But I believe you are not working for Bill and you may have the guts to bring him down," said Abraham.

Then he stood with great difficulty and walked toward an old cabinet. He found an old chocolate box, removed the lid, and searched inside until he found a pendant. He brought the pendant with him as he came back to his seat.

After catching his breath, he told Richard, "Actually, I don't have anything on Bill. I tricked him into believing I had the recording of him killing Robert. If I really had the recording, I would have sent it to the feds and put him in jail. Emanuel was recording Bill and his people while on the phone with me. He described their movements in detail. Then Bill killed Emanuel right after Emanuel hid his phone in a crack in a tree trunk. I called Bill and told him that Emanuel had sent me a recording of Robert's murder. First, Bill did not believe it, but I described the events in detail, exactly how Emanuel had told me, and then he believed me. I searched for Emanuel's phone. I found the tree and the crack in the trunk, but I could not find the phone. Every time I asked Bill not to kill someone, I was afraid Bill might get fed up and kill me, too. But what I am going to tell you may cause many people to die if Bill finds out. No one knows that Bill killed Gabriel's father," said Abraham. "Gabriel is also Bill's confidant. He is aware of everything that goes on in Bill's mansion. And I hope that he will have access to the information you need: the blackmailing documents as well as all the bribes he paid to politicians, judges, district attorneys, police, city staff and others, that he uses to control people in power. So, you have to approach him very carefully, prove to him his real identity before he blows the whistle on you. Gabriel's father was a deputy of Kiki Coto; his name was Fernando Dominguez. He was one of the few officers who Bill could not buy, who stood by Kiki to the end and got killed. Bill killed both him and his wife. I arranged for a couple I knew to adopt Gabriel. But I did not tell them who he was so that Bill wouldn't find out. Later, Bill hired the husband as a driver. After a rival gang killed the adopted parents, Bill brought Gabriel to his mansion. He even let him go to school for several years. For Gabriel, Bill is more than a father. He is his hero. He adores Bill, and Bill is fascinated by Gabriel. From a young age, Gabriel was in charge of staff, some much older. He is accurate and very well organized with an excellent memory, just like his father. Even George is sometimes jealous of Gabriel."

"How do you think he can help?" asked Richard.

"Many years ago, Bill did some extensive renovations in his mansion, all underground. He used an equivalent of a high-rise building cement in his mansion. But you can't see anything from outside. I am hoping there will be a lot of interesting and useful information that Gabriel can provide you, including hopefully all the evidence of Bill blackmailing many people, including your judge."

"Why don't you talk to him and tell him about his real parents and the fact that Bill killed them?" asked Richard.

"He won't believe me. I intentionally did not tell him so that he wouldn't get into trouble. He couldn't have done anything with this information before, other than confronting Bill and being met with Bill's rage. He could have been killed."

"What do you suggest?" asked Richard.

"I've thought about it a lot," replied Abraham. "Somehow, I was expecting you would show up. I have a pendant with a photo of Gabriel with his real parents. I think Gloria should show it to him and tell him the truth. Because if you talk to him, he won't believe you, and that will only cause more problems."

"You said that Gabriel was three years old when Bill killed his parents. Gloria was only two years old. How could Gloria remember better than him?" asked Richard.

"The issue is not if Gloria or Gabriel will remember something or not. I have been to Bill's mansion several times. I have seen how Gabriel looks at Gloria. Gloria will at least have a chance. Gabriel will be getting a lot of shocking information at once. If you break the news to him, he will become overwhelmed and will either not believe you and tell Bill what a crazy idea you have, or he will believe you, and before you know it, he will be chasing Bill to kill him. But he has known Gloria for a long time. He will have more trust in her than you or me. And don't forget, he likes her, at least I think he does. Don't underestimate the power of love. Gloria can control his rage better than anyone. You should meet Gloria and tell her all about Gabriel and his real parents beforehand, and the fact that their parents were close friends and most probably they were playing together as children as well. You see, Gabriel's face has not changed since childhood. You would recognize him from the photo. You can see a small patch of white hair at the edge of his hairline above his forehead on the left side. If he is convinced that the child in this photo is him, he will realize that the woman must be his real mother and the man in the officer's uniform, his real father. And when he hears about Gloria's real parents, and he is told that Bill murdered both their parents, only then might he believe you and be willing to help. But under no circumstances should Bill know who Gloria and Gabriel really are. Otherwise, he won't hesitate to kill them both."

Abraham gave the pendant to Richard and told him to be careful.

"Good luck and keep in touch. If you need help, keep me informed. Hopefully, I will see Bill going down before I die."

CHAPTER THIRTY-EIGHT

Richard was in the visitor's room waiting for Gloria. As Gloria entered the room, Richard stood and greeted her. After inquiring about her well-being, Richard asked Gloria how well she knew Gabriel. Hearing Gabriel's name, Gloria at first blushed, but then felt sad, remembering that she was stuck in prison for the rest of her life and she should not make wishes that wouldn't come true.

She was serious and emotionless and said, "We were colleagues at Bill's place."

Richard picked up on Gloria's vibe when he mentioned Gabriel's name and hoped that Gabriel would have a mutual feeling but pretended he had not noticed Gloria's initial reaction.

"I met Abraham before coming here. He saved both your lives after Bill killed both your parents," replied Richard.

"A different gang than Acabar's murdered Gabriel's parents," replied Gloria.

"His adopted parents were murdered by a different gang, yes, but Bill murdered his birth parents. Of course, he does not know that. Nobody knows that except Abraham, who arranged his adoption. His adopted parents were working for Bill. And after the rival gang murdered them, Bill brought Gabriel to his mansion, and the staff took care of him. From a young age, Gabriel was very organized, meticulous and detailed, just like his real father, Fernando Dominguez, who was the deputy of your father, Kiki Coto."

Tears ran down Gloria's cheeks when she heard her father's name. Then realizing that there was no use being emotional behind bars, she wiped the tears and returned to her emotionless state.

Gloria asked Richard, "Why are you asking about Abraham and Gabriel?"

"Gabriel may have some information and documents that could be useful to us," replied Richard.

"A judge found me guilty of first-degree murder. How can any information or document exonerate me?" asked Gloria.

"Let me tell you something. I don't know what I am looking for. I don't know how it will happen, but I am one hundred percent certain you will be exonerated," said Richard.

Richard's deep conviction and faith shook Gloria a little, and she replied, "Okay then, tell me what I can do. But consider the fact that Gabriel will defend Bill with his life."

"Not if he knew Bill killed his family," replied Richard.

"Then why don't you tell him?"

"I'm afraid if I talk to Gabriel before I can convince him who he really is, he will blow the whistle on me, and Bill will kill him along with you and many others. But if you talk to him, show him this pendant and ask him not to tell Bill, even if he does not believe us, and give himself a chance to investigate the truth, he may listen to you."

"What pendant? Can I see it?" asked Gloria.

Richard handed over the pendant to Gloria. As soon as Gloria opened it and saw the photo inside, she started crying out loud. This time, she could not control her emotions.

Richard was very surprised and told Gloria, "You must have been around two the last time you saw Gabriel or his parents. How can you remember them?"

"When I saw Gabriel in Bill's house for the first time, he looked very familiar, like an old friend. I thought that maybe I was mistaking him for someone else. Now I remember where I know him from. What do you want me to do?" Gloria eagerly asked.

"I think you should call and tell him that you have some very important information you want to share with him. Ask him to come and visit you, but not to tell anyone. When you find out when he is coming, let me know, and I will be here with you. Do you have his number?" asked Richard.

"Yes, and I will call him and let you know," replied Gloria.

Before leaving, Richard asked Gloria one more thing. "When we meet Gabriel, tell him first about your real parents, the hero called Kiki Coto who stood for justice and gave his life for what he believed in. Then talk about his brave deputy, Fernando Dominguez, without mentioning that he was Gabriel's father. Fill in the dots and tell him that Fernando was Gabriel's father and they were both killed by Bill. This way, we will make sure that

Gabriel will not leave in the middle of the story from disbelief."

That evening, when Gloria thought that Gabriel would not be busy, she called Gabriel and asked him to visit her. She begged him not to tell anyone about the call and warned him that if he did, her life would be in danger. Gabriel agreed and told her that when he knew when he could visit, he would call her. A couple of days later, Gloria called and gave Richard the time that Gabriel was to visit.

Richard went a couple of minutes early to wait for Gabriel's arrival. But to his surprise, Gabriel was already sitting with Gloria. Richard considered it a good sign, greeted them, and sat down. Gloria had told him that Richard would be coming and did not discuss the issues with Gabriel, but seeing Richard made Gabriel feel anxious and guilty, like he was betraying his best friend, Bill.

Richard asked Gloria to tell Gabriel about herself. Before Gloria told Gabriel the story, she made Gabriel promise not to tell anyone about the conversation and the information he would be receiving. Gabriel agreed, and Gloria started telling Gabriel the story.

While Gloria was talking about her father, Richard would sometimes complement her description of her father by saying things like, "Her father knew he could have cooperated with the gangsters and lived a wealthy life, but he chose righteousness over material gains," and "He knew he could lose his life, but still, he did not give in to evil."

Gabriel looked at Gloria with adoration and pity, thinking that her life would be different if her father had not been killed. Then Gloria told Gabriel about Kiki Coto's deputy, Fernando Dominguez, and how he died helping his friend try to defeat the evil.

"He must have been as righteous and brave as Kiki Coto," she said.

"I have his photo." She handed the pendant to Gabriel.

Gabriel took the pendant curiously.

As he was about to open it, Gloria said to him, "Wait a minute. No matter what you see, or how upsetting it is, please do not get too excited and try to control yourself."

Gabriel got even more excited, but without listening to what Gloria was saying, he said, "I promise."

He opened the pendant.

"What is this? This is me, but these are not my parents!" exclaimed Gabriel while moving a couple of feet backward. "My parents were Alvaro and Yolanda."

"They were not your biological parents. They had adopted you when you were a child. They were your adoptive parents," replied Gloria.

"How can you be so sure? If this were true, my parents would have told me, "said Gabriel.

"They did not know who your real parents were," Richard jumped in.

"So, nobody knew they were my real parents, and yet here we are, and you are telling me that they were?"

"Abraham gave you up for adoption, and he did not tell them who your real parents were. Your adoptive parents would probably have told you that you were adopted once you were older, but still, they did not know who your real parents were," Richard explained.

Gabriel said, "Abraham," while deep in his thoughts, trying to figure things out. Then he said, "If Abraham knew, then Bill should have known and would have told me."

"All his life, Abraham tried very hard to hide the truth from Bill."

"Bill is like a father to me. Why would Abraham try to hide the truth from Bill?" asked Gabriel.

"Because if Bill had known you were Fernando's son and that Gloria was Kiki's daughter, he would have killed you both," said Richard.

"You are both crazy. Is this a sick joke? Bill is your uncle. How can you talk behind his back like this?"

"If it weren't for Abraham, I would not exist either," replied Richard.

"You are really crazy. I am not going to listen to you anymore," said Gabriel. Then he turned to Gloria and said, "Him, I don't know. But how could you say these things about Bill? You know how much he tried to help you."

"Bill's assistant, Doug, killed Earl, and Bill framed me for the murder. Bill killed my parents and yours," said Gloria.

"You'll regret this," said Gabriel and left without paying any attention to Gloria's cries to wait and listen. But he returned after walking only a couple of steps. He very angrily told Gloria, "Because I promised not to tell anyone about this stupid story, I won't, but I don't want to hear about these absurd accusations against Bill anymore. You and Richard must have gone through a lot of work editing this photo and coming up with this ridiculous story. Why? What did you want to accomplish?"

Gloria was crying quietly with her head down while Richard replied, "If you want to know the truth instead of blindly believing in Bill, you can easily go to Juarez yourself and ask the people, young and old, about your parents and who killed them. I did the same thing for Gloria and found the truth."

"I am not going on a wild goose chase and wasting my time. I don't know what your agenda is, but I am out of here," said Gabriel.

"I wouldn't lie to you, Gabriel. If I lied to you, I could not look into your eyes anymore. Go to Juarez, and if you find out that what we told you is not true, I promise I will never look into your eyes again," said Gloria.

Gabriel was a little taken aback. He became quiet and was looking for words, but Richard jumped in and said, "I will go to Juarez with you if you want."

"That wouldn't be a good idea," replied Gabriel.

"Why not?" asked Richard.

"Because Bill will find out and wonder what we are doing travelling together."

Gloria stopped crying. She realized that Gabriel was considering going to Juarez and was a little relieved.

Gabriel said, "I will be in touch."

Before he left, Richard asked, "Do you want my number?"

"I have your number," replied Gabriel and left very agitated.

Richard was visibly worried. He was not sure of Gabriel's next move.

"Are you sure he will keep his promise and not tell Bill about our conversation?" asked Richard.

"Yes, one thing that you can count on with him is keeping his promise. I am sure he will investigate and get back to us," replied Gloria.

"I could have gone with him. I already know people there. I would take him to the right people," said Richard.

"That is exactly why he didn't want you to go with him, so you won't set him up with people you know," replied Gloria.

Every day that passed, Richard became more anxious and worried, wondering if Gabriel would go to Juarez and investigate or if he simply did not believe Gloria and him and would tell Bill about their conversation.

A week later, Gloria called.

"Gabriel has taken several days off to visit his parents' grave. He did not tell Bill which parents."

"How do you know?" asked Richard.

"One of my friends told me, "Replied Gloria.

"Let's hope he is in the right city," replied Richard.

CHAPTER THIRTY-NINE

After several more agonizing days, Gabriel called Richard from a burner phone in the middle of the night and asked for a meeting.

"How about we go to see Gloria and meet there?" asked Richard.

"You know the warden reports all visits to Bill's assistant. Once they will consider a coincidence, but if we meet there more times, they will get suspicious," replied Gabriel. "You know San Pedro? There is a church there that I visit once a week to bring leftover food for the homeless. I will send you the address. It is quite a distance, but I enjoy the quiet sometimes. Wear some worn clothing so that you can blend in with the residents. I will see you there at 9:00 p.m. tomorrow."

The next evening, Richard bought some clothing that was a little bigger on him and torn in several places. He wore a fake beard and a cap and very nervously went to the meeting place. He tried to get there on time, but since he was very anxious to hear what Gabriel had to say, he arrived half an hour early. He walked around, then sat on a plastic milk box and realized that an older man was looking at him strangely. He looked the other way, so he wouldn't make him angry but heard him calling.

"Hey, you! Who are you? What do you want in here? You don't belong in here!"

"I am meeting someone," replied Richard.

"Are you meeting Gabriel?" asked the man, while others started looking at him.

Richard became more nervous, but before he could reply, the man continued. "You can be spotted from a kilometer away. Get in this and keep quiet."

The man directed Richard to a big cardboard box with a mattress and a couple of plastic milk containers for seats. As Richard nervously sat on one of the containers, Gabriel drove up and gave his car keys to the man talking to Richard. The man pointed to the cardboard box where Richard was sitting and told Gabriel that his guest had arrived.

Richard realized that Gabriel was not the same person anymore. Before, Gabriel was in control, calm and composed. Now, he was angry and agitated.

As soon as Gabriel sat down, he asked Richard, "What can I do to help?"

"Did you find out the truth? Do you believe me now?" asked Richard.

"If I hadn't, we wouldn't be talking. It is like I was killing my parents every day by working for and protecting their murderer. In Juarez, everybody knew the truth. Now I do, too. Tell me, what do you need from me?" asked Gabriel.

Richard suddenly felt very uncomfortable and asked Gabriel, "Do you want to discuss the issue right now, in here?" He looked at their surroundings.

"I've been coming here for years now. I was being followed for a long time. I guess Bill's security got tired of following me to the same location all the time. No one is following me anymore. But I was very careful today to make sure that no one followed me. This is the safest place. Start talking," Gabriel instructed.

"A lot of judges, public prosecutors, lawyers, court clerks, police, and many politicians are cooperating with Bill."

"Get to the point. What can I do to help?" Gabriel asked with a sense of urgency.

"Well, some of them are on Bill's payroll and will always stay loyal to him. Others wouldn't cooperate with Bill if he did not have something on them to blackmail them," replied Richard.

"So that's what that shit is!" exclaimed Gabriel.

"What shit are you talking about?"

"There is a big safe under the house. Actually, it is not under the house. It's underground beside the house but in the property parameters. I think what you are looking for is in there," replied Gabriel.

"How can I get my hands on it?"

"Get in my car and let's take a tour," replied Gabriel.

By then, all the food was out of Gabriel's trunk and given to the homeless people. Gabriel drove past Bill's mansion, stopped at a street curb about half a kilometer away, and got out of the car.

Richard followed his lead and got out, looked around, and asked Gabriel, "Why did we stop here?"

"The sewer opening," replied Gabriel. "You have to get to the safe and remove the contents through the sewer pipe. There are guards, employees and cameras all over the house. There is so much stuff in the safe that it will be impossible to carry it through the house. There are several underground tunnels that Bill built many years ago as security. In case of a police raid, he can enter the tunnels and get out from a safe opening in a completely different location. The safe opens through the tunnel that opens to this sewer. There is another tunnel on the other side of the house that opens to one of those houses on the other side of the highway. Of course, now that he has the entire police force on his payroll, he does not pay much attention to these tunnels, and they are just some old constructions he thinks won't be needed anymore. I have the safe combination as Bill opened it several times while I was with him.

But there are two problems we have to overcome. First, there is a sensor on the safe door, so when it opens, the security gets a signal. Bill would usually notify the security before opening the safe. The second problem is the sensor on the concealed door to the tunnel. If I open the door, the security will know. While the general area has many cameras, there is no camera looking at the door. I can pass by the cameras without raising any alarm. However, if I open the door, the sensor will trigger. You have to find a way to disable these two sensors.

There is a section on the concrete sewer pipe where the concrete has been ground to a thin layer in a rectangular shape. It will break with a good kick. You can see the ground lines from the tunnel but not from the inside of the sewer. But the area is reinforced by a very thick layer of curved metal that connects the tunnel to the sewer pipe in the shape of the pipe. This way, in case the ground area breaks accidentally, it won't cause a flood in the tunnel and people won't be able to enter from the sewer.

In addition to the metal reinforcement on the sewer pipe, there are a couple of insulated thick metal doors in the tunnels that are locked from both the inside and outside. If you can disable the sensors on the concealed door and the safe, I will get into the tunnel, open the metal doors and the sewer reinforcement. I will do it when I know you are in the sewer on the other side. I will knock on the rectangular ground section so that you can mark that section. You can come later with some help, break the sewer pipe at the marked location, get in the tunnel, open the safe and remove all the contents.

To mark the sewer opening, I will call you when Bill is away during the day or in the evening. But for you to enter the tunnel and the safe and remove the contents, I will call you when Bill is away for at least a couple of days."

"Why a couple of days? How many documents and evidence are there?" asked Richard.

"I don't know, but the contents will probably fit a twelve-foot truck," replied Gabriel.

"How am I going to remove so much stuff, and how am I going to transport it?"

"I just told you, you need a twelve-foot truck."

"Very funny. Tell me, how can I remove so much stuff?"

"You need several very trustworthy people," replied Gabriel.

"How can I find several trustworthy people?"

"When we first met, your biggest problem was to have access to the incriminating material Bill has on different people. Now that you can have access, you keep asking 'how can I' all the time. Just think about it and find a way. I am putting my neck on the line here," Gabriel said. Before Richard could answer, Gabriel added, "I know how. I have several good friends with those homeless people. I can ask them for help. But first, you plan everything. Buy or rent whatever equipment you may need. Let me know when you are ready, and I will tell my friends to help you."

"Did Renzo set up the security, or was it someone else?" asked Richard.

"These tunnels and safes were constructed before my time. I'm not sure if it was Renzo. But another company took over after Renzo went to prison, and the new company updated the whole system, except the basement. I guess Bill didn't think that he would need them," replied Gabriel.

"I am going to pay another visit to Renzo."

Gabriel handed over a piece of paper with a telephone number written on it and asked Richard to call the number when he disabled the sensors.

"This is a burner phone number. I will use each phone for one call only and destroy it soon after. I will give you another burner phone number every time we talk."

CHAPTER FORTY

Richard flew to Chicago the following morning to visit Renzo. This time, Renzo was not as defiant and angry as before. He was aware that Richard was fighting against Bill. He still thought it was a losing battle, but he appreciated Richard's courage.

"Did you set up the security system in Bill's house?" Richard asked.

"I did, but I heard they upgraded some sections after I went to prison."

"They upgraded almost the entire house, except the basement and the tunnels," Richard explained.

Renzo was surprised at Richard's knowledge of the tunnel system. "So, what can I do for you?" he asked.

"I need two things: instructions on how to bypass or neutralize the two sensors, the one on the concealed door to the hallway for the safe, and the sensor on the safe door," Richard said.

"I assume you have the code for the safe?" asked Renzo.

"Yes, I have it," replied Richard.

"You just mentioned that the basement security system has not been upgraded, so it is what I installed. Why

338

wouldn't Bill upgrade the basement?" Renzo wondered out loud. Then he said, "You know, there are things you do, and you don't know why you are doing them, but you just do them anyway. Well, I was doing lots of those things that didn't make sense then, but now I know why I was doing them."

"Whatever it is, it sounds promising. What is it that you were doing?" asked Richard.

"Well, for every sensor I made, I set up a built-in bypass," replied Renzo. "But you know, you will only get one chance. If you fail the first time, that will be the last time you will be trying. I will be dead the next morning and probably you and many others, too," he continued.

"I'm willing to take that chance for myself. He does not have to know you were involved," replied Richard.

"But he will," said Renzo and continued explaining that the instruction to bypass every sensor was in a book with a blue cover at his home. "I hope my wife did not throw it away."

"Can you call and ask?" asked Richard.

"She does not talk to me," replied Renzo.

"How am I supposed to get it from her?"

"You have to ask her," replied Renzo with a laugh. "When you get the book, follow the instructions to get into the system and enter the sensors' numbers. They will stay disabled until you activate them again or Bill enters the safe and the security realizes the sensors are not working. But you have to be in the house when you are disabling the sensors."

"I can arrange that. I will pay a visit to George," replied Richard.

CHAPTER FORTY-ONE

Richard returned home and informed his mom that he had to visit Terza and get a book from her.

For a moment, Cathy was taken aback but then became calm and answered, "Why not? Let's go and pay her a visit."

Cathy and Richard went to Terza's apartment the following morning and rang the bell.

"Who is it?" Terza asked through the intercom.

"It's Cathy. I am here with my son, Richard. Please open the door."

"I have nothing to say to you," replied Terza.

"But I have something to tell you, and I think you would like to hear it," replied Cathy.

Reluctantly, and without saying anything, Terza buzzed them up.

When Richard and Cathy got to Terza's apartment, Cathy told Terza, "You were not the only one who lost a loved one because of Bill. He also killed my father."

"How could he have killed your father? He is your brother, isn't he?" asked Terza.

"He was my brother. I've disowned him since I found out what kind of a monster he is. Now, can you help us to make him pay?" asked Cathy.

"How can I help you?"

"I met your husband yesterday and . . ." Richard began.

Before Richard could finish what he was saying, Terza asked with surprise, "You were in Chicago yesterday? You saw Renzo? How is he?"

"Yes, I saw him. He is okay, considering. He asked me to pick up a blue book from you."

"I threw away a lot of his stuff. I hope I did not throw the book away. I will bring his stuff, and you can go through it," replied Terza.

"If you want, just show me where it is, and I will go through it. You don't need to carry it," replied Richard.

Terza led Richard to a small storage cabinet and showed him the boxes. Then she returned to Cathy. She was much nicer to Cathy now. She felt they both had suffered from Bill. They started chatting while Richard started going through the boxes.

Cathy asked about Danny.

"Thank God Bill did not go after Danny, too," Terza replied. "Sometimes, I think Robert sacrificed his life to save Danny. Otherwise, I suspect Bill would want to draw Danny into his claws."

"Are you keeping in touch with Renzo?"

"It has been a long time since I talked to him, but I'm thinking about giving him a call."

Richard returned fifteen minutes later with an old blue cover book tucked under his arm.

"Would you like a cup of coffee?" Terza asked Richard.

Cathy asked Richard to have a seat for a little while longer, and she continued re-bonding with Terza while Richard was flipping through the book.

At home, Richard started a careful review of the contents. He entered a summary of instructions into his device.

CHAPTER FORTY-TWO

Richard called George and asked him to go for a drink that Friday evening. They met in their usual location and started drinking. Richard kept ordering drinks until close to midnight. When the time came to leave, Richard offered to order a ride for both of them and told George that after dropping him off, he would continue to his place with the same ride. George was too drunk to understand what exactly Richard was saying.

On the way, Richard asked George when the last time was that he had played pool.

"It's been a long time," replied George.

"I bet you are so drunk that I can beat you," said Richard.

George remembered that Richard would beat him even when he was not drunk, and so he looked at Richard curiously but didn't make a big deal out of it and replied, "You're on."

They arrived at Bill's mansion and went to the basement game room, and started playing. Richard tried very hard to lose, but he won just short of embarrassing himself for missing too many easy shots. They continued drinking until George fell asleep. Richard took out his device from his backpack, connected it to the house security, and disabled both sensors. Richard then ordered a ride and went home.

The next day, Richard called Gabriel.

Before telling him that he had disabled the sensors, Gabriel told him, "Good job, the sensors are off. Since you have to make some changes to the truck, you should buy a used truck. Make a hole at the bottom around the middle and wait for my call. I will call you when they are out."

Richard looked up several used truck dealers and went to the nearest one to purchase a truck. He then bought a circular saw and cut the bottom of the truck. He attached eight straight brackets to the cut piece to cover the hole and remove the cover whenever necessary and waited anxiously for Gabriel's call.

Gabriel also told Richard that Julio, the homeless guy he talked with last time, was aware of the situation and had agreed to accompany Richard when he went to mark the section of the sewer that should be removed. He also agreed to be there during the extraction of the material with four to five of his friends.

After a couple of days, Richard received the call from Gabriel. He went to the location with Julio, and while Julio stayed in the truck, Richard covered the sewer opening with some cardboard boxes, extended the ladder down the sewer, entered the sewer, and marked the section where Gabriel banged from inside.

Driving back to drop off Julio, Richard found out that Julio had been a sound technician but had started using drugs. He lost several jobs because he could not concentrate on his job. Shortly after he had lost his job, his wife separated from him, and with no job or income, he became homeless.

CHAPTER FORTY-THREE

Richard was waiting anxiously for Gabriel's call to inform him when the coast was clear. After about ten long days, Richard's phone rang.

Gabriel said, "The monkey is out of the cage and will be out for three days."

With the truck full of duffle bags, Richard drove toward Julio's location. Julio was expecting him.

"How many people do you need?" asked Julio.

"The more, the better. But everything must be done in a synchronized manner and very quietly. I don't want anyone to cause trouble and get us caught," replied Richard.

"Do you think you can give each individual a small bonus payment?" asked Julio.

"I will give them hourly payment for as many hours as it takes. Gabriel said three or four people is enough, but I think even double that many will be okay," replied Richard.

Julio turned around and gave some names to the guy standing behind him. In a minute, six more individuals appeared in front of Richard.

One of them said, "Anything for Gabriel."

Richard had brought several plastic boxes fastened to the inside railing of the truck that could be used as seats. He had also purchased several cases of bottled water. They went to a fast-food place and bought food for everyone. They parked in a parking lot near a park and took their time eating and chatting until it became dark. Then he slowly drove to the sewer opening. They put a cardboard box around the hole, so no one would see what was going on. One of them stayed in the truck, and the rest went down, each carrying as many bags as they could carry. Richard was nervous but very focused.

When they arrived at the marked section of the sewer, Richard told the gang, "If something goes wrong, nothing will happen to any of you, but Gabriel and I will be dead for sure."

Everybody assured him they would not cause any problems. Richard took a deep breath and kicked the marked area. Nothing happened. Before he tried again, one of the guys, a big man, asked Richard to let him do it.

"Be as quiet as possible," Richard said.

He kicked in the marked area. As Gabriel had described, there was a heavy metal door at the sewer opening and another one about ten feet inside. Both were left opened by Gabriel.

"We are eight people in the sewer. We should stand apart so we cover the distance between the safe and the truck. When I open the safe, I will hand two bags to the person nearest me, and we'll hand the bags down the line to the truck.

They got to the safe. Richard checked his phone, entered the password, and cautiously turned the handle while holding his breath. It clicked, and the safe door opened. There was not much room to maneuver in the safe. There were shelves and filing cabinets all over, full of documents and different electronic devices.

At first, Richard was overwhelmed with the overload of documents inside the safe. Then he remembered that Gabriel had said he would need a twelve-foot truck, and now Richard understood why.

Julio was in awe. "My God. We have to move all this stuff through the sewer pipes?" he asked.

Richard told Julio, "Maybe I will only take the memory storage units and not the paper documents." But then he said, "What if they are as important as the memory storage units? We will try to take them all. Let's get to work."

Julio and Richard started filling the bags. After several hours, they had removed most of the stuff from the shelves and got to the filing cabinets. Richard and Julio opened a couple of cabinets and found they were not completely full. They became more hopeful and continued the hard work.

It was past midnight when Julio tried to open a filing cabinet and realized it was locked.

"There must be very important documents in this one if it is locked within the safe," said Richard.

"Or maybe it is what I think it is, in which case, you don't need to pay us anymore," replied Julio.

Julio was struggling to open it. He was moving and banging the filing cabinet against the floor and making noise.

"Keep quiet," Richard told Julio. "Tell people in the chain to get a tool from the truck to pry open the cabinet."

Julio was too excited to even listen to what Richard was saying. He kept on struggling, and finally, he put his foot against the filing cabinet to hold it still and pulled the handle with both hands. The drawer came out and banged against another filing cabinet, making a very loud noise, and then a lot of cash was scattered around inside the safe.

Julio got very excited and exclaimed, "It is our payoff time!"

"We're not taking the money," said Richard.

"You might not be, but I'm sure taking the money."

A guard was patrolling the basement close to the underground safe and heard the loud noise. To his amazement, there were no doors or rooms in the area, only a couple of built-in fancy wall units. He wanted to ignore it, but the noise was very distinct and loud. Gabriel was also in the same area, pretending to work while keeping an eye on the area. He also heard the big bang and noticed the guard was investigating.

The guard approached him and asked, "Did you hear that noise?"

"Yes," answered Gabriel. "I think it was from upstairs. I will go and check."

"I am sure it was from inside this wall. I'm calling my supervisor," replied the guard.

Gabriel casually walked away while the guard started talking to his supervisor. Gabriel stepped out of the house and tried to call Richard several times. But there was no answer. He realized Richard was in the safe where there would be no phone reception. He took his car and drove to the truck. He asked the guy in the truck to inform Richard that someone may check the safe. He instructed that the safe door and the door immediately after the safe should be closed for a while and there should be no noise.

"When the coast is clear, I will call you so you can inform Richard," Gabriel told the individual in the truck

He returned to the house and went downstairs. The security had seen him go out and come back, but Gabriel had high clearance, and nobody ever asked him where he went or would suspect him of any wrongdoing. He was the boss when the boss was not there. Usually, he was much more concerned than the guards. He saw that the head of the night security was going down toward the concealed door where the guard who heard the noise was standing.

The head of security jokingly told the guard, "Did you see a ghost? Where exactly did the noise come from?"

The guard pointed to the built-in wall units.

"I think it was from upstairs," said Gabriel.

The head of the security opened the door to the wall unit and pushed up a couple of shelves at the same time. The wall unit moved open. He went inside, checked the safe door, came back and said that everything was in order, and agreed with Gabriel that the noise must have come from upstairs. The guards went their own way. Gabriel took a deep breath, realizing how close they were to getting caught. This time, he turned on a nearby TV and pretended to be watching it while monitoring the area. The head guard went into the security room and told his colleague that he had checked the safe in the tunnel and everything was in order.

His colleague replied, "It didn't show on the screen that the concealed door was opened. The sensor didn't trigger."

Gabriel was slowly relaxing in front of the TV, thinking how lucky they were to avoid the danger in time, when he saw the head of the security pass by him in a hurry, heading toward the concealed door.

He jumped and asked, "What happened? Where are you going?"

The head of security replied, "The sensor did not trigger. I'm checking to see what's wrong."

Gabriel was sure the guards would find Richard and others in the safe and tunnels, which would result in certain death for Richard, him, and his friends.

Gabriel did not consider running and saving himself, not even for a second. He imagined his father decided to stay and help Kiki Coto, knowing too well they would most probably be killed. While looking at the tunnel opening, Gabriel asked God to make Richard and the others invisible to the guards. He felt God's presence and was completely convinced that his prayers would be answered.

The security guard opened the concealed door again while talking to his colleague inside the monitoring room and asking him if the sensor was working?

"No," he replied. "It is like the door was never opened."

Meanwhile, Gabriel peeked inside the tunnel and saw the safe door closed and no one to be seen. He was relieved. He thanked God for answering his prayer, but he started to wonder what he should do next.

"Okay, write a report to the technician to come and check tomorrow morning," the head of security told the guard in the monitoring room and went back.

What Gabriel did not know was that when one of the guys approached Julio and told him that a guard might come out to check the concealed door and the safe, Julio went toward the safe to ask Richard to get out of the safe and close the door. Then he heard the concealed door opening, jumped inside, and closed the safe door while they were both inside. The rest of the gang stayed behind the partition door in the tunnel, and after a while, they returned to the truck.

Richard and Julio were stuck inside the safe as they could not open the door from the inside and could not call anyone as there was no reception for their phones. Gabriel became worried. Usually, the technician arrived early in the morning. He may find that the safe door sensor was also not working. He did not know if Richard had completed the extraction. He wanted to go inside the tunnel and check things out but was afraid the security guards would become suspicious.

But then he thought, *maybe Richard needs help, and if I don't check it out, Richard may not complete what he came for. And then not only will Gloria not have any chance of being exonerated, but we also won't get our revenge by putting one of the worst kinds of criminals behind bars. And if Bill finds out about our plan, he will kill us all.* He decided that the ramifications of not checking things out and making sure that everything was okay were much more serious and frightening than to do so.

I am the manager, after all. Everyone answers to me. I have the right to check things out, and no one can question me, not yet anyway, he told himself, trying to build his confidence. He called the guard and told him casually that he was going to recheck things and that he would keep an eye on the area until the technician arrived in the morning.

Gabriel opened the concealed door, entered the tunnel, and saw everything was quiet. He opened the safe door, and while there was still half of the stuff remaining, there was no one to be seen. He quietly called Richard's name. Richard and Julio appeared from behind the cabinets.

"What happened?" asked Gabriel, and then he said, "Never mind. We don't have much time. Early tomorrow morning, a technician will come to check the door sensor. Hurry up."

Before he left, Julio called him and showed him the two bags full of cash and told Gabriel that Richard wanted to leave them behind.

"Why, Richard? It's blood money. The blood of people like my parents and Gloria's parents." Before Richard could answer, Gabriel told Julio to take them. "Just hurry up. We don't have much time. Leave by 6:00 a.m., even if you have not removed everything," cautioned Gabriel.

They started working harder, running back and forth through the sewers. Now they had a better incentive in the form of two large bags of cash. By 6:10 a.m., they were in the truck with no sign of any activities in the tunnels.

Gabriel entered the tunnel one more time to make sure that everything was okay. He opened the safe again and was happy to see that all the shelves and cabinets were empty. Despite everyone wearing gloves, he wiped all the metal or shiny surfaces inside the safe and the tunnel partition doors.

In the meantime, Richard drove very carefully toward the bridge where his helpers were staying.

When they reached the bridge, Julio told Richard, "We can't take the money with us. We want you to keep it for us and return it when we ask for it. Of course, you can keep your share and give us the rest." And just as they were ready to leave, Julio asked Richard, "Will you need our help going through all the stuff?"

"Of course, I will. That's a very good idea," replied Richard. "Let's get some breakfast, go to a quiet place and go through it all together. I need the documents related to all the dirty judges. Any document that says 'judge' on it, separate it, so I can choose the ones I need. After I confront Judge Éclair and other judges involved in Gloria's case and make them come clean, I'll hand over the rest of the documents to the feds."

Richard purchased breakfast for everyone, then drove to a quiet street, parked the truck, and each took a bag and started going through the contents. They would read the names of famous judges and politicians out loud.

Around noon, one of them yelled, "Bingo! I found it, Judge Éclair."

"Thank you," said Richard. "But there may be more than one item on him."

After a while, another yelled, "I found a Thomas Éclair! But it does not say judge on it."

"Put it with the judges' pile. Maybe it is before he was selected as a judge."

It took them all day to go through the documents. On the way to drop off the gang, Julio told his friends to dig a deep hole in the secluded area of the park near the bushes and wait for him. Then Richard and Julio drove to a storage unit that Richard had rented. They moved all the evidence into storage, except two bags of cash and the bag containing judges' evidence. Richard drove to the park where Julio's friends were waiting, dropped off Julio with the two bags of cash, and drove home.

Richard started going through documents and electronic devices where Judge Éclair was in them, starting from the earliest dates. In the first several documents, he was a lawyer getting paid by Bill's associate to fold his clients' cases. He did this either by telling his clients to plead guilty despite winning chances or by agreeing with opposing counsel to suppress crucial evidence and then giving his clients excuses for agreeing with the other lawyer.

In another tape, a lesser-known associate of Bill's was making an agreement with Éclair. He promised to help him get elected as a judge by advertising for him through different news media, publishing positive articles about him, and giving positive interviews in many news media. Additionally, he would publish negative reports about Éclair's opponents. In exchange, Éclair promised to follow his orders whenever he asked, either regarding his case or someone else's case that he had agreed to help for a fee. Éclair had to repeat clearly that he agreed to follow Bill's orders anytime he asked, whether the order was to suppress evidence or any other order. The interviewers were with Bill's associates who were not officially and directly working for Bill, so they would not be connected to Bill if he had to use the videos. A couple of times, Éclair brought up Bill's name by saying that he would follow Bill's order whenever Bill asked. The interviewer would get mad and yell at Éclair, reminding him that he should not use Bill's name, and then they would do it all over again.

Richard found similar pieces of evidence for the appeal judges and many other judges. Richard copied everything onto different electronic devices and gave it to Julio.

"If anything happens to me, give these to the feds," Richard said.

CHAPTER FORTY-FOUR

He took several copies of the important sections of the conversations between Thomas Éclair and different associates of Bill and went to see Judge Éclair. A security guard did not let Richard enter Éclair's office. Richard gave him a sealed envelope and asked the guard to give it to Éclair.

Éclair opened the envelope and read: *I have Bill's recordings, where in exchange for money, as in taking bribes, you openly and eagerly agreed to fully cooperate with Bill and let murderers and drug dealers go free and put the innocent in jail.*

Éclair came out from his office very frightened and asked Richard to come in. Richard played several clips of different recordings for Éclair.

"That son of a bitch. Why would he record all of our conversations? I have cooperated with him all the time. He did not need to keep these recordings," said Éclair. "Are you suicidal? You know he will kill you and your family. Maybe you want to die, but did you ask the rest of your family if they want to die, too?"

"You have one chance only," said Richard. "You call for a news conference with all the media outlets right here in your office and confess to your crimes, confess that for money received from Bill and other criminals, you suppressed evidence and let murderers free and put the innocent in jail. In which case, I will not give the personal documents that Bill has on you to the media, or by 4:00 p.m. today, all the documents will be given to the media first and then to the feds."

Before Éclair could say anything, Richard continued. "You know, some of these documents are very dirty and very compromising for you and are personal in nature. They have nothing to do with bribery or any legal case. They are only related to your personal preferences, which, if released to the media, will devastate your family. Bill just accumulated these documents as means for blackmail, in case you decided not to cooperate with him, or you decided to work with other criminal organizations, especially Acabar's rivals."

"You know, Bill made me a wealthy man over the years. How much will satisfy you?" asked Éclair.

"Not a penny of your bloody money will satisfy me," replied Richard. "You destroyed hundreds of innocent lives, and you want to get out of it with your bloody money?"

"Then what do you want?" asked Éclair.

"I want you to make it right for all the innocent people you put behind bars, including that innocent girl you charged with murder," replied Richard.

"Which girl are you talking about?"

"You know well who. The one whose case was destroyed by rejecting all the evidence, including the recorded confession by Bill's associates and guards that Doug committed the murder and not Gloria."

"Oh, that case. But it is a closed case. There is nothing I or anyone else can do," replied Éclair.

"Yes, there is. I'll call all the media and invite them here, outside your door in the hallway, and you will confess to all the crimes you committed over the years. When you get to Gloria's case, you will describe everything in detail, all the evidence you rejected and the phony evidence you accepted. Either you agree to do it right now, or I will give all the documents to the media and the feds. As soon as they see these and hundreds of other documents, they will free Gloria. I am giving you the chance to come clean, to confess in front of the media and later in court in front of a real judge that you know Earl was killed by Bill's assistant, Doug, and that you suppressed crucial evidence and found Gloria guilty. An innocent girl who Bill enslaved. If you do that, I won't hand over those documents that are completely personal in nature. There is a lot of blackmailing evidence against you. In most of them, you agree to take bribes and let a murderer walk or put an innocent individual in prison. However, some are completely personal. The feds must have evidence related to bribes. But if you confess and let Gloria free, I will not give the personal evidence to the feds."

"I have two questions: why do you want me to confess in exchange for not giving the personal evidence to the feds? And the second question: what guarantee do I have that after I confess, you won't still provide all the evidence to the feds, including the personal ones?" asked Éclair.

"The answer to the first question is that I don't know how long it will take for the feds to process these documents and make the information public and retry Gloria's case. It may take months or even years, or it may become a political issue, and they might never reveal the truth. That is why I will give the documents to the media first. Even then, it may take months for Gloria to be released. As for your second question, I am an independent human being and a man of my word. I am not a criminal like you, who's a puppet for a criminal organization and has to follow orders and cannot make any decision of his own or make any promises," replied Richard.

"Watch your language. I am still a judge," replied Éclair.

"You are not a judge; you have never been a judge. You are a lying bastard who for money puts innocent people in jail and lets murderers go free."

"Let me think about it," said Éclair.

"No time to think. You either agree to confess so I can call the media or by 4:00 p.m., the media and the feds will get all the documents. Don't even think about calling your filthy boss. Even if Bill kills me, the media and the feds will receive all the documents. My friends have them, and there is no way you or your boss can find them in time to stop them."

At this moment, Richard realized that Éclair had put down a gun in a drawer and closed it.

While sweating and trembling heavily, Éclair picked up the list and asked Richard, "So, if I tell the media that Gloria is innocent, you won't give the personal documents to the feds or the media?"

"That's right," replied Richard. "But there is one condition. You must be convincing enough that Gloria will be freed very soon."

"Then give me a couple of hours, and I will get ready."

"I know you could call Bill to send someone to kill me right now. I am ready to die. But regardless of whether I die or not, the media and the feds will receive all the documents."

"I am not going to call Bill. Just my family," replied Éclair.

Richard went outside Éclair's office and sat on the bench, wondering if these were the last minutes of his life.

Éclair sat quietly, deep in his thoughts. Then he called his wife and informed her that he had to make things right in the murder case of Earl Murphy and told her that he would not be coming home that night. He then called his children and said goodbye to them.

Then, he prepared his statement to read to the media. While he was writing his statement, he experienced a sudden realization about the severity of the crimes he had committed. Then Richard saw the different news people and journalists arrive outside Éclair's office one by one.

At 3:30 p.m., Éclair came out of his chamber and started reading the statement. He described all the crucial evidence he had dismissed following Bill's orders. He gave explanations about why the evidence should have been admitted. He talked about the confession by Bill that his assistant, Doug, killed Earl. He spoke about the clock on the wall contradicting Gloria's photos and how Gloria was seen on another side of the building at the time of Earl's death. He revealed how Bill asked the coroner to break Earl's ribs and how the shoe was replaced with a smaller one by Bill's buddy, Chief Scott Timmins. He told the truth about collusion between both Gloria's lawyer, Andrew Ramstone, and District Attorney Sean Wilderson, and many other issues.

After reading the statement, he added that it was his true judgment that Gloria was innocent of killing Earl Murphy, and he had firsthand knowledge that Bill forced her to pose beside Earl's dead body for photos. Then Éclair looked at Richard for approval. Richard nodded.

While the news media started asking questions, Éclair took a gun from his pocket and shot himself in the head. The news of Éclair's death was on all media. Thousands of people no one suspected of being in Bill's gang turned out to be members, including judges, politicians, police, and government administrators. They all started scrambling to destroy evidence and hide from authorities. The streets became busy immediately.

Richard, while shocked as he did not expect Éclair to kill himself, was very disappointed to see him dodge the hammer of justice and not stand trial for the atrocities he had committed during the years he cooperated with Bill posing as a judge. Richard was hoping that Éclair would testify in court and free Gloria without further delay. He was not sure what would happen now that Éclair was gone.

He quietly left the chaos. He called the feds while walking to his car and asked for an agent.

He started explaining the documents he had in storage, but the agent immediately asked, "Is it related to the events in the courthouse and Éclair's death?"

As soon as Richard confirmed that it was related, the agent asked for the address and told Richard to meet him there.

"Bill may flee. You should also go to his house to arrest him," Richard warned them.

The agent replied, "A task force is already at Bill's house."

Richard told the agent about the underground tunnels and said the task force should talk to Gabriel about the locations. The agent thanked Richard and called the task force's head to talk to Gabriel about the escape routes in Bill's house.

When Richard arrived at the storage unit, about twenty agents had already opened his storage and were collecting all the evidence. Richard approached and asked for the agent he had talked to. The agent came forward and asked Richard to go to their headquarters to make a statement.

"Was Bill captured?" Richard asked.

"Police surrounded the house and blocked the tunnel exits, but Bill escaped through a tunnel that nobody knew existed, not even his staff manager, Gabriel, who was shot by Bill while he unsuccessfully tried to stop Bill from escaping," the agent replied.

Richard got worried about Gabriel and asked, "Is Gabriel's injury serious?"

But the agent replied that it was not.

The following morning, all news agencies announced that Bill was still at large. He had escaped through an elaborate underground tunnel system. Bill's assets were confiscated.

CHAPTER FORTY-FIVE

That evening, Richard was with his family, including Flore, and they all went to see Gabriel, who was recovering in hospital.

"There was another tunnel branching out from the tunnel underneath the highway that was concealed. It was a continuous concrete wall, ground from the outside. Only if you knew the exact location could you kick it open like the one in the sewer," Gabriel told Richard. "I tried to stop Bill from escaping, but Bill shot me without hesitation and continued running."

When the feds were chasing him in the tunnel, Bill had kicked the concrete open, went into it, and locked a metal door behind him. The feds found out later that the tunnel surfaced into a house one street over.

The chief of police, Sean Wilderson, Andrew Ramstone, and many other officers, lawyers, politicians, and judges were arrested.

The word on the street was that Bill was operating his criminal organization from the underground.

The next day, Richard and Phil asked the court to free Gloria on bail until the official court proceeding for her complete exoneration.

Richard called Abraham to give him the good news, but the maid informed him that Abraham had died the night before in his sleep, just after hearing the good news of Gloria's release.

In another court proceeding, they asked the court for Cathy's share of her father's assets. During the proceedings, a clerk walked in and gave a small package to the judge and told him that the person who gave him the package had told him it was related to this case. The judge granted recess and opened the package in his chambers in the presence of both counsel and the district attorney. It was the recording of Bill killing his father that Emanuel had hidden in the crack of a tree trunk.

Julio and other homeless people bought a house with the money they found in the safe. All the homeless moved into the house and stayed there until they could find a job and move out. Occasionally, they would come back again and stay for a while longer.

A couple of months later, the court of appeal exonerated Gloria of all charges. Shortly after, in another courtroom, Cathy was granted half of Bill's assets inherited from his father. Phil opened a court case for compensation for Gloria for all her suffering resulting from a corrupt justice system and won. With the compensation proceeds, Gloria bought a farm for her parents and sent her brother and sister to university.

Cathy hired a lawyer in Chicago to appeal Renzo's case. It was confirmed that Renzo was set up as bait and was forced to go to Chicago. The court in Chicago considered Renzo's part in unfolding one of the biggest criminal organizations, and his sentence was reduced to time served, and he was released. Cathy bought a house for Renzo and Terza and set up an educational fund for their son, Danny. She also started a charity for the homeless in her father's name.

In yet another court, it was determined that George and his mother were not involved in Bill's illegal activities and were granted the other half of Bill's inherited assets. Many employees and friends testified that Bill's wife and son were never involved in his illegal activities.

All the assets that Bill had accumulated through illegal activities were confiscated by the feds and were assigned to a fund for victim compensation. Richard opened a court case for all the abused employees of Bill who were forced into slavery.

A couple of months after Gloria was freed from prison, Gabriel proposed. At their wedding, while Gloria's father, Jose Luis, was walking Gloria down the aisle on her left side, Gloria stopped in the middle of the aisle and called Richard to walk with her on her right.

As they started walking, Gloria looked to her right and saw Kiki Coto, in his full police chief uniform, walking along her side, looking at her with adoration and in heavenly bliss.

THE END